Gone to Dust

ALSO AVAILABLE FROM LILIANA HART AND POCKET BOOKS

The Darkest Corner

LILIANA HART

Gone to Dust

POCKET BOOKS

New York   London   Toronto   Sydney   New Delhi

Pocket Books
An Imprint of Simon & Schuster, Inc.
1230 Avenue of the Americas
New York, NY 10020

This book is a work of fiction. Any references to historical events, real people, or real places are used fictitiously. Other names, characters, places, and events are products of the author's imagination, and any resemblance to actual events or places or persons, living or dead, is entirely coincidental.

First Pocket Books paperback edition July 2017

POCKET and colophon are registered trademarks of Simon & Schuster, Inc.

For information about special discounts for bulk purchases, please contact Simon & Schuster Special Sales at 1-866-506-1949 or business@simonandschuster.com.

The Simon & Schuster Speakers Bureau can bring authors to your live event. For more information or to book an event, contact the Simon & Schuster Speakers Bureau at 1-866-248-3049 or visit our website at www.simonspeakers.com.

Interior design by Bryden Spevak

Manufactured in the United States of America

10 9 8 7 6 5 4 3 2 1

ISBN 978-1-5011-5005-0
ISBN 978-1-5011-5006-7 (ebook)

To Scott—I'm glad I get to do life with you.
I'd choose to marry you and be your ezer all over again.
I love you always.

CHAPTER ONE

She'd captured his heart.

This woman of noble birth—a queen—who'd traveled across vast lands to bring him gifts, to seek his wisdom and knowledge. But it was she who was wise, and her intelligence and cunning personality enticed him. Never had he met a match such as she. Her presence was greater than any gift she'd laid at his feet.

"You're quiet, my lord," she said.

He lay on a pile of furs, naked except for the amethyst ring on his finger—a ring of kings that bore his seal. A soft breeze stirred the air and cooled his overheated skin. The thin linen sheet couldn't hide his desire as she walked through the shadows of his chambers and came to stand before him, bathed in the soft glow of lantern light.

Her beauty stole his breath—her skin dark and smooth—her eyes black as the rare diamonds she'd presented to his kingdom. The white silk of her robes was tied at each shoulder and plunged deeply, displaying the *fullness of her bosom—the material so thin he could see the jeweled adornments covering her nipples. The silk was slit up each side so every step she gave him a glimpse of the heaven he knew was hidden beneath. Her hair was her glory, rich and full, and she'd unpinned the crown of curls so it flowed almost to her feet.*

"You leave on the morrow," he said, his heart pierced with sorrow.

His body was rigid and stiff with pride. He was king. And he would beg for no woman to stay. But he wanted to.

"I am queen," she said, her smile sad. "My kingdom needs me. My people need me."

"I need you," he rasped, his hand knotted in a fist at his side.

"And you shall have me," she said, moving toward him.

She released the ties at her shoulders and the white silk slithered down the length of her body, leaving her bared before him. His phallus throbbed and his chest burned with desire. She was exquisite. Never had he wanted another woman as he wanted her.

The days had turned to weeks, and the weeks to months since her arrival to his lands. But never had she offered herself. The desire had burned between them, the flames fanning hotter and higher as time passed, but he'd respected her wishes to remain chaste in her own bed, though he could have taken her, as was his right as king. And now she honored him by giving him her body.

"You are more beautiful than all the treasures in my kingdom," he said, his gaze lingering on her full breasts, the lantern light reflecting off the diamond adornments that sent fractals of light glittering across the floor.

"I am your greatest treasure. Long will you remember me. Long will you love me."

He knew the words she spoke were truth. She knelt next to the bed and bowed her head, submitting herself to him. And then she said two words that made him rage at the injustice their positions had wrought.

"My king," she whispered.

"As you are my queen," he said, voice hoarse with sorrow and desire. "We could rule together, combine our lands."

She looked up at him, knowledge and wisdom in her eyes, and his hand moved to her cheek, stroking it softly. "Do you forget the lands between us?" she asked. "That which is ruled by another?"

"I do not forget," he said with a sigh. "And I know you are right. Those are lands not ours to take. To conquer would bring wars we cannot fathom."

"Then tonight we will give our bodies to each other. And when dawn comes and I take my leave, you shall know you are well loved."

She took his hand and kissed it softly, and then she joined him on the bed, sliding the sheet from his body and moving over him, so she was poised to take him into her. Their hands clasped and their gazes met, and he knew *this would be a spiritual experience, that they would truly meld—mind, body, and soul—with their union.*

His jaw clenched and sweat beaded on his skin as her heat enveloped him. And then her head fell back with a moan as she sank down on him. The world spun away as pleasure unlike he'd ever known surrounded him.

His vision dimmed and the incessant chime of a doorbell rang in his ears.

"A doorbell?" Miller Darling said, shaking herself out of the scene she'd been writing. "What the hell?"

She snarled and her head snapped up at the interruption. She was going to kill someone. No jury would convict her. The sign on the front door clearly said "Do Not Disturb."

She hit save on her keyboard and headed out of her second-story office, stubbing her toe on a box of books she didn't remember putting directly in the walkway. Her footsteps pounded heavy against the stairs as she raced toward the front door and the unsuspecting victim who continued to ring the bell.

The *click* of the dead bolt seemed unusually loud as she unlocked it with indignant righteousness and jerked the door open, only to have it catch on the chain. She closed it again and undid the chain, muttering under her breath at the wasted opportunity to make a real impact on the intruder.

Miller stared into the startled eyes of the UPS man, ready to flay him alive. He was tall, thin, and pale, his sandy hair thinning on top, and his cheeks were red from the blistery wind and cold. He held a package and an electronic clipboard in his hands.

She was pretty sure she growled at him. The last week of a deadline was the *wrong* time to disobey the instructions on the door.

"Geez, lady," he said, eyes wide. He took a step back and beads of sweat broke out over his upper lip. "Are you sick or something?"

"Or something," she said, eyes narrowed.

She wasn't sure when she'd showered last, but she was pretty sure she'd been wearing the same clothes for at least three days. Maybe longer. Her gray sweats had coffee stains on them and what might have been a smear of jelly from a PB&J she'd slapped together— minus the peanut butter because she hadn't had time to go to the store.

She wasn't wearing a bra, but it was hardly noticeable beneath the fuzzy red bathrobe her best friend Tess had gotten her for Christmas about a dozen years before. There was a small package of Kleenex in one of the pockets and a mega-size box of Milk Duds in the other.

"The sign says 'Do Not Disturb,'" she said.

"You've got to sign for the package." He shrugged as if he hadn't just ruined her entire day, then held out clipboard for her to sign.

She ignored the gesture and took a step forward.

He took another step back. "I'm not sure you understand what I'm saying. I don't care if you're delivering gold bullion or the electric pencil sharpener I ordered three months ago and never received. The sign says 'Do Not Disturb.' Do you know how long it's going to take me to get back in the mood?"

His eyebrows rose and his mouth opened and closed a couple of times. "No?" he said, phrasing it like a question. He was starting to look scared. Good.

"That's right. You don't know," she said. "Lovemaking like that can't just be performed on a whim. It takes preparation and the right frame of mind. I had the candles lit and the music playing, and she was about to ride him like a stallion. You've set me back hours at least. How would you like it if someone kept ringing the doorbell right before you were about to have an orgasm?"

He swallowed hard and dropped his clipboard. "I . . . I wouldn't." He bent down to pick it up and then shoved it and the box at her once more. "I'm sorry for interrupting. But you're the last house on my route. I've got to get it delivered and signed for so I can go home."

She sighed and scribbled her name in the little box and then took the package. "Next time, do us both a favor and sign it for me and put it in the rocking chair. I won't tell anyone if you don't. And I also won't want to kill you, which is what I want to do now."

"I appreciate your restraint," he said, swallowing again. "Sorry about that. I guess I'll, uh . . . let you get back to . . ." He gestured with his hand, and she realized what he thought she'd been doing and what she'd actually been doing were two very different things.

"I'm a writer," she said by way of explanation.

"Right," he said, looking skeptical.

She ran her fingers through the rat's nest on her head and two pencils fell on the porch. Her shoulders slumped in defeat and she turned back into the house, leaving the pencils on the ground and dead-bolting the door behind her. The UPS man was still standing there. He was probably reevaluating his career choices.

There was no point trying to get back to work. The moment was broken and the mood was gone. Besides, she'd had the opportunity to smell herself and feel the rumble in her stomach. A shower was in order, followed by whatever she could find to eat in her kitchen. Writing wasn't a pretty profession. When she was in the trenches of a story she often forgot to tend to day-to-day life. Sometimes, the story took hold of her and wouldn't let go, and that's where she'd been the last several days.

She tossed the package on her entry table on top of the mail that had been accumulating for the past week. Her housekeeper, Julia, came in every Tuesday and Friday, but she knew better than to knock on her office door and disturb her, so she put the mail on the table and cleaned around her office. She also made sure Miller didn't leave the coffeepot or stove on and burn the house down.

The mail was the least of her worries. The bills were all done automatically online, so she assumed anything in the stack wasn't urgent. She caught her reflection in the mirror as she headed back up the stairs and had to do a double take because she thought a stranger was following behind her.

"Yikes," she said, grimacing.

She looked bad, even by her usual definition of deadline crazy. She needed desperately to get her roots done and have her color touched up. It was rare she kept it the same color for a long stretch of time, and it was currently black with bright blue highlights. She looked like a cross between the Cookie Monster and Don King.

Her face was pale and there were dark circles under her eyes. She couldn't remember the last time she'd been out in the sun or to the gym. And, Lord, her eyebrows needed a pair of tweezers.

Since work was over for the moment, she decided to do damage control and transition back to human again. Maybe that was just what she needed to get back into the groove of things and not leave her poor characters on the verge of orgasm. She'd been there. It wasn't a fun place to be.

Maybe that's what she needed to get back in the mood. It had been weeks since Elias Cole had left her high and dry, and her pity party had lasted long enough.

Maybe he was married.

Except where was his wife? Because she'd certainly never seen him or any of the others with women. He'd most definitely been interested in her, and boy, had there been chemistry. There'd been no doubt in her mind that the hardness pressing against her hip had been one hundred percent Elias Cole. He'd been her one rebellion. Or at least that had been the plan.

She wasn't an idiot. She recognized when a man was interested. He'd given all the signs, and there'd been no doubting the sexual attraction between them. Then he'd disappeared without an explanation or so much as a goodbye. The big jerk.

Whatever. Sex was sex. It was a natural human function, and surely she could find someone to scratch her itch. Except that she wasn't a fan of one-night stands, and she was unbelievably picky when it came to being intimate with a man. The tribulations of being a romance writer.

It didn't matter that the only person who came to mind was Elias. She knew her own ego well enough to understand that the reason she couldn't get him out of her head was probably because they'd never done the naked tango. Fine. He'd changed his mind and it was time to for her to move on.

She hurried the rest of the way up the stairs, her mind on him instead of the work she was abandoning, despite the mental pep talk she'd just given herself. The majority of her adult life had been spent writing the romances women dreamed about, but Miller was more practical than that. The kind of love she wrote about—that soul-deep connection to another person—wasn't something she expected to find for herself. It wasn't something she *wanted* to find. That depth of love could be devastating, and it wasn't worth taking the chance. She much preferred for her relationships to be fun while they lasted, for the sex to be great, and to part as friends in the end. She'd never had her heart broken, and she had no plans to.

Her parents had loved each other with the same focused obsession that they'd loved the treasures they'd sought their entire married life. From her earliest memories, the stories of King Solomon and the Queen of Sheba were part of their daily conversations. Her bedtime stories had been filled with tales of adventure and temples of treasure. And of the love of two people who spent their earthly lives knowing they could never be together.

It had broken her heart as a child to think of what it must have felt like to know a part of their soul had been missing. Her father had always told her that's how he'd feel if he had to go through life without her mother, and Miller had decided as a young child to never subject herself to that kind of heartbreak.

Her parents had spent their marriage traveling the world, searching for the treasures of the lost temple and piecing together a history that the greatest books in the world hadn't achieved. And it was her older brother who'd been burdened with the responsibility of taking care of her. He'd been four years older, and probably the last thing he wanted to do was babysit his younger sister, but that's exactly what he'd done. He'd been her only stability as a child, an adult long before he should've been, and they'd always been close. He'd never shown her outwardly that he resented the fact he'd been stuck home with her when he'd wanted to be hunting treasure alongside their parents. But she'd known. Every once in a while she'd catch a glint in his eyes that told her he'd rather be anywhere other than Last Stop, Texas.

She could admit her abandonment as a child was one of the reasons she had trouble with long-term commitments and ideas of her own family. She could never do to her own child what her parents had done to her and her brother.

After a few weeks, her parents would come back full of excitement and stories of their adventures. And more often than not, they'd have some trinket that had supposedly been housed in the temple where King Solomon kept his treasures. She had a box full of them in her closet. It was sad to think her best memories of her parents all rested in that box.

Her brother had eventually left home and joined the military, much like her father had at his age, but the obsession with a three-thousand-year-old king and the queen who would never be his must've been hereditary, because Justin had taken up the search, and it had only intensified after their parents were killed when their small plane went down.

Their obsession with each other and the love of two people in history had led to their death. Her brother was the only family she had left, and she only saw him on holidays, and only then if he wasn't on a mission or involved in training. When he got the occasional leave time, he spent it searching for the same treasures and obsessions that had killed their parents.

All she knew was that kind of love and obsession had left her without her parents and with a cynicism she worked hard to keep out of her books. People left. Even when they loved you. It was the way of things, and it was why she much preferred to end her books with a happily ever after instead of seeing where her characters ended up ten years down the road.

She had a good life, and normalcy was very important to her—at least as normal as one could be when she made her living from making stuff up. To say she was a control freak was probably an under-statement, but she liked knowing she was responsible for her own happiness and achievements. Her work fulfilled her. And the occasional relationship satisfied her.

It wasn't often she found a man she was intrigued enough by to invite to her bed. She was damned picky, actually. She wrote romance novels, for crying out loud. So what if she wanted great conversation, a smoking-hot body, and great sex? She'd never seen the point in settling. And since she didn't believe in the happily ever afters she wrote about, she figured her chances with a man like Elias Cole were a done deal.

He hadn't seemed like the kind of man who was interested in happily ever afters either. He'd all but ravished her on her front porch and then calmly walked away, leaving her more sexually frustrated than she'd ever been in her life. He'd hardly acknowl-edged her existence in the weeks since the incident, and in place of the happy-go-lucky smile was a per-petual scowl.

She shivered as she walked into her bedroom and turned up the thermostat on her way to the bath-room. At some point during the last three days, it had gotten colder outside, and she hadn't noticed through the deadline fog or the warmth of her bathrobe.

Her bedroom was tidy—the king-size bed neatly

made and all her clothes folded and put away. She hadn't felt the mattress beneath her in days. She'd been taking catnaps, crashing on the couch in her office when she needed to recharge.

Miller loved color, and the bedroom reflected that. The bed was like a white cloud, but pillows in cobalt, teal, and turquoise added vibrancy, along with a crocheted throw using all the same colors at the foot of the bed. The large canvas on the wall was an abstract ocean scene using thick layers of paint, her bedside lamps were blown glass in the same bright blue, and the cozy chair in the corner was yellow with thick blue stripes.

It was her favorite room in the house, and that was saying something because she loved all of her house. She'd painstakingly redone every room exactly as she'd wanted it. But this was *her* room, and it was perfect—from the reading chaise she'd found at a flea market that sat beneath the beveled windows to the large walk-in closet that had originally been the nursery that attached to the master bedroom. *Perfect.*

Most people in the small town of Last Stop, Texas, considered her eccentric, and many of them had much more creative names for her. She hated to not live up to people's expectations, so when the Gothic home on the corner of Elm Street and Devil's Hill had gone on the market, she'd snapped it up in a heartbeat. And she'd gotten it for a steal too, because Realtors couldn't even get clients to go inside of it.

It was the house that had scared the bejesus out of every kid in Last Stop for the last century. It was the house that sat dark and looming, so people made it a point to always walk on the *other* side of the street instead of passing directly in front of it. It was the house with the creaking gate and the overgrown rosebushes, and it looked spectacular at Halloween.

She never passed up the opportunity to help solidify her reputation by adding a little graveyard in front or sticking a voice box in the bushes that let out horrible moans. The house was rumored to be haunted by Captain Bartholomew T. Payne and his wife Annabelle, after old Bart had decided he'd rather see his wife dead than have her leave him for another man.

Miller had always been fascinated by the story, even though she'd yet to feel the presence of the original owners of the house. She rarely had visitors other than her friend Tess or her cleaning lady, so the outside was rather deceiving. Even with fresh paint and repairs done to the sagging porch and leaking roof, it still gave off a menacing presence. But like with all great things, it had a story, and she'd always been drawn to a good story.

She loved every square inch of it, and she would *never* move. The house fit her personality like a glove, and she cackled every time she peeked out her office window to see kids scurrying across the street and staring at the house in wide-eyed horror. It was the little things in life that brought joy.

She sighed as she passed the bed. The soft sheets were looking a little too enticing. She couldn't afford a comfortable sleep. Not until the book was done. If she got in that bed it might be a week before she woke up. It was important she keep her energy high, so she'd shower and dress, and then she'd get out and talk to actual people instead of the ones in her head before sitting back down at her desk and getting back to work.

She stripped out of her clothes and considered throwing them in the trash instead of subjecting Julia to laundering them. Julia was a single mom to five boys. She not only cleaned Miller's house, but did a few other houses as well. Then she cleaned the schools on Saturday, and the church on Sunday evening. Miller could only hope that the laundry of five boys was worse than that of a writer, though she wouldn't have bet money on it.

The pipes creaked as she turned on the water in the claw-foot tub, and while she waited for it to heat up she found an extra box of black hair color under the sink so she could tackle her roots. By the time she'd gotten the color on and her head wrapped in plastic, the water was hot. She lit the candles on the window sill and dimmed the lights, and then she tossed a bath bomb in the water and hoped the smell of roses was strong enough to overpower the smell of deadline.

An hour later, her skin was pruny, her roots were dyed, and she smelled a whole lot better. She blow-dried her hair, moisturized her face, and put on double the concealer she normally would because she could've slept in the bags under her eyes.

By the time she was done, she was exhausted. And talking to real people didn't sound as exciting as it had before. Where was she going to go? Happy hour? By herself? Maybe Tess would come with her. But she was married now, and there were rules about things like that. She'd somehow talked herself out of a big night out, and she found it wasn't as appealing as she'd first thought. Mainly because her mind was still stuck on Elias Cole.

"Ridiculous man," she muttered.

What she needed was to clear her mind with a good friend and conversation, and Tess was three blocks away with a fully stocked wine fridge. Maybe they could have a girls' night in like they used to, but there were those marriage rules that had to be observed. Since Tess's marriage to Deacon Tucker, Miller had learned dropping in unannounced was never a good idea. They were still in that honeymoon phase of their marriage where they were almost always naked. It made the funeral home a really interesting place to visit after office hours. And sometimes *during* office hours.

She put on black leggings, a sports bra, and an oversized gray shirt that warned people if they annoyed her they might end up in one of her novels. People always laughed, but she'd been known to kill off the occasional annoyance in one of her books. Comfort was the name of the game for the evening's activities. She'd give her brain a quick break, and then get back to business.

Miller hopped on the bed and struck a quick pose propped against a mound of pillows, and then she held up the latest release of one of her good friends. She took a selfie with the book and then uploaded it to Facebook, pimping her friend. The great thing about social media was no one would know she'd worked ninety-plus hours in the last few days, eaten nothing but carbs and chocolate, and drunk an unhealthy amount of coffee. She wouldn't change things for the world, though she needed to hit the gym very soon so her behind wasn't as wide as her chair. When it came to her readers, she'd continue to put on double layers of concealer so they'd see the fun and glamourous life they thought a bestselling author should live.

She stuck her head into the massive master closet and dug out a pair of neon-fuchsia running shoes with lime-green laces. Tess told her they made her eyes hurt, but Tess hated everything to do with running, so her opinion hadn't influenced Miller's decision to buy them. She grabbed up her dirty clothes and robe, embarrassed to leave them for Julia to find.

Her stomach rumbled again and she bounded down the stairs, making a stop at the laundry room and dumping the clothes in the washer. She hummed as she measured the soap and turned on the hot water, and then she added a little extra soap just to be safe.

The pile of mail on the entry table caught her attention and she again scooped it up, taking it with her to the kitchen. Everything about the kitchen was functional, from the hidden cabinets where she kept her small appliances, to the wine refrigerator in the big butcher-block island, to the pot filler over the stove. Unfortunately, she didn't get to actually *cook* in the kitchen very often, mostly due to the fact that when she was working, she frequently forgot to eat. Besides, what fun was cooking for one? When she did cook, it was to make emergency brownies or comfort mac 'n' cheese. She figured if she was going to torture herself by working out, she might as well have a good reason.

She dumped the mail on the island, then opened the refrigerator. A bottle of ketchup and a cold pack she sometimes used on her eyes were the only things on the shelves. It'd been a while since she'd had a real meal, and even longer since she'd been to the grocery store.

She closed the refrigerator door and saw the note beneath the magnet in Julia's handwriting.

You need everything. This is no way for
a grown woman to live. You'll get scurvy.
Make me a list and I'll get what you need
when I come on Tuesday.

"It's Friday," she said, and then thought about it a second. "I think," she corrected. "I could be dead of starvation by Tuesday," she said.

She'd just have to wing it. She wasn't opposed to eating fast food until the fridge was stocked. The only things worse than going to the grocery store were visiting the gynecologist or getting bad book reviews.

She went through the mail quickly, discarding most of it as junk, but the last envelope had her brother's familiar block handwriting on it, so she put it aside and then turned to the package. It was a plain brown box, no bigger than the length of her hand, and just as wide. There were several layers of brown tape, so she grabbed a knife from the block on the counter.

Justin had taken up the habit of sending her trinkets that had supposedly belonged to Solomon after he'd joined the military, but they hadn't come in a while. She slid the knife under the layers of tape and lifted the flaps. The box was crammed with newspaper, and she noticed the headlines were written in Spanish. That was certainly odd. She pulled it out and then tilted the box over. Something weighty and wrapped in more newspaper fell into her hand, but it was the *clank* of metal hitting the counter that grabbed her attention.

She picked up the heavy ring with the large purple stone. Within the stone was the carved insignia of the king she'd been told stories about her whole life. And despite her resentment of the tales and adventures that had broken her small family, the obsession had become hers. Because now she was writing the story of the great and troubled king and the woman he'd loved more than any treasure, hoping that putting it on the page once and for all would finally give her freedom.

It was her brother's ring, given to him by her father, as it had been given to him by his father, passed down from generation to generation. A ring made in the image of the one Solomon had worn during his reign. A ring that had been one of twelve that Solomon had given to each of the prophets of the twelve tribes of Israel.

If her information was correct, and she had no reason to believe it wasn't. In the chest with the trinkets and letters was a small book with her family history written on the pages, and tucked inside it were papers and letters, many of them museum quality that she needed to have protected between glass. It was on her ever-growing to-do list. But her history was there, dating back to the prophet that Solomon gave one of the rings to.

What wasn't written between the pages of her ancestry was the reason why her parents had been the way they'd been. There was no explanation for their obsession, other than pure academic fascination of a legend. Her father had been in the military before getting his degrees in ancient civilization. He wrote papers and taught graduate-level classes at the university so they could pay their bills, never really had to be in class much since most of the graduate-level study was research and writing papers. And her mother had spent most of her days planning the next trip, scattering maps across the dining room table and following leads.

Before her parents had left on their last adventure, her father had taken Justin into his study and talked to him for a good while. She remembered how jealous she'd been of that time they'd spent together, of the attention she craved but never received. She'd been in bed when they'd finally finished their time together, but she'd been awake, listening for Justin's bedroom door to close. When she'd gotten up for school the next morning, her parents were gone and Justin was wearing her father's ring. The ring she was now in possession of.

There was nothing in this world that would've made Justin send her his ring. It had been passed down from father to son for more generations than she could count. And if Justin never had a son, it would go to her son if she ever had one. The ring was priceless. And it was always to be worn by the living male heir. Which meant for Justin to not be wearing it was more awful than she could imagine.

Cold fear clutched at her belly and her hands shook as she took the tissue paper in her hand and slowly unwrapped it. When she got to the contents inside, her mind couldn't process what she was looking at.

She dropped the package and took a step back, her hands clammy and bile rising in the back of her throat. In the middle of the tissue paper was a human finger. She had a sinking feeling she knew why her brother no longer wore his ring.

CHAPTER TWO

Miller wasn't someone who panicked in a crisis. But there were always exceptions.

"Not a panicker," she managed to croak, just to reinforce the sentiment. "I'm sure there's an explanation. I have no idea what it could be, but I'm sure there is one."

It wasn't unheard-of for her to get unusual packages or gifts. She'd even dealt with a stalker early on in her career. Maybe this was someone playing a sick prank, and the finger wasn't even real. That didn't explain the ring though, but it was at least a workable theory.

There was only one way to find out if it was, in fact, a real finger, and it didn't involve her getting a closer look at it. Spots danced in front of her eyes as she hurriedly rewrapped the finger and tossed it back in the box. Then she shoved the newspaper back inside and closed the lid. She put the ring on her thumb, grabbed her purse and keys, and then headed to the carport at the back of the house where she kept her bright red Range Rover.

The wind cut like a knife, and she sucked in a breath of surprise at how much the temperature had dropped since the last time she'd been outside, not counting her encounter with the UPS man earlier that morning. Her anger had kept her plenty warm during that exchange.

Texas falls and winters were always unpredictable, so it was best to just be prepared for anything from an ice storm to temperatures in the nineties within a twenty-four-hour period. It made dressing every morning interesting. Which was just another reason she was grateful she didn't have to put on real clothes and go to an office job every day.

She didn't want to waste time going back inside to grab a jacket, so she forged ahead. Her teeth chattered, but she wasn't sure if it was because of the weather or the contents in her hand.

She put the box in the passenger seat, determined not to think about what was inside. The clock on the dashboard said it was just after five in the afternoon, and in another half hour it would be completely dark. Hopefully, Tess would be done with work for the day. And if she wasn't, she was about to get one a hell of an interruption.

Tess Sherman was the director of the Last Stop

Funeral Home—an unfortunate name in Miller's opinion—and her best friend. In a town of only a couple thousand people, the funeral home didn't get a whole lot of business. Which was great for the town, but not so great when you were trying to keep a business afloat. And certainly not reason enough to have five incredibly attractive employees who were driving the women of Last Stop crazy with lust.

The new owner of the funeral home had been sending hot men to Tess at pretty regular intervals the last couple of years. Miller had never understood how a small funeral home could afford to hire that many full-time employees, and she couldn't imagine how bored they must be. Tess had never understood it either, but since she wasn't the boss there was nothing she could do but take them in like they were contestants on *The Bachelorette*.

The men stood out like sore thumbs in a small town like Last Stop. Miller's imagination had run wild at the thought of all that testosterone occupying the same space, and she'd come up with several new book ideas. And so what if her last two heroes had looked and acted an awful lot like Elias Cole? He was most definitely romance novel material. Except for the fact that he'd left her hot and bothered, with her shirt flung over the porch railing and her jeans halfway to her knees before he'd run off like his pants had been on fire.

The funeral home was only three blocks from her house, and she made it there in record time, running two stop signs and squealing into the driveway on two tires. She was relieved to see there weren't any cars parked in the side lot and the Suburban that hauled the bodies was housed in the multicar garage.

She parked behind a black Hummer that belonged to one of Tess's many ridiculously hot employees, and a motorcycle that belonged to Tess's husband. Miller wasn't sure what kind of lottery Tess had won to end up with a group of testosterone-driven alphas all under the same roof, but she wouldn't mind buying a ticket for herself.

Miller looked at herself in the rearview mirror and noted the lack of color in her face, and that her eyes were wide with shock. Her teeth had stopped chattering, but her hands shook as she grabbed her bag and the package and pushed the car door open, getting out and then bumping it closed again with her hip. She didn't bother to lock it. Getting to Tess was a priority. She needed her friend.

ELIAS COLE TOOK a long swig of beer, and then held the cold bottle against the bruise forming on his cheek. It throbbed like a bitch.

It had been one hell of a long day. It had started before sunup, when he'd done a ten-mile run, and then he'd gotten to the funeral home in time to change into old work clothes so he and Deacon could dig a grave for the guest who would soon be occupying a plot at the cemetery. Despite the cool temperatures, it was hard, sweaty work, and he'd been ready and grateful for a shower by the time they'd gotten back.

Once the funeral home business was finished for the day, there'd been training to take care of. Daily training was essential in their line of work. They had to stay sharp, and they were constantly running different scenarios.

They all came from different backgrounds and had different training and different specialties. It was what made them unique and what made them a force to be reckoned with. He was a SEAL sniper, and he kept his skills honed. Levi was Mossad, and Dante had been with MI-6. Deacon had been CIA, and Axel had been his Australian counterpart in ASIS.

The technology the Gravediggers were provided was unparalleled, and that included their training. Virtual reality and holograms put them through real-time simulations, and there were never two the same. Some of the sims needed military skill. Others needed stealth and subterfuge. Some even called for explosives. Which was why he was nursing a bruised cheek with a cold beer bottle. Aches and pains were all part of the training process.

"Cheer up, mate," Axel said, setting bowls of pretzels and chips on the table. "It could've happened to any one of us." He took a drink from his own beer and sat on the opposite side of the table.

It was Friday night. The work and training were over, and it was time to let off a little steam with beer, poker, and bullshit. They were all gathered, minus Deacon, at the glass-top kitchen table in the carriage house behind the old Queen Anne funeral home. A replica of an English rose garden sat between the two structures, and there were benches and a fountain so mourners could escape viewings when the funeral home got too crowded. When there weren't mourners invading their space, it was a nice area to look at or spend time in. Axel could usually be found at sunset most evenings on one of the private corner benches.

The carriage house was like Fort Knox, only with better security. The kitchen, living area, and gym were on the first floor. No one ever used the living area, but the kitchen and gym looked out toward the garden and the back of the funeral home. Gravediggers headquarters was on the basement level, but only those with the access codes could enter. The top two floors had the bedroom suites—two on each floor—but only Levi and Axel were sleeping at the carriage house. Like Elias, Dante had chosen to live off-site, though he'd picked a high-rise apartment in Dallas instead of the simple ground-floor apartment Elias had chosen just a few blocks away.

"Well, it didn't happen to any one of you," Elias said sulkily. "It happened to me." His pride stung. He hated letting anything get the best of him. Even a piece of shrapnel that was completely out of his control. "Damn block of wood could've taken my eye out."

"Then we could call you One-Eyed Cole," Axel said cheekily. "You'd sound like a pirate. Very intimidating."

"Fuck off," Elias said, but his lips twitched with a smile.

"If I recall," Dante said, shuffling the deck of cards and then dealing, "when I took that knee to the chin a couple of months ago when we were doing lift drills, I believe it was your maniacal laughter I heard ringing in my ears."

Elias grinned, feeling the pull of his bruised cheek. "That wasn't my laughter you were hearing," he said. "That was the little Tweety Birds fluttering over your head. You got your clock cleaned. It's a good thing your head is so hard."

"Maybe you ladies could stop talking about your injuries and play cards," Levi said.

Elias let out a whistle and settled back in his chair to look at his cards. "For a man we practically had to drag into this game, you sure are eager. You must have a hell of a hand."

"Or maybe I've got better things to do on a Friday night than hear you two whine over your injuries. If it's that bad, maybe we should just take you out in the field and shoot you."

"Believe me," Elias said, "if you did, that bitch Eve would find a way to bring me back from the dead again."

"Someday, brother," Axel said, "you're going to have to explain about the hatred you have for her."

"Faking our deaths and ripping us from our lives isn't enough?" he asked. "I can't imagine you feel too kindly toward her knowing you have a wife who is living her life without you."

Elias felt a twinge of guilt for bringing it up, but it was true. Axel was the only one of them who'd had a family, and his wife had been just a few months pregnant when she'd received the news of his death. She'd lost the baby shortly after.

"It wasn't Eve's decision to put me here," Axel said. "She gave me the choice. And it was one I can only blame myself for making."

Elias finished off his beer and reached for another out of the cooler. "Well, at least she gave you a choice. Now someone put some damned money on the table. This ain't no therapy session."

They played the first hand, but Elias's mind wasn't in the game. Which was probably why he lost twenty bucks right out of the gate. What he did notice was that Dante had checked his watch about a dozen times in the last ten minutes.

"Either you've got some kind of cheating system rigged up on your watch, or you've got a hot date," he said to Dante.

Dante smiled, and Elias wondered how anyone ever thought that smile reassuring. Anyone looking at Dante would've thought he was a successful businessman with extremely refined taste and wealth. The British accent helped. He could charm anyone to his way of thinking. And he had skills that often blew Elias's mind. He moved like a ghost, and he could get in or out of any situation.

"As a matter of fact, I do," he said. "It's my weekend off, and my plans include only leaving my bed to get my lady friend more champagne so she doesn't get dehydrated."

"Borr-ring," Elias said, rolling his eyes. "You know you can have sex in places outside of the bed, right? You've got to pull that British stick out of your ass so your lady friend doesn't spend the weekend yawning."

"I'm not a caveman," Dante said. "There are things women appreciate. They like romance and attention. They like to be seduced. And they like soft sheets."

"That's old married sex," Elias said, making Axel snort just as he was taking a drink. "Women like to have their worlds rocked. They like spontaneity and adventure. You've got to live a little while you're still in good enough shape to do it. You've got the rest of your life to have old married sex."

"Believe me," Dante said, "I manage to make things spontaneous and adventurous from the comfort of my bed. I've never had any complaints."

"Do you have a Facebook page or something?" Elias asked. "What's your average review?"

"Shut up and put your money where your mouth is," Dante said.

Elias was feeling better after that exchange, and he decided to double his bet. Then he heard the squeal of tires in the driveway, and the slam of a car door. He saw a flash of color through the window as Miller raced across the stone path and through the kitchen door in the ugliest shoes he'd ever laid eyes on.

"What the hell?" Axel said.

"Ignore her," Dante said. "She's crazy. Hot . . . but crazy. Have you ever tried to have a conversation with her? It's like trying to grasp a rainbow. She's all over the place."

"She's smart," Levi said. "Some men think that's sexy. Her mind goes a hundred miles an hour all the time."

"I like intelligent women," Dante said. "But Miller is just a little too much . . . everything. She's got all this worldly knowledge, but there's an element of naïveté to her. She's hot as hell, but there's part of her that doesn't recognize it, so she detracts from it by constantly changing her hair."

"That's a fascinating analysis, Dr. Phil," Elias said.

"How about we get back to the game, and the two of you get your mind off Miller? She's Tess's best friend."

"You didn't used to have such problems with us talking about Miller," Dante said, his brow raised. "I believe it was you who used to lament over every sweet curve of her ass."

"Who the hell uses the word 'lament'?" Elias asked, shaking his head. "And don't talk about her ass, or you'll be getting another knee to the chin."

"Civilized people use words that have more than one syllable," Dante said, his attitude very upper-crust British all of a sudden. "And I think your sudden disinterest screams of interest."

"You're crazy," Elias said, tapping his cards on the table impatiently. "Because that makes no sense. Sure, she's a beautiful woman. And she's smart as hell, and interesting to talk to. But that's where it starts and stops."

"Turn on the monitor," Levi said. "Maybe something is wrong."

"Or maybe y'all are a bunch of nosy old women," Elias said.

But the comment was in vain. Axel had already switched on the TV monitor that was mounted in the corner of the kitchen, and he changed the channel to connect to the cameras they'd placed around the property.

CHAPTER THREE

Tess was in the kitchen uncorking a bottle of wine when Miller burst through the back door.

"I was just thinking about you," Tess said, without taking her attention from the bottle. "I figured you had to be pretty close to a break. Usually three days is your limit without seeing me or taking a shower. It's always good to know when I'm right."

She and Tess had been friends since grade school. They'd been thick as thieves all the way through, and they'd even roomed together in college, though their schedules had been on opposite ends of the spectrum, so they'd hardly ever seen each other.

Miller had made it to her senior year at the University of Texas before calling it quits and deciding college wasn't for her. Writing term papers wasn't near as exciting as the stories she'd been putting on paper since childhood. Her love of the written word had consumed her, and going to class seriously cut into her reading time. She'd once pretended to have the flu and taken two weeks off of school when several of her favorite authors had released books on the same day. She had a sickness, all right, but it wasn't the flu.

So she'd spent her last year of college waiting tables and writing like a madwoman, trying to sell her manuscripts. Her first book had been sold the week before she should've graduated. She'd followed her passion, and by sheer determination and blind luck, it had worked out in her favor.

Tess was a good few inches taller than Miller, and she was wand slim. She had a mass of bright red hair that was mussed, though she'd piled it up on top of her head, and she wore one of the soft button-down dress shirts she preferred and a pair of leggings.

It had been a running joke between the two of them since puberty that Miller would be more than happy to give Tess some boobs since she had plenty to spare. In fact, she had plenty of *everything* to spare. And she wasn't complaining. She'd learned to love her body, and she worked hard to keep it in shape. But working out was one of those things she'd always have to do because she was just naturally curvy. Plus, she liked dessert, so running a couple of extra miles was worth it.

Despite the panic building inside of her, she needed the illusion of normalcy. She could count on

Tess like she'd never been able to count on anyone. Her heart raced and fear clutched her gut, but she took another steadying breath and took a good look at her friend.

"You've got beard burn," Miller said, dropping the box and her bag on the kitchen table.

Tess smirked and poured two glasses of wine. "Yep. And it's *everywhere*."

"No one likes a braggart, Tess."

"Sure they do. I have the wine."

"You're right," Miller said. "I love a braggart. Pour my glass to the rim."

"That doesn't sound good. Book not going well?" she asked, filling the glass to the top as requested.

"The UPS man interrupted my love scene."

"Do we need to get rid of his body? Let me know before the guys go off for the evening. I've found the density of a prone male body isn't easy to lift."

"No body," she said vacantly as she dropped down in the seat. "But I scared the bejesus out of him."

She'd always read about people having out-of-body experiences, but she'd never had one herself. That's what she felt like. As if she was watching some horrible movie of her life play out while her emotions—the ones that wanted to scream and yell and cry—floated somewhere in the ether so she couldn't connect the two parts of her body.

"Good job," Tess said.

Miller watched Tess move around the kitchen with familiarity. Her friend couldn't boil water, but she knew how to put snacks together like a champ. She pulled hummus and veggies from the fridge, and then she grabbed a bag of potato chips from the pantry and some dip. The rule was they had to have equal servings of healthy and junk food.

Miller couldn't hold it in anymore and took a gasping breath. Tess looked up at her, and her focus sharpened.

"What's wrong? What happened?" She put down the armful off food she had on the table and came to put her hands on Miller's shoulders.

Miller crumpled and she dropped her face into her hands as the tears started to fall. She never cried, at least never for herself.

"I don't even know where to start," she said.

She stared at the box she wished she'd never opened.

"You're freaking me out," Tess said. "Please tell me what's going on. The last time I saw you like this was after your parents died. Drink this."

Tess pushed a glass of wine into her hand and then took the seat next to her. Miller took a small sip, but her stomach was roiling, so she pushed it aside.

"Ohmigosh, are you pregnant?" Tess asked.

"What?" Miller said, sputtering. "Are you crazy?"

"I've never actually seen you push wine away before. It's the only reason I could think of that you'd do something like that."

"I'm not pregnant. Good grief. Last time I checked, sex was a necessity for that to happen. I'm going through a dry spell."

"It's because you work too much. You need to take a singles cruise or something and have a sex adventure."

"That sounds super safe. I'll get right on that," Miller said, raising her head to look at Tess. "Right after I finish this book that's due in a week and figure out if the finger I got in the mail today is real."

Tess's mouth dropped open. It wasn't often she caught her friend off guard, but apparently, the mention of dismemberment did the job.

"I'm sorry. Did you say someone sent you a finger in the mail?" she asked.

Miller took the box and pushed it toward her. "I was hoping you'd be able to tell me whether or not it's real. Maybe someone is playing a horrible prank." And using her brother to do it, she added silently.

Tess had a background in mortuary science, and she knew dead bodies better than anyone. She took the box and emptied the contents much like Miller had earlier until she found the newspaper that held the finger.

The wood floors of the old house creaked, and Miller assumed it was Tess's husband, Deacon. A few seconds later he appeared in the kitchen, freshly showered, and he came and kissed his wife on top of the head before making his way to the coffeemaker to start a new pot.

Never in her life would she have matched Tess with someone like Deacon Tucker. He was big and brooding and mysterious, but Tess was nobody's fool and she'd told Miller that there was more to Deacon than met the eye. He was a couple of inches over six feet and his dark hair brushed the tops of his broad shoulders. The only thing that mattered to Miller was that he looked at Tess like she was the most amazing woman on earth.

"How's it going, Miller?" he asked.

"I've been better," she said. "Someone sent me a finger in the mail. But thanks for asking."

He paused and looked at her, considering whether she was joking or not, and then he looked at the package his wife was unwrapping.

"Pissed anyone off lately?" he asked.

"No more than usual. I thought it might be fake. Like those ones you can get at the Halloween store."

"Definitely not fake," Tess said, using the newspaper to touch the finger since she didn't have gloves.

Spots danced in front of Miller's eyes, and she dropped her head to the table. "I think it's Justin's," she said.

"What?" Tess asked.

"Who's Justin?" Deacon asked.

The kitchen door behind her opened and she froze. She didn't have to turn around to know Elias stood there. Her body recognized him, as if they were tethered by some invisible string, and she'd know the scent of him anywhere. The soap he used was distinctive—clean—and even in her dreams it wrapped around her as if he were really there.

She caught his reflection from the corner of her eye in the wall of windows that looked out over the garden, but she didn't turn to face him.

"Justin is my brother," she answered Deacon.

He came over and took the seat next to his wife, looking at the finger in her hand.

"What makes you think it's your brother's finger?" Elias asked, coming to take the seat beside her, as if he were welcome in the conversation.

Her shoulders stiffened and she felt the heat of fury rush through her. It only intensified when he took a pair of gloves out of his pocket and put them on before reaching for the box.

"What are you doing?" she asked between gritted teeth. "You always carry gloves in your pocket?"

"Tools of the trade," he said, not sparing her a glance.

"Right," Miller said.

She was curious by nature. It was just part of the job territory because she never knew when a single sentence might spur the idea for an entire book. And while Tess was always open with her work and answered any questions she might have, the men who worked for her were not. But she could concede that a mortuary assistant might always keep an extra pair of gloves on him. Just in case.

He wore old jeans and a white T-shirt, and it was a stark contrast against the tan on his sinewy forearms. She knew Elias preferred to spend most of his time outdoors, and she'd overheard on a couple of occasions that he escaped to his boat whenever possible. His dark blond hair had a tendency to curl slightly at the sun-bleached tips, and she'd noticed he hadn't bothered to shave in a couple of days.

His green gaze was direct on hers, but she didn't look away. Even through the trauma of what was happening with her brother, shame washed through her as she thought of their last encounter. She felt the heat rush to her cheeks at how he'd rejected her so cruelly, and it made her even angrier that he'd inserted himself into her personal troubles.

"Best to keep extra prints off everything until we know something for sure," he said, taking the finger and the newspaper it was wrapped in from Tess. "Why do you think it's your brother's finger?"

"Because of this," she said, taking the ring from her thumb and holding it up so they could see.

Tess gasped. "King Solomon's ring?" she asked.

"King Solomon," Deacon said skeptically. "Like from the Bible?"

"The Bible, the Qur'an, the Talmud, and pretty much every other historical text you can think of," Miller said without bitterness, reciting the life of a man she knew by heart. "He was the son of David, and considered the wisest and wealthiest king of all Israel. His temple is legendary. The riches unimaginable."

"It's where they kept the Ark of the Covenant," Tess said. "Among other things."

"You're telling me that ring is a couple thousand years old?" Deacon asked, taking the ring from her so he could get a closer look.

"Yes, and it's been passed down in my family from father to son since then."

Deacon let out a long low whistle. "That's a hell of a legacy you have from your family. Most people have trouble tracing back a few generations. You're very fortunate."

Miller felt the lump form in her throat. She didn't feel fortunate. A lineage written on fragile paper didn't bring her parents back.

Deacon turned the ring slowly under the light. The band of gold was wide and there were several small dings in the material. But it was the emerald-cut amethyst that caught the eye. It was the most beautiful shade of purple she'd ever seen—deep and rich and vibrant. And carved from beneath the stone was the seal of King Solomon, similar to the star of David, who was his father, but with only a slight change in the star's design.

"This ring is supposed to have been in the temple?" Deacon asked.

"No," Miller said, staring at the ring. "At least that's not the story that was passed down through my family. What Justin and I were told was that Solomon made twelve rings, identical to the one in your hand. They represented the twelve tribes of Israel, and Solomon gave one ring to a prophet from each tribe before his death. God was angry at Solomon and told him that after his death, his kingdom would dissolve. After Solomon's death, the united nation of Israel fell apart when they refused to swear allegiance to Solomon's son, so they divided into twelve nations."

"I didn't know you were Jewish," Elias said.

"By ancestry, yes," she told him. "By practice, no. That's not exactly something a teenage boy is going to teach his younger sister. If my parents ever practiced, they never spoke of it. But the Bible stories were the ones they read to us when they were home, so I'm familiar with my heritage."

"How long since you've seen your brother?" Deacon asked.

"He joined the navy right out of high school," she said, shrugging off the hurt of his abandonment.

"He'd come home on occasion, but after he became a SEAL those visits became few and far between. I only see him at either Thanksgiving or Christmas, depending on his deployment. But he's always sent letters, usually three or four a year. It's always been our thing."

"Your brother is a SEAL?" Deacon asked, his brow arched in surprise, and then he looked at Elias.

"He was," Miller said, looking back and forth between the two of them. "In the last letter he sent me, he told me he'd retired from active duty. I haven't heard from him since then." And then she remembered the letter that had been in her stack of unopened mail. She'd left it at the house.

"I haven't seen him since we were in high school," Tess said. "He was always so serious. And built," she said, waggling her eyebrows. "Those broad shoulders and dark eyes. All the girls at school had crushes on him."

"All the girls?" Deacon asked, looking at his wife.

Tess grinned sheepishly. "I've always had a thing for brooding men with dark good looks."

"It's true," Miller said. "She went through a Johnny Depp phase her junior year of college that bordered on unhealthy."

"Shut up," Tess said, shooting her a look.

Miller grinned, but it wobbled at the corners as she thought of her brother. "He was handsome. He looked so much like my dad it was almost like having him home." She toyed with her wineglass but still couldn't bring herself to drink it.

"His letters are always filled with the same story, different location. I lost my brother to the same obsession as I lost my parents. We both had to grieve and cope with their deaths in our own ways. I think he feels like if he keeps searching for Solomon's treasures as they did, he'll eventually find out what really happened to them. I've spent the last fifteen years trying to get as far away from the tales of King Solomon as I could."

Except now she was writing her own story. Giving herself the same kind of closure Justin was looking for, but in her own way.

Deacon looked at the ring one last time and tried to pass it to Elias, but he shook his head. He was focused on the newspaper that had been crumpled in the box with the finger.

"The newspaper is in Spanish," Elias said. "It's dated four days ago."

"You think he's in Mexico?" Miller asked.

"Doubtful," he said. "This is the *Telegraph*. It's a South American newspaper."

"And you'd know that how?" she asked him.

"I'm well traveled," he said dryly. He began straightening out the crumpled newspaper and a white sheet of folded paper fell to the table.

Miller grabbed it before anyone else could and opened it up.

"What is it?" Tess asked, leaning over to see.

"Wow, that's terrible handwriting," Miller said, squinting at the words. "And it goes back and forth between English and Spanish."

"Let me see," Elias said, taking the letter right out of her hands.

Miller almost snatched it back, but he'd started to read it and she was curious. But boy, once he was finished she was going to give him a piece of her mind. He'd done nothing but wreak havoc in her life, and it was time he knew he had no right to her life and no place in her life.

"It's signed by someone named Emilio Cordova," he said, looking up at Deacon. "Sound familiar?"

"Not that I can recall, but it's an easy enough search," Deacon answered.

Elias read through the letter silently, and Miller tapped her fingers on the table impatiently.

"Cordova sounds like another treasure hunter," he said. "Apparently, Justin stole a priceless artifact from him."

"Because I'm sure this Emilio character got the artifact on the up-and-up," Miller said, rolling her eyes.

"Hey, I didn't write the letter," Elias said. "I'm just reading it. If you'll stop interrupting."

"By all means," she said, narrowing her eyes. Her anger was reaching volcanic eruption levels, and she noticed Tess kept pushing her wineglass toward her. Apparently, she had more pent-up anger at Elias than she'd thought, because she was *really* pissed.

He stared at her for a second out of those cool green eyes, but there was no shame or embarrassment over the way he'd treated her. There was certainly not the spark of interest that had been in his gaze only a couple of months before. He just sat there assessing her like she was a bug on a microscope slide.

He confused the hell out of her. He was brash and bold, good-natured. He had the kind of devil-may-care attitude she sometimes envied in those who never seemed to have any real responsibilities. If she had to categorize him, she'd say he'd probably been one of those boys in school who was always the center of attention. The kind of guy who was voted most popular and was probably the star jock. He had an easy smile for everyone, and that laid-back attitude that made him seem like he hadn't a care in the world.

She wished she could get him out of her head. Get his *kisses* out of her head. The not knowing was driving her crazy. Their bodies would've fit perfectly together if he hadn't stopped. Why had he stopped? She needed to put the whole mess behind her and move on, but it seemed that was easier said than done.

She'd had enough. The blood was pounding so hard in her ears from her anger she could barely hear, and she reached over to take the letter from him, but he began to read aloud.

My dearest Miller,
*   Your brother has taken something that is priceless to me. I'm sure you are familiar with the table of King Solomon. Your brother is most knowledgeable about that era. I knew your parents as well, so I can only assume that it is a family obsession that you share in.*

Miller felt the bottom drop out of her stomach at his words, and she withdrew her hands to her lap, lacing her fingers together tightly.

"How could he know my parents?" she asked.

"I'd think people with interests as specific as the treasures of King Solomon would run in a pretty small circle," Tess said. "There's only so much treasure to go around."

"I can't believe he's claiming Justin was in possession of King Solomon's table," Miller said. "There's no way. It's one of those artifacts that's the hope of treasure hunters worldwide. Like the Holy Grail."

"Should I assume it's more than a regular dining room table?" Deacon asked.

"It depends on who you ask," she said. "There are

plenty of legends about what actually happened to the treasures in Solomon's temple after it was destroyed by Nebuchadnezzar. But in the fifteenth century, when Spain held so much power and they were making conquests and sending out explorations, it's said they conquered Muslim nations and took the majority of King Solomon's treasure from them. If you ask the Muslim nations, however, you'll hear it was them who conquered the Spanish and *kept* the treasure. The table is supposedly made of solid gold, encrusted with diamonds, sapphires, rubies, emeralds, and pearls."

"Sounds gaudy," Tess said.

"Its beauty is supposedly breathtaking. The gold tabletop like a shimmering liquid pool. Its power is as coveted as the riches laid within the gold. Those who see their reflection in the gold tabletop see their true selves. They either see an inner beauty that is enhanced by looking at the table, so the viewer becomes goodness and light, more Christlike. Or they see an inner darkness that will multiply tenfold. You can imagine what could happen if it fell into the wrong hands."

"And they think your brother has it," Tess said. "That's not good."

"No," Elias said. "That's not good."

"I can't imagine Justin hauling a table around trying to get off an island," Miller said. "And he's missing a finger. It doesn't make sense. The weight alone would take more than one man could handle. What else does the letter say?" she asked Elias.

> I can only assume it's a family obsession you share in. Justin was unwilling to compromise and tell us the location of the table when we finally crossed paths. I'm sure you'll notice we sent you a trinket or two, so you know Justin is here in my presence.
>
> Despite our best efforts, he's remained silent, but while searching through his belongings we came across a photograph of you and a half-written letter, along with a single leg from the table. It is truly magnificent. But the power the table wields is useless unless it is whole.
>
> Does your brother always send you clues to treasures he's found in his letters? I bet he does. Just like in the one he was currently writing he was sending you clues to the location of your parents' plane crash. I've confirmed this hunch by telling your brother exactly what we plan to do to you if you don't help us find the treasure. He was most displeased, and he took out his anger on two of my best men. I've learned to never underestimate a SEAL. I believe he regrets the fact that he inadvertently involved you in this little quest for glory and riches.

Please accept our invitation to join us. A friend will meet you at the airport in Baltra. And from there, you'll travel by boat to see your brother. We're not unreasonable. We understand you'll want to guarantee his safety before you lead us to the treasure. If you choose not to be our guest, I'll unfortunately have to keep sending you packages in the mail until you can be convinced. Bring the ring.

"Ohmigod, I hate boats," Miller said, taking the paper from Elias and reading the last part for herself. "This can't be happening."

"What?" Elias asked. "You mean your brother getting himself mixed up with the wrong people and then dragging his innocent sister into the pit of hell with him?"

"Listen, you . . ." Miller said, reaching her boiling point. But Tess interrupted before she could unleash her fury.

"Deacon," Tess said, "why don't you and Elias give us a few minutes so no one gets hurt and none of our furniture gets broken. Last time I saw Miller this mad, she drove her VW Bug right through Carl Jansen's fence. She took the clothesline with it. His drawers were scattered all over town for days."

Elias opened his mouth to say something, but Deacon clapped him on the shoulder. "Take your time," he told his wife, kissing her on top of the head. He gathered the finger, the newspapers, and the box. "Let me know when we're safe from flying furniture." And then they both left.

It took Miller a second for the red haze of anger to fade before she realized what he'd done. "He took Justin's finger. And the ring. Your husband is a dirty thief."

Tess snorted out a laugh as Miller got up to follow after them. "He's not a dirty thief," she assured her, pulling her back down to her seat. "You know better than that. But he does have contacts and resources that might be valuable in finding Justin."

"If you say so," Miller said, wondering what kind of contacts a gravedigger and mortuary assistant could possibly have. "But if a picture of that finger shows up on Deacon's Facebook page, we're going to have a problem."

"I think you're safe on that front," Tess said. "Now drink your wine for some liquid courage so you can tell me what the hell is going on between you and Elias. And then we need to decide what you're going to do about this mess."

CHAPTER FOUR

The wine helped. A lot.

They'd moved the wine and snacks into the parlor area of the funeral home. Tess had never been a big fan of the overly formal room done in shades of cream, but Miller had always liked it. She imagined the original lady of the house, corseted in her finery, serving tea to all the other ladies of Last Stop in front of the grand marble fireplace, ornate moldings, and stained glass. There was a story to be told in this room, and she always appreciated a place that had a story. She paced back and forth across the thick Persian rug, while Tess lounged back on the couch and waited patiently for her to get it all out. Her anger had only intensified since she'd left the kitchen, and she knew from experience she just had to let herself wind down. Her temper didn't make itself known very often, but when it did it was best to steer clear of anyone who might become collateral damage.

She'd tried to go home to work off her mad on her StairMaster, but Tess had snatched her keys before she could walk out the door. Tess was tricky like that. Fortunately, she was also a good friend and Miller knew she could trust her with anything. She hadn't had the courage to talk to Tess about Elias up until now because she was so damned embarrassed about the whole debacle.

"The nerve of that man," she said, for probably the dozenth time. "How dare he just barge in here and butt himself into my personal business. And after what he did to me."

"You still haven't explained what that was," Tess said, moving from the couch to start a fire. She stacked the logs neatly and lit the kindling beneath. Tess was always much better at getting a fire lit than she was. It probably had something to do with the fact that Tess was a hell of a lot more patient and methodical.

"I mean, how dare he insinuate that Justin's caught up in dirty dealings," Miller said, continuing her pacing. "He doesn't even know Justin. And Justin wouldn't purposefully put me in danger."

"Baby, you have to admit it's a bad situation," Tess said softly. "Justin didn't meet these guys at a church potluck. No one is perfect, and you said yourself that Justin was as obsessed as your parents were."

"All I know is I'd trust Justin any day over someone like Elias Cole."

"Correct me if I'm wrong," Tess said, "but a couple of months ago, you two were setting so many sparks off each other I thought you were going to catch fire. You went home with the man, and then wouldn't mention him again. What happened?"

Miller paused in front of the fireplace and put her hands on her hips. "He didn't want me," she said.

"What?" Tess said, outraged, coming to her feet. "What an idiot. There's no way that man didn't want you. I saw it with my own eyes."

"I don't know what happened." She shrugged and continued her pacing. "We could barely keep our hands off each other the whole drive to the house, and then once we got there, who knows how long we went at each other in the front seat of my car. The neighbors probably got an eyeful."

"You live next door to Betsy Danforth," Tess said. "You know she can't see once it gets dark, and she's deaf as a doornail. You could've had the most cataclysmic orgasm of your life on your front lawn and she'd miss the whole thing. Mama has told her for years she needs to go get hearing aids."

Tess's mother, Theodora, had once owned the Clip n' Curl hair salon in town, and she'd been considered the hub for gossip and bad advice. She'd recently turned over the running of the Clip n' Curl to her protégé so she could go live with Tess's grandmother in a fancy retirement community. The two of them hadn't killed each other yet, much to everyone's surprise.

"I guess it's a good thing," Miller agreed. "By the time he got me to the front porch I was half-naked and would've done anything that man had asked, because holy moly, he knew exactly what to do with his mouth. And then it was like someone flicked a light switch. He set me down and pushed me away. And then he turned his back and walked away without a word."

"You're kidding me," Tess said, wide-eyed.

"I wish I were. I'm pretty sure no one in their right mind would make up a story like that."

"He didn't say *anything*? Not 'goodbye,' or 'my house is on fire'? Nothing?"

"Nope. Not one single word. And he had to walk home because he'd been driving my car. I don't know how he managed to walk three blocks with a hard-on the size of Nantucket."

Tess giggled and slapped her hand over her mouth, her eyes filled with mirth. "That was going to be my next question. I was thinking maybe he couldn't—"

"Oh no," Miller said, arching a brow. "He most definitely *could*. But I've got my suspicions. I think he's married and he had a change of conscience."

"I'm pretty sure he's not married," Tess said.

"Then that's even worse. That means he just up and changed his mind as soon as he saw me almost naked. If I weren't so awesome, that kind of rejection could play hell with my self-confidence."

"Your body is awesome. And I've never known you to have issues with your self-confidence unless you're talking about your books. Writers are so weird."

"Thank you." Miller dropped down on the couch and wrapped her arms around a pillow. "I'm just pissed off, but I'll get over it. I've never felt that kind of chemistry with a man before in my life. I don't have time to analyze it to death. Clearly, I've got bigger issues to deal with than Elias Cole. He can go straight to the devil for all I care. Justin is my priority. This Cordova guy sent a finger, so there's a chance Justin is still alive. And Justin's a SEAL. He knows how to survive."

"It's too bad you couldn't see that half-written letter Cordova said he found in Justin's backpack. What do you think he meant by saying there were clues in the letter?"

Miller stood up suddenly and let the pillow drop to the floor. "Justin's letter," she said. "There's a letter at the house. It came in the mail a couple of days ago, but I was working, so I just saw it on the table this morning. I've got to read that letter. I need to go."

"I'm coming with you," Tess said, leaving the food and drinks on the coffee table in a very un-Tess-like move. "You still haven't mentioned how you're going to handle Cordova's offer to help him find King Solomon's table."

"Well, I'm going to go home and read Justin's letter," she said. "And then I'm going to pack a bag so I can go find my brother."

"I'M GOING TO get in huge trouble for this," Deacon said, pulling up the camera for the parlor when Tess and Miller had moved from the kitchen.

"Afraid of your wife?" Elias asked. His stomach was in knots. He'd spent the last two months trying to forget Miller Darling ever existed. He'd been doing an admirable job until he'd seen the terrified look on her face when she'd walked into Tess's kitchen.

"You bet," Deacon agreed, grinning. "I don't like sleeping alone. I'm just saying I don't like intruding on their privacy like this."

They'd escaped to Gravediggers headquarters below the carriage house, and Levi and Axel were already downstairs, waiting for them. Dante had left for his weekend of debauchery.

"That was certainly an unexpected turn of events," Axel said once they'd coded their way into the secure room. He and Levi were already at the computers, the poker game clearly not of as much interest as the information Miller had given.

"No kidding," Deacon said. He immediately went to one of the high-tech computers and took the finger from the box. He pressed it to the scanner and waited as the fingerprint image was displayed on the computer screen so it could find a match.

"Justin Darling," Elias said, shaking his head. "That son of a bitch."

"Know him?" Deacon asked.

"Very well. We were both on the same SEAL team. Went through BUD/S together. He's got the training, but being a SEAL wasn't his first love. He enjoyed the allure of Solomon's treasure like his parents did. He missed a couple of ops that got called early because he was off doing God knows what. Nothing like going into a high-tension situation with a man down. He'd get called on the carpet, and he lost rank a couple of times because of his irresponsibility, but it never made much of an impact. He did his own thing. And now he's dragging his sister into it."

Axel whistled. "Mate, after seeing the way she treated you just now, she's going to be right pissed when she finds out you knew her brother and didn't say anything."

"I didn't have anything nice to say," he countered. "Besides, I couldn't blow cover by letting her know I was a SEAL. She's too damned curious. She'd want to know how I ended up at a funeral home in the middle of nowhere."

"Somebody turn up the audio on the surveillance," Levi said. "All I can hear is Miller's mumbling."

Deacon winced, but turned up the volume. Elias knew Tess wasn't a fan of the surveillance system inside the funeral home, but she also knew it was a necessity, just like the dozens of cameras they had on the exterior, and the main entry points of Last Stop so they'd always be aware if they were under attack.

"Tess is *not* going to be happy about this," Deacon said. "We made a deal never to listen during private conversations."

"There's always an exception to the rules," Elias insisted. "Miller might know something she didn't say in front of us at the table. Justin has gotten her into a hell of a mess."

"No kidding," Axel said. "Listen to this."

His fingers moved quickly across the keyboard and an image of a man came up on the big screen. He looked like someone you'd never want to cross. He was distinguished, his black hair peppered with gray and his mustache trim and neat. He might pass for handsome if it weren't for his eyes. Anyone who had a lick of sense and saw those eyes would run the other direction.

"Emilio Cordova, age fifty-one, born in Portugal. Mother is the only one listed on birth record. No father. Was in and out of juvenile detention until the age of sixteen. Then seemed to get smarter because he didn't get caught again until he was twenty-two.

Minor drug charges. Theft, battery, assault. And then at twenty-nine years old he meets a woman named Ana Cortez."

"You're fucking kidding me," Deacon said. "The Black Widow?"

"One and the same," Axel said. "If Justin has put Miller in the Black Widow's line of sight, she won't have a chance. She needs protection."

"Don't look at me," Elias said. He'd never felt panic, even during the most harrowing missions, but the thought of being alone with Miller for a prolonged period of time was enough to send him right over the edge. "She hates my guts."

"I noticed," Deacon said. "I don't suppose you want to shed some light on that. The last time I saw the two of you together it was everything I could do not to tell you to go get a room."

To make things more awkward, Miller's voice rang loud and clear through the monitor, and Elias dropped down into one of the seats at the conference table. He should've gone with his gut and turned the monitor off the second Miller had driven up. He'd still be playing poker without a care in the world.

"All I know is I'd trust Justin any day over someone like Elias Cole."

"Correct me if I'm wrong, but a couple of months ago, you two were setting so many sparks off each other I thought you were going to catch fire. You went home with* *the man, and then wouldn't mention him again. What happened?"*

"He didn't want me."

Three pairs of eyes turned in his direction and stared incredulously. He didn't squirm under the scrutiny, but he felt his skin flush hot. It would do no good to try and explain why he'd done it. It wouldn't matter that walking away from her had been the hardest thing he'd ever done. All that mattered was that he *had* walked away.

"Any other information about Cordova?" he asked. "He said Miller would be met in Baltra. What's the connection there?"

Axel quirked a brow, but he didn't say anything about the conversation happening inside the funeral home.

"A few years back, the Black Widow and the Sinaloa Cartel in Colombia had a territory disagreement that led to millions of dollars in missing drugs and a hell of a lot of dead bodies. She ended up with a price on her head, so she fled to Europe and has mostly stayed there since then. But she instructed Cordova to move the organization and do whatever he had to do so they became the most powerful drug cartel in the world. He's damn near accomplished that goal too. Cordova is a hell of a businessman.

"He moved their main operation to the Galápagos Islands. It's run by the Ecuadorian government, and they need the money the cartels can bring in. And the thing is, the Ecuadorian people love him. He's like Robin Hood. And the islands aren't over-run by tourists, so they don't have the U.S. Embassy breathing down their necks if the occasional tour-ist goes missing. The island airports make it easy for drugs to come in and out and be dispersed where they need to go. They've basically got control of the entire country, and several other pockets of South America."

"*. . . I don't know how he managed to walk three blocks with a hard-on the size of Nantucket.*"

Elias groaned at the sound of Miller's voice again. Tess's laughter was easily heard through the speakers, and there were various snorts of laughter from his brothers as they stared at him again like he'd grown a second head. Assholes.

Tess's next comment just added insult to injury.

"*That was going to be my next question. I was think-ing maybe he couldn't—*"

"*Oh no. He most definitely could. But I've got my suspicions. I think he's married and he had a change of conscience.*"

"*I'm pretty sure he's not married.*"

"*Then that's even worse. That means he just up and changed his mind as soon as he saw me almost naked.*"

"I'm throwing a punch at the first person to say one word," he said.

"I agree with Tess," Deacon said, grinning unashamedly. "I think you're an idiot."

"I've got my reasons, okay? Just leave it alone. And leave me out of this whole mess, come to think of it. Justin and Miller Darling aren't my problem."

"... I'm going to go home and read Justin's letter. And then I'm going to pack a bag so I can go find my brother."

"Of course she is," Elias said, closing his eyes and shaking his head. "Because it makes total sense for her to walk into cartel territory with that body and smart mouth, without any viable survival skills. I'm not getting involved in this mess. I'm going to take my boat out and go fishing."

"Keep telling yourself that, brother," Deacon said. "In the meantime, I'm going after my wife. I'd rather not find out the hard way that Cordova doesn't trust Miller to come to him of her own free will."

Elias dropped his head back against the chair, and then did it again for good measure. "Well, fuck," he said.

CHAPTER FIVE

Miller and Tess hunkered together on the floor of her closet, a box of her brother's letters in front of her and the newest one still sitting unopened.

There was something comforting about being in there with Tess. They'd done the same thing as girls, playing in closets and anywhere else their imaginations had taken them, whether it was Narnia or Alice falling down the rabbit hole.

The carpet was soft and they leaned against the long, padded bench that sat in the center of the closet. Clothes hung from every available rod. She didn't wear most of them—with the exception of the large section dedicated to yoga pants and muscle shirts with pithy sayings, also known as the writer's wardrobe. She had an equally impressive shoe rack, but most of her Jimmy Choos had unscuffed soles.

She really needed to get out of her comfort zone more. Working her ass off was all fine and good. She was a bestselling author and she was more than financially solvent. But she wasn't exactly experiencing life by heading to the city for the occasional girls' night out or to the gym a few days a week. Of course, she didn't really have time to experience life for the next year and a half. At least not until she'd fulfilled all the books in her contract.

Besides, with as much research as she did, it was almost like she was living the adventures she wrote about in her books. Only she didn't have to worry about things like getting seasick or dysentery, or losing her passport. Or getting robbed by gypsies, which had happened to another author friend of hers.

Her gut clenched at the thought of even attempting to rescue her brother—a SEAL—who couldn't even manage to rescue himself. She'd barely been out of the state of Texas, much less out of the country.

"It was a good idea to bring the wine," Tess said, pouring the last of the bottle into their glasses. "I've never drunk wine in a closet before."

"I have," Miller said. "Sometimes I like to think in here. It's pretty cozy."

"Do you still try to find the passage to Narnia behind your coats like you did when we were kids?"

"Every damned time," she said with a sigh. "It's a real disappointment. Adulthood sucks."

"I'll take it over high school any day," Tess said. "I

think I'm a little buzzed. You should open the letter while I can still think coherently. This carpet is really soft, and I kind of want to take a nap."

"It's a good napping place," Miller agreed, feeling a little buzzed herself. "My thinking sessions usually turn into naps. That's one of the good things about being an adult. I can take a nap in my closet if I want to. And I can dream and let my imagination run wild, without getting robbed by gypsies."

Tess looked over at her quizzically. "I was with you up to that point. I didn't realize closets were being targeted by gypsies."

"I have an unusual fear of being robbed by gypsies," she said.

"You have an unusual fear of quite a few things," Tess said. "But it's good that you recognize these things. And chances are you'll be mostly safe from gypsies in Last Stop. Now open the damned envelope and stop stalling."

"Fine," she said.

She picked up the letter that had Justin's neat block lettering on the outside, and tried to ignore her shaking hands. There was no reason to be nervous. It was just a letter. She slid her finger under the flap and the glue gave way easily. She pulled out the paper and unfolded two sheets. And then she read aloud:

Hey, Sis,

Sorry it's been a while since I've been home. Retirement has been interesting, and I needed to take some time and understand what life was going to be like outside the military. I think I'm at that point where realization has sunk in and I don't know what the hell to do with myself. I'm thinking of coming home for good, but there are some things I need to do before I can.

I've gotten the opportunity to travel to a lot of places in the past couple of months. Meet a lot of people. Discover things that Mom and Dad could only dream of. I found their plane in the Galápagos Islands.

"Ohmigod," she said.

The blood drained from her head and when her lungs started burning she realized she was holding her breath. She sucked in air and the words on the page blurred. She felt arms around her and realized Tess was holding her tight. At some point, hot tears had started falling down her cheeks.

"That can't be right," she said. "They told us their plane went down somewhere in the West Indies. They'd gotten information that part of the temple had been taken by the Spaniards and carried with them on their voyages to discover the new world.

"He's got to be wrong. Authorities never found

the wreckage. They said they either crashed in an area that was too deep to see the wreckage, or they crashed somewhere off course from their flight plan. There was no sign of a crash on any of the surrounding islands. The Galápagos Islands are nowhere close to the West Indies. What would they even be doing there?"

"Keep reading," Tess said.

I always thought they were crazy for going on that last trip. It seemed like an impossibly wild-goose chase. Why would King Solomon's treasures be hidden in a group of Spanish islands? I thought for years that maybe they hadn't been telling me the whole truth when it came to that last trip. They'd received information from somewhere, and they were secretive about it, and I don't know if you remember, but they left in a hurry. That was the night Dad gave me the ring. I asked him where they were going, but he wouldn't answer me. He just told me to take care of you and to let you know they'd be back soon. Of course, they never came back.

I went back and looked at their journals and notes, but there was nothing I could find. Just uncharted maps, made distinctive by the crude landmarks drawn on them. Dad knew how important the secrets of Solomon's treasure were, and that others would kill for the slightest bit of information. He was always very careful with his journals and findings. You might remember he only recorded things in his journals that were easy enough to prove.

The history of Solomon's people and his treasure are well recorded in many texts. God brought chaos to Israel after Solomon's death, but chaos can only last so long before there is complete destruction. Years later, Solomon's temple was destroyed by Nebuchadnezzer, many of the treasures stolen, including the Ark of the Covenant. But there was significance in the rings Solomon passed to the leaders of the twelve tribes. Those who held the rings were said to be prophets and protectors. It was an inheritance of great importance and sworn to upon the price of death. And it was a lineage to be passed for generations.

These protectors were able to hide many of Solomon's treasures, through the destruction of Babylon and the conquering by Alexander the Great. By then, there was no united Israel, and the chosen had fled for their lives. Many adapted to other ways of life, other cultures, just to survive, but they never forgot their promise to their king and their God.

Many of them joined the ranks of Alexander the Great. His people were great seafarers and sailed the earth long before the Spaniards. Their journeys took them to far-off lands, where they settled and continued their legacy.

Do you remember when we were kids and you and Tess would try to follow me when I took LeeAnn Hooks out to the field to park? I could hear y'all a mile away, and see your wide eyes through that crack in the rock. You were always a horrible spy.

"I don't know how he could hear us a mile away," Tess scoffed. "LeeAnn Hooks sounded like a cat that got her tail stepped on every time she got close to an orgasm. Your brother was hot, but he always had horrible taste in women."

"I don't think that's the point of that trip down memory lane," Miller said. "Remember what Cordova said about clues in Justin's letter."

"Right," Tess said. "Keep reading."

Did I ever tell you I read one of your books? You're a hell of a writer. I especially enjoyed The Pirate's Cove, *though the guys gave me a hell of a time for reading it. And I've got to admit, they might have convinced me to read it out loud, though I had to let someone else read the* love scenes. A guy named Rocket wants to meet you. Hope you don't mind that I gave him your number. Where'd you learn all that stuff? Never mind, I don't want to think about it.

Your portrayal of island life was spot-on. In your book, you call them the Triangle Islands, but I've seen them for real. They exist by another name, and everything is just as you described it, right down to the waterfall. You must've spent a lot of time doing research.

I know you remember the stories Mom and Dad told us as children. They haunt me sometimes, almost as much as the memories of the things I've done and seen as a SEAL. Needless to say, sleep for me is rare. But what the hell, I can sleep when I'm dead, right?

Dad always told me I had a purpose far greater than anything I could hope for. I'm not sure I've lived up to that expectation. But the stories have stayed with me.

Do you remember the miniature replica of the temple we built that summer? I'd have much rather been outside playing, but every day, like clockwork, Dad would have us gluing those little pieces together and following the diagram. Remember how hard it was to place the pillars just right? They kept falling over, and I think the one on the right eventually stayed that way.

You should know Mom and Dad were never just treasure hunters. They had to leave us for good reason. They'd found their higher purpose in life, and died trying to fulfill it. I've known my higher purpose since the day Dad pulled me into his study and gave me King Solomon's ring.

If I've learned anything in this life it's that evil exists. My one wish for you is that you never experience that. I've tried to keep you protected from my life. Take my advice: if anyone ever comes looking for me, start running and ask questions later. It's better to be safe than sorry.

I'll see you soon, kid. Stay out of trouble, and lay off the sex scenes. It's gross to think of my sister writing that stuff.

Justin

"I think I'm going to need another bottle of wine," Miller said. "How the hell am I supposed to know where to start by reading that letter? Do I just show up in Baltra and start looking for waterfalls and big rocks with cracks in them? I'm sure that'll be easy to do with henchmen on my back."

"Take a chill pill, Carmen Sandiego," Tess said. "You know I love you, so I can say this, but this is pretty much the worst idea you've ever had."

"Opening another bottle of wine?" she asked hopefully.

Tess didn't even crack a smile. "You cannot be serious about flying to the Galápagos Islands to meet with a bunch of strange men who are threatening you and your brother. They might shoot you in the head the minute you get off the plane."

"No, they won't. They need me to decipher Justin's letter and lead them to the treasure."

"And you think once you do that they'll just let you and Justin leave?" Tess asked.

"Of course not," Miller said. "I'm not an idiot. I just haven't figured that part out yet." Miller could practically feel Tess's frustration. Her redheaded friend wasn't good at concealing her emotions, especially when everything she was thinking played out across her face.

"You need help," Tess said. "Professional help. And not the mental kind, though I wouldn't rule that out altogether yet."

"Very funny," Miller said. "What I need is Rambo. Or at the very least, John Cena."

"A plan would be nice too. You can't just get on a plane and head straight for the eye of the storm. Do you even have a passport? You've never been out of the country before. You'll stick out like a sore thumb."

"Of course I have a passport," Miller said, undaunted by Tess's logic. "Where am I supposed to get professional help and a plan? Oh, I know, I'll just do a Google search and I'm sure someone with those qualifications will pop right up. Though now that you've put the thought in my head, I'm kind of leaning toward John Cena. Holy moly, I bet that man could go all night."

"I'm going to be smug right now because Deacon is like John Cena on steroids. And he can go all night *and* all day."

"Have you always been such a bitch?"

"Your jealousy is showing. But because I'm such a good friend, I'm not going to mention it."

"You *are* a good friend."

"Damn straight I am," she said. "Since I'm being such a good friend today, I should probably tell you I know the perfect professional for this little expedition."

"Is this going to be like the time we were in college and you accidentally hired a stripper instead of the Santa Claus we needed for that fundraiser?"

"No, but you have to admit we got a lot more donations with the stripper than we would have with the real Santa Claus."

Miller shook her head in disbelief. "We got fined by the campus police."

"This guy is better than the stripper," she said. "I promise. I'm going to get more wine."

Tess hoisted herself from the closet floor, and Miller held up her hand so she could be pulled to her feet.

"I'll come with you," she said. "I need chips."

"I saw the state of your pantry when I was getting the wine," Tess said. "Unless elves magically filled it while we were up here, the only thing you have to eat is a can of tuna and a disproportionate amount of barbecue sauce."

"I can't ever remember if I have any when I go to the store," Miller said with a sigh. "How are we supposed to get our nourishment and soak up the wine?"

"That's one of the good things about being married," Tess said, her smile a little wobbly. "If you call and ask for snacks, they have to bring them to you. It's a rule."

"So many damned rules," Miller said, as they opened her bedroom door and went into the hallway. It opened up into a small landing, and the second they reached the top of the stairs, that's when all hell broke loose.

The windows at the front of the house imploded, sending shards of glass flying in every direction. A yellowish smoke filled the air, and Miller's eyes burned from the acrid scent. She sucked in a deep breath and held it as she lost complete visibility.

"Go," Tess yelled, pulling her back and shoving her toward the bedroom.

Miller didn't have to be told twice, but then she thought of the laptop sitting on her desk and the almost-finished manuscript. She detoured to the left into her office, and she could hear Tess's curses behind her. She slapped the lid of her laptop closed and held on to it for dear life, tripping again over the boxes she'd set in the doorway as she ran out.

Footsteps crunched over broken glass, and she heard the crash of what sounded like a table being knocked over. Things could be replaced. She and Tess couldn't be.

They raced across the hall and into her bedroom, slamming the door closed and locking it for good measure. Though a good kick would be all that was needed to gain entry. Surely Mrs. Danforth had called the police by now. Unless she was sleeping. And it's not like she could hear anyway.

She had no idea who the men were invading her home, but her best guess was they were sent by Emilio Cordova. Apparently, he wasn't too confident in her accepting his request to meet in Baltra.

Tess let out a scream as a large boot crashed through one of the bedroom windows. Miller's beautiful, beveled, hundred-year-old windows. She was going to kill someone.

"Hold this," Miller said, shoving her laptop into Tess's hands, and she ran to her nightstand, where she kept her .9mm.

Her hands weren't as steady as she'd have liked them to be. But it wasn't like she was one of the heroines she wrote about in her books. Stuff like this didn't happen in real life. She'd taken the gun classes for research. She'd never expected to actually use the thing.

By the time she got the gun out of the drawer and pointed at the window, Deacon was standing there holding Tess in his arms and Elias was right behind him clearing shards of glass out of the way.

"Let's roll, Annie Oakley," Elias said. "Axel and Levi are kicking ass downstairs, but we need to get out of here so they can do a clean sweep. The last thing we need is the sheriff breathing down our necks."

"You climbed up my tree," Miller said, dumbfounded. Elias took her wrist and easily disarmed her. She'd forgotten she even had the gun in her hand.

"Yep, and we're going to climb right back down and run like hell to my place."

"Why are Levi and Axel kicking ass downstairs?" she asked. "Someone should call the police. You broke my beveled window. That's going to be a bitch to replace. I don't understand what's going on."

"They were spying on us," Tess said, narrowing a look at her husband.

"Good thing too, sugar," Deacon said. "Or y'all would be in a hell of a lot of trouble right now."

"We're going to talk about this later," Tess said.

Footsteps were loud in the hallway, and something big banged against the wall and dropped to the floor. Miller was guessing a body.

"Let's go," Elias said again.

"The letters," she said, running toward the closet to grab the small shoe box she kept of Justin's letters.

Her bedroom door shook as someone rammed against it, but the frame held.

"They don't make things like they used to," Deacon said. "That's a good, solid door."

Miller felt like she was in the middle of a weird dream—the kind where nothing but chaos flitted in and out of the subconscious until you woke up wondering what the hell had just happened and if you'd had too much to drink the night before. Which maybe she had, though usually half a bottle of wine didn't affect her quite like this.

Elias was back out the window in a flash and straddling one of the larger tree branches with his hands held out to her.

"Come on," he said. "I'm going to swing you down to one of the lower branches. Just wait for me there and I'll help you get the rest of the way down."

She looked to the grassy area below and felt her heart jump in her chest. Gnarled roots of the old tree stuck up from the ground. It was a *long* way down, and it was going to hurt if she fell. Heights weren't her favorite thing.

She tried to say something sarcastic to cover her fear, but all the spit had dried up in her mouth. She felt the push behind her, and Deacon all but picked her up and tossed her out the window to Elias. He grabbed hold of her hands, and just like he'd said, he swung her down to a lower branch.

She didn't have time to catch her breath before Tess was right next to her, her pale skin like a beacon in the darkness.

"Where's my computer?" Miller whispered.

"Deacon's got it," Tess said. "He almost left it behind, but I told him you'd kill him very slowly and painfully."

Miller let out a shaky breath and squeezed Tess's hand. It was all she could do. She wasn't sure she'd ever been so terrified in her life.

"Down," Elias said, putting an arm around her and lifting her when he needed to as they shimmied down the tree.

She heard nothing but breaking glass and chaos from inside the house, and she was devastated at the thought of what would be left of her home when the smoke cleared.

"Damn, it sounds like they've got a real fight on their hands," Elias said.

And the man almost seemed giddy about it. As if he wanted to run back inside and join them.

"I know," Deacon said, sounding a little disappointed himself. "It's been a while since we had a good hand-to-hand."

"I feel like I'm being pretty patient here, but I'll ask again," Miller said. "Who the hell are you people?

This is freaking Last Stop, and sexy gravediggers don't just bust into houses like G.I. Joe and save the day."

"Sexy?" Elias asked.

Miller couldn't keep a coherent thought in her head. This was so far out of her comfort zone she wasn't sure where reality started and stopped. This kind of action in real life was nothing like her books. She couldn't decide if she wanted to hyperventilate or vomit.

"Oh God," she said. "Mrs. Danforth is going to hate me after this. She'll say I'm bringing down the property value on the street."

"She already thinks you're eccentric and weird," Elias said. "And you'll give everyone something to talk about in the morning. Now get that fine ass in gear and start running."

He pushed her forward and she ran. She didn't have another choice. The apartments where he lived were only a couple of blocks away, and she wasn't at all surprised he took them through people's yards and through concealed areas instead of staying along the street side.

"Thank God for my treadmill," she said, feeling her lungs burn as she ran at a full sprint.

She was happy to note that she maintained pace with Elias. Tess and Deacon were right behind them, and she could hear Tess's occasional curse, which would've normally made her smile. Tess *hated* running. Or really, any kind of cardio workout. Which was why she stuck strictly to yoga.

The only apartment complex in Last Stop wasn't exactly prime real estate. It was dimly lit, and the beige building was a long rectangle of three floors, with an alleyway and stairs right down the middle.

Elias lived on the bottom floor in a corner unit at the back of the building, and it was darker there than anywhere else, as if he'd purposefully put everything in darkness. She wouldn't have felt at all comfortable knowing that anyone could be lurking in the shadows while she was inside, but maybe Elias didn't worry so much about that since anyone who broke into his place would have to be a complete idiot.

Elias didn't lead them to his door, but instead he hit the keyless entry on a black pickup truck that was parked at the back of the lot. Miller rarely saw him driving the truck. He woke early and ran for several miles before going into the funeral home for work. He showered and dressed for the day there, at least according to Tess after she'd casually asked. He had no need for the truck unless he was going out of town. Not that she'd admit how she knew his schedule so well, but she made it a habit to peek out her office window in the mornings as he ran by with his shirt off. Though, to be fair, Mrs. Danforth always seemed to be out on her front porch drinking her coffee when he ran by too.

Elias had backed his truck into the parking spot, and it reminded her of Justin. He was always paranoid about being able to get out quickly if the need arose. She guessed for SEALs, the need probably arose more often than it would for a romance writer, but it seemed a bit paranoid for a gravedigger.

He clicked the key fob and the lights flashed twice, and he hoisted her into the backseat of the cab before she could tell him she was fully capable of doing it herself. Tess climbed in the other side next to her, and Deacon got in the front.

Elias put the truck in gear and was moving out of the parking lot before they got their doors closed.

"Wait! Where's my laptop?" she asked, unable to keep the panic from her voice.

"Relax," Elias said, passing the thin silver rectangle back to her. "It's just a computer. You can replace it."

"You couldn't possibly understand how ridiculous a statement that is," she said, taking it gingerly and putting it in her lap. "This is my lifeblood. There's nothing replaceable about it. I've got less than a week to finish this book. I'd have let those bastards take me before I left the computer in the house to be destroyed at their hands."

"That's a little dramatic," Elias said.

"You try being on deadline and having a hundred pages left to write in a week, and tell me how dramatic you are."

"All right, crazy lady," he said. She could practically feel his eye roll from the backseat.

"We going in the back way?" Deacon asked.

"That's probably best," Tess said. "It's almost the middle of the night. We'll draw more attention to ourselves if it looks like there's a lot of activity at the funeral home. Cal's not an idiot."

Cal Dougherty was the town sheriff, and he definitely wasn't an idiot. He was a hometown boy who'd gone off and spent some time in the military and did several years at a big-city police department before moving home and winning the coveted sheriff's position. And while he wasn't an idiot, he had limited resources and even more limited experienced officers, so that worked in their favor.

"He's not nearly as interested in what's going on at the funeral home now that you're married," Deacon said to his wife.

"Will someone explain what's happening here?" Miller asked again. "Anyone can answer. Really. I don't care who the explanation comes from." Then she turned to Tess and said, "And why do you seem to know so much? What's the back way? Who are these people?"

"Lord, you ask a lot of questions," Elias said.

"I'm a writer. You'll get used to it," she shot back.

They sped along bumpy back roads to the outskirts of Last Stop and took a sharp right onto a graveled one-lane road. There was an electric gate in front of them, but before she could squeeze her eyes closed in fear of hitting it, it swung open and they drove right through.

"Look on the bright side," Deacon said. "At least the two of you are speaking again."

Miller narrowed her eyes at him. "He just flung me down a tree like Tarzan and his chimpanzees. I'm about to start speaking a whole lot."

"Team Alpha to Bravo," Deacon said into the high-tech watch at his wrist. "Status report."

"Copy, Alpha. Scene is secure. One Tango in custody. Five others in flight. Looked like a simple snatch and grab. They're all carrying tranq guns. Sirens on the way. We've got your vehicle and will circle around. ETA fifteen minutes to HQ."

"Copy," Deacon said. "On our way."

"My house," Miller demanded. "Ask about my house. Is it destroyed?"

Deacon relayed the question and she breathed a sigh of relief when she heard someone on the other end say there was minimal damage.

"Don't worry," Deacon said. "The Shadow will have things back to normal before too long. The local cops will think it was a burglary attempt gone wrong and that will be that. You'll need a cover story to feed the sheriff once he starts looking for you."

Miller cut her eyes to Deacon and pursed her lips.

"Like what?" she asked. "That I'm escaping for a long weekend with my Latin lover after we met on Facebook? I guess I picked a hell of a time to have a social life. I'm sure the sheriff won't notice that at all." She made sure the sarcasm was thick.

"I told you to stay off Facebook," Tess said, clucking her tongue in disappointment. "Nothing but creepers and old flames. Neither one is good for you."

"Thank you," Miller said dryly. "That's very helpful."

"It's easy enough to create a cover story," Deacon said. "A night out on the town. A weekend secluded away with no cell or internet so you can finish your book." He shrugged. "Just pick something."

She tapped her fingers nervously on her leg, the full meaning of Deacon's conversation sinking in. "Those men were going to kidnap me?" she asked.

"Looks like it," Elias said. "But we'll confirm once we get the Tango in for questioning. Levi will break him in no time."

"Levi," Miller said, sound barely coming out of her mouth. Little pieces of the puzzle started clicking together and she turned to Tess with a startled gasp.

"Ohmigod," she told her friend. "How could you have kept this from me all this time? You're like freaking M from James Bond. You're using the funeral home as a front and then you have all these ridiculously hot agents pretending to be your employees. I can't believe you didn't tell me. We've known each other since first grade. How did I not know you became a spy? When did they recruit you? College? Is that why you changed your major to mortuary science instead of sticking with premed?"

"Again with the questions," Elias said.

She felt like she'd just had the rug pulled out from under her. It was as if everything she'd ever known had been a lie. Added to what she'd already found out about her brother and that her parents' plane had been found, she was thinking this day in particular would go in the books as extra shitty.

"Whoa,"Tess said, wide-eyed. "I think your imagination is running overtime. I'm not a spy. And I'm not like M from James Bond. That would be an incredibly scary lady named Eve Winter. I'm sure you'll meet her. She's going to hate you, so be prepared. The rest of it you're pretty much right about."

"Are we going into the Bat Cave?" Miller asked.

"How many movies are you going to mix together?" Elias asked.

"It depends," she said. "Do any of you have a big hammer or turn green when you're angry?"

Elias snorted out a laugh. "You left yourself wide open for big hammer jokes. I'm not even going to take the bait."

Miller scowled as they picked up speed along

the one-way road. Rocks shifted beneath the tire treads and Elias seemed as if he knew exactly where they were going. He came to a sudden stop, and she started to reevaluate that opinion. They were in the middle of nowhere, and there was nothing to be seen from her viewpoint.

"Tess, if you weren't sitting right beside me I'd be a little worried about being taken out in the middle of an empty field by men who are clearly armed and dangerous."

Tess patted her on the arm and said, "Don't worry. They probably won't kill you." Miller's eyes widened and Tess said, "I'm kidding. Take a breath."

The men got out of the car, and Tess followed, so Miller opened her door and stepped out into the chilly night air. The rocks crunched beneath her feet, and she shivered as the frigid night air snaked down her shirt. She looked around at the bleakness of the area—the tall winter grass that shushed eerily with the wind, and the starless sky that had no beginning or end. And when the truck's headlights went off, they stood shrouded in blackness.

She felt someone touch her hand, and she jumped at the contact. There was a reason she wrote romance instead of horror. If she didn't keep her imagination in check, she'd be jumping at every shadow. Her heart pounded and the blood rushed in her ears, and then she took a deep breath and mentally told herself to get a grip. Tess would never lie to her. Except about being a spy, apparently, but other than that, she trusted Tess with her life.

"You're safer here than you'd be anywhere else," Tess said. "I can promise you that." A high-powered flashlight flicked on and she felt herself relax. "If you need help finding your brother, you've come to the right place."

Elias snorted again, but it wasn't with good humor this time.

"Listen, buddy," Miller said, turning only to realize he'd been standing close behind her. She'd almost walked right into his chest. That ridiculously hard, chiseled chest that had taunted her dreams for weeks. Too bad it was attached to a real horse's ass.

"I've about had it with your attitude," she said. "You barged into my business and now my home, breaking a window I might add, after you had the nerve to leave me half-naked on my front porch. The least you could've done is let me have an orgasm first before you ran off, you big jerk. There weren't enough batteries in the universe to fill that order."

His eyebrows rose almost to his hairline and he opened his mouth to say something, but she poked her finger against his chest and he shut up.

"I don't need your stupid attitude or your stupid machismo. I need someone man enough to help me find my brother without running off with his tail tucked between his legs at the first sign of impending orgasm."

Tess snorted out a laugh, but Miller was too mad to care about the fact that they had an audience.

"I don't need a grown man baby right now," she continued. "I need someone who is trained. Someone who can understand my brother and his thought processes. And someone who's going to give me good advice and support so I don't die in the middle of some godforsaken island. I need freaking John Cena. So unless you can provide those things, kindly shut up."

He reached up and calmly took her finger and removed it from his chest. She could feel the vibrations coming off his body, and his eyes looked like hard, black marbles. She swallowed hard, but didn't back down. Never show weakness. And if you feel weak, at least bluster your way through it so no one knows the difference.

"Actually," Elias said, "I *can* provide those things. I'm trained. And I know Justin's thought processes better than all but a few people on this earth. He was one of my SEAL brothers. Still want my help?"

If Miller had been a teapot, she figured that would've been the moment where steam would pour out her lid and she'd start whistling.

"Umm . . . maybe the two of you could do this inside," Tess said. "I'm cold and I've had to go to the bathroom for twenty minutes."

Miller was so mad she could barely see through the haze of her anger, so she turned her back to Elias, deciding it was probably best to pretend he wasn't there. He had to be lying. How could Elias have been a SEAL? There was no way he could know Justin. And if he did, why hadn't he told her?

Her temper still boiled, but she watched with fascination as Deacon parted the tall grass and a palm plate came into view. He placed his hand on the metal plate and then it lit up with a bright white light beneath his palm, eventually turning green as his hand was scanned.

The ground rumbled beneath her feet, and she took an involuntary step back, directly into the hard chest she'd been avoiding, and the ground rose into a hill in front of her. She quickly took a step forward to break contact.

"Holy crap," she said, heart pounding in excitement. "That's pretty much the coolest thing I've ever seen. Can I take pictures? That's going into a book. Where does this thing lead? Please tell me you have the Batmobile in here."

"Sorry to disappoint," Deacon said. "Just a couple of GEM cars and a three-mile stretch. And no, pictures would not be a good idea. And you really can't put this in a book. In fact, I need you to swear to secrecy that you won't speak about anything you're about to see to anyone. If you don't, the consequences won't be pleasant."

"Yikes," she said. "What about Tess? Can I talk about it with her?"

Deacon's hands were on his hips and he just stared at her a few seconds and sighed. "Yes, you can talk about it to Tess."

"I'm good, then," she said. "I never confide in anyone else anyway. No one can keep their mouth shut in this damned town."

Lights came on in rapid succession all the way to the end of the tunnel. Miller wasn't sure what a GEM car was, but by process of elimination she figured it was the two space-age-looking golf carts. They each had seats for four, and when Deacon got in the driver's seat and started the engine, she realized it was electric. She couldn't even hear it running.

"We'll leave the other one for the others," Elias said. "They're right behind us. Get in and hang on."

She wasn't left with much choice. She got in the backseat next to Tess and took hold of the grab bar just as Deacon pressed the accelerator. They took off with a speed that had her teeth snapping together.

"Definitely going in a book," she said.

They came to a stop with the same jaw-snapping motion, and Deacon and Elias were already out and up the small ramp that led to a large metal door before she could get her wits about her.

"Come on," Tess said. "This is the cool part. You'll like it."

"It gets cooler than what I just saw?" she asked. "You realize my mind is exploding right now. I just thought of about forty-two new book ideas as we were driving through the tunnel."

"I figured as much," Tess said. "You always tap your index finger on your thigh when you're thinking. Or when you have a good poker hand."

Miller looked at Tess in shock. "Are you kidding me?"

"Nope, you've done it since we were kids."

"Why the hell didn't you tell me? No wonder I never win at poker."

"Now you know," Tess said encouragingly.

"I haven't bothered to ask," Miller said, "but is this one of those moments where if I know and see too much I'll end up dying peacefully in my sleep or my car will accidentally run over a cliff with my charred remains inside?"

"Don't be ridiculous," Tess said. "You know as well as I do there are no cliffs around here."

"Not very reassuring, Tess."

Tess patted her on the shoulder and they walked toward the door. She decided to ask the question again later, just to make sure, but she couldn't imagine Tess pledging to spend her life with a man who'd snuff her out if she walked in on the wrong thing. It was all bizarre. And for anything to make sense, she decided she needed some coffee and sleep. In that order.

There was an embossed gold trident in the center of the solid metal door, and she watched in fascination as Elias typed in a code on the small keypad next to the door. A screen popped out, and much like the one they used to get into the tunnel, a palm plate slid out and Elias put his hand down for the scan. But the door didn't open. Another section of the wall slid open and what looked like a fancy version of military-grade goggles came out of the wall. Elias stepped up to them, and Miller realized it was a retinal scan.

"See? I told you," Tess said.

"I hope this high-tech factory has coffee and a bed," she whispered. "I've got to get a few hours' sleep before I can think of the best way to get to Justin."

"You're the only person I know who uses coffee to help her get to sleep. It's not normal. And I keep telling you, you don't have to figure out what to do about Justin on your own. You're in the same room as some of the best trained agents in the world. I promise, their ideas are probably going to be better and more efficient than yours at this point."

"What do you mean by *some* of the best trained agents?" Deacon asked his wife with an arched brow.

"Stop fishing for compliments. You and Elias are classified as *some*. The rest of the best trained agents in the world are a few minutes behind us. And wherever the hell Dante is. I notice you didn't mention him."

"It's his weekend off, but I called him back in," Deacon said. "He's not going to be happy."

There was a series of clicks as locks were undone, and the metal door slid open with a smooth *whoosh*. Miller didn't realize how cold she'd been until she walked into the warmth of a sterile white corridor. There was a set of stairs that led up to another metal door, this one without the trident. But they didn't take the stairs.

"What's up there?" she asked Tess.

"The carriage house," she answered.

Miller's brows rose. "The carriage house at the funeral home?"

"Yep, that's the one."

"I'm sorry," she said. "You're telling me we just took a twenty-minute road trip to end up three blocks from where we all started." And then it dawned on her. "Oh, wow. So this is what they were doing when they did the renovations a couple years ago."

"Yeah, pretty incredible, isn't it?"

"I'll say. I can't believe you found contractors to work that fast and keep it all a secret. I couldn't get my contractors to show up on time or stop peeing in my rosebushes. I tried to see behind those big tarps they put up every time I came over."

"I know." Tess grinned. "The Shadow aren't like regular contractors. They get things done, and they get them done quickly and quietly."

"Good. I hope they can find matching hundred-year-old windows to replace the ones that were destroyed."

Elias led them to the other metal door to the left end of the hall, this one with the same gold trident as the one they'd just come through. The security ritual was the same, and she wondered if you had to go through the same process to get out. She didn't like the idea of being stuck at the whim of another person, especially if that person was an overbearing alpha male who held a grudge against her brother.

"Y'all have mentioned The Shadow a couple of times. Who are they?" she asked Tess.

"It's hard to explain. But they basically get shit done. They're both prep and cleanup. And sometimes there's a hell of a lot to clean up."

"Not a very original name," Miller said, wondering how she could tweak it for a book.

"I'll make sure to pass that along," Tess said, rolling her eyes.

"The logistics of all this is blowing my mind. No one in town has a clue what's going on right under their noses. I can't even imagine the headache of trying to dig a basement in Texas."

"That's part of the reason they picked Last Stop," Deacon said. "The soil here is different from all the limestone that's found in surrounding areas."

"I can't believe I never figured this out," Miller

said. "I'm usually so observant. And Tess is horrible at keeping secrets."

"To be fair," Tess said, "you've been on deadline, and you tend to not pay attention to anything else when you're buried in a book."

"I notice how you didn't disagree with me about you keeping secrets," Miller said.

"Which is why I've also been glad you've been on deadline and not so observant. It made it easier to keep it from you when you stopped coming around the funeral home a few weeks ago."

"I stopped coming around the funeral home so much because you've clearly been training for the newlywed sexual Olympics, and I was never quite sure when you were in competition mode, so to speak. But from the frequency of the 'Closed' sign on the front door for long lunches and the amount of unexplained broken furniture around the house, I figured you'd at least made the semifinals."

Elias choked on a laugh.

"Shut up, both of you," Tess said, her cheeks flushed red. "We're not that bad. And we only broke the one chair. And it was an ugly chair, anyway."

"Well, in that case . . ." Miller said.

Locks clicked on the door, and then with a quiet *whoosh*, it slid open. There was a gold insignia of the trident on the white tile floor, but as soon as she turned the room opened up into a large conference room. The carpet was industrial-grade blue and the walls a soft ivory. There was a wall of monitors to her right as she walked in, and she noticed the different images from around town and inside the funeral home.

There was a large conference table in the center of the room surrounded by leather office chairs, and then there were individual workstations spread around the perimeter of the room with multiscreen computers. On the far wall, facing the conference table, there were three large screens.

"You might as well come on in and get comfortable," Deacon said. "There are drinks and snacks in the little kitchen area off to the side. I have a feeling it's going to be a long night."

"Why do I feel like I'm about to face a firing squad?" she asked.

"You've got good instincts, sweetheart," Elias said, pushing past her to make his way to the small kitchen.

"Don't call me sweetheart," she said automatically, and followed him. The kitchen was long and narrow, but everything was top-of-the-line, especially the coffeemaker. She could put up with anyone for a good cup of coffee, even Elias Cole.

"Right," he said. "After that tongue lashing you just gave me, 'sweetheart' is probably the last thing I should call you."

He moved in a little closer, and she could feel the

heat of his body, even though they weren't touching. She tilted her head back so she could see directly into the depths of his green eyes. The slow flush of arousal heated beneath her skin as he moved his head toward her, his breath feathering against her lips.

"You know what I think?" he asked softly.

"Not a clue," she said, her gaze dropping to his lips for just a split second.

"I think you wouldn't be so mad at me if I'd made you come that night," he said. "All that anger is nothing more than pent-up sexual frustration."

Her eyes snapped back to his and she took a step back. "Wow, your ego must be super heavy to carry around all the time." She leaned a little closer and kept her voice low, because she'd noticed it had gotten awfully quiet in the other room. "And just so you know," she said, the corner of her mouth quirking in a smile, "I didn't need you to make myself come that night. I managed just fine on my own."

"Liar," he said, but she sensed the change in him, and she would've bet money he was hard as a rock thinking about her pleasuring herself. "Left you hot and bothered, did I?"

"More like lukewarm and irritated," she said, taking another step back.

She needed to get herself under control. She didn't know what his game was, but he'd obviously made up his mind that he didn't want to sleep with her, while at the same time he'd decided to insert himself back in her life with Justin's disappearance.

He poured her a mug of coffee and then one for himself. "Sure, baby," he said, handing her a mug. "Whatever you say. Cream is in the fridge."

He started to walk off, but she said, "Thank you, but I drink my coffee black. And, look, let's just forget about what happened between us. It was meaningless." She smiled what was known in the South as her company smile, and she felt pleasure as his eyes narrowed.

Her smile turned into a look of sympathy and she patted his shoulder. "And bless your heart, you shouldn't worry about or be embarrassed by what happened. Some men just can't perform. I hear it's a very common problem."

She turned and walked out of the kitchen, and she could feel his eyes boring into the back of her head. "Oh, thanks for the coffee," she called over her shoulder.

CHAPTER SIX

Miller had mistakenly thought that sitting at the conference table next to Tess would make things feel more normal. But in reality, she felt like she'd been placed in the middle of someone else's story, and she was waiting to see what was going to happen next.

She didn't know any of the men who worked for Tess well, though she'd spent her fair share of time ogling them with the rest of the women in town. When men like that dropped into a place like Last Stop, people were bound to notice.

Before Tess and Deacon had married, the men had been a great source of entertainment, especially at the Clip n' Curl, which was pretty much gossip central for Last Stop. The women in town were relentless in their pursuit of Tess's five sexy gravediggers, coming up with outrageous stories and opportunities just to be in the same vicinity.

Dorothy Whitmire hid behind the trash cans at the funeral home one morning and then jumped behind the Hummer as it was backing out of the driveway. The way she carried on and lay down in the driveway, you'd have thought they'd backed over her at full speed. And she'd almost hyperventilated when Axel picked her up and brought her inside the funeral home.

Tess had told her Dorothy's behavior had been shameful, the way she kept undressing them all with her eyes. And she wouldn't let Axel put her down. Thank goodness Tess's grandmother had come in and summed up the situation pretty quickly, because she told Dorothy she was making a fool of herself, and that she should let Axel put her down because it looked like she'd put on a lot of weight. Tatiana Sherman didn't suffer fools lightly.

Since Tess and Deacon's marriage, the relentless pursuit of the remaining bachelors had grown to unknown heights. As Wanda Carmichael had so rudely stated, "If someone like Tess Sherman can bag a hottie like Deacon Tucker, then there is hope for us all."

Miller's feelings toward Wanda had never been very warm—not since high school, when Wanda had entertained herself and most of the other students by the lies she wrote on the bathroom stalls. And Miller had killed off someone in one of her books who looked and acted suspiciously like Wanda, though she'd go to her grave denying it.

Miller had a tendency to stand back and observe people in their natural habitat. Their quirks, sayings, facial expressions, and the way they talked about other people fascinated her. It's how she researched characters in her books. So she'd always seen herself as outside the fray of fascination when it came to the men. Or maybe it was just because her close friendship with Tess gave her everyday access that most people didn't have. Either way, she'd gotten to know them since they'd arrived. At least, as well as they allowed themselves to be known by anyone.

And now, to find out they weren't what everyone believed was just mind-boggling. Though she had to say it made a hell of a lot more sense now that she knew the truth. The Gravediggers. She supposed the name was apt enough since they did, in fact, dig graves for Tess, along with a myriad of other interesting jobs that required latex gloves. Tess was going to have a lot of explaining to do once she got her alone.

Miller looked at the larger-than-life men sitting around the conference table. They dwarfed her and Tess, and she wondered how they breathed with all the raging testosterone. The fight had obviously been a good one, as Axel and Levi both had a few cuts and bruises already forming, and they'd recounted the action that the other two had missed in a pretty graphic play-by-play.

Levi Wolffe was the newest recruit to Last Stop, and Miller had only seen him a handful of times in the past couple of months. He was the one Elias had said was an expert at getting information out of people. She shuddered to think how, exactly, he went about getting that information. But looking at him now, it was hard to imagine. He was quiet and watchful, his soft brown eyes taking in every movement and every word. He was tall and lean, but powerfully built. He was the most classically handsome of all the men. Between his chiseled face and body, swarthy skin, and dark eyes, he'd given the ladies of Last Stop a whole lot to talk about since his arrival.

Because *she* was observant, she'd also noticed he didn't quite see himself as part of the team yet. He held himself off from the others, sat pushed slightly back from the table so he could see everyone—a part of the group, but not really. He didn't joke or banter with the others. He was there to do a job, and nothing more.

She'd gotten to be friendly with Axel Tate. He'd been around almost as long as Deacon, and he seemed to be second-in-command. He looked to be a few years older than the others, and had a maturity and wisdom that seemed ingrained.

His Australian accent slipped out the longer he

was in conversation with someone, and he reminded her a bit of an untamed lion. He moved like a predator, smooth and graceful for someone of his size. He was built like a brawler and had the inherent good looks that most she'd met from down under seemed to share. It was a country of beautiful people. And if you could get past the heartbreaking sadness in his eyes, the clearness of the blue would take your breath away.

He'd always been friendly, and whenever she'd run across him the last couple of years he'd always been busy doing *something*. He was one of those types of men who couldn't stand to be idle. It was also curious that of the five of them, he was the only one who wore a wedding ring, though she'd never heard him speak of his wife. It was something she planned to ask Tess about later.

"We need to decide how we're going to extract Justin from the islands," Deacon said. "I think we'll all agree that going in full force is going to put us in unnecessary danger. Those islands and the surrounding areas are cartel owned. We'd be flying into the lion's den."

"A one-man operation would be enough," Axel said. "Slip in and out as a tourist. Extract Darling and we'd pick you both up in one of the stealth aircraft."

"It's doable," Elias said. "It's just figuring out where he is."

"Which is why it's going to be a two-man operation instead of a one-man operation," Miller said. "I'm going too."

Elias looked at her and then back at Deacon. "I'll pass," he said. "Anyone here is capable of going and getting the job done."

Miller tried not to let it sting that he'd rejected her. Again. The level of dislike he had for her was unexplainable.

"I'm grateful for the help from anyone," she said, the hit to her pride making her voice stiff.

"I hope you mean that," Deacon said. "Because it's going to be Elias. No one has experience on the water like he does. And this is a mission where saving a few seconds in the water might make a difference between life and death."

"I said I pass," Elias said again.

"You don't always get to make that choice," Deacon said. "There's no one better to go find a SEAL than another SEAL. Justin is going to use the water to his advantage, just like you would. And it'd be easier for the two of you to slip under the radar of Cordova's men, posing as a couple, than it would for you to go alone."

"Nope, nope, nope," Elias said, shaking his head. "She's a romance writer, for Christ's sake. She's never even been out of the country. What's she going to do if we get shot at or get stranded in the jungle? *Write* her way out of it?"

"Hey, I'm not an idiot," Miller said. "Just because

I haven't experienced the same kinds of things you have doesn't mean I don't have the knowledge. Besides, you're going to need me to find Justin. He left clues to the treasure in his last letter to me."

"You keep assuming I'm going to be with you," he said. "I can assure you I'm not." Then he turned back to Deacon. "I can't spend a couple of weeks in close quarters with her. She's inexperienced and she could get us both killed. I'll go in alone or not at all."

Before Deacon had a chance to respond, there was a series of beeps and the coded door that led back toward the tunnel opened and Dante Malcolm stepped into the room. He didn't look happy to be there.

He was dressed in what looked like a cashmere sweater and a pair of charcoal slacks. He'd obviously had plans for the evening that had been interrupted. He looked at the group of them sitting around the table, and then his gaze landed on her.

"This should be interesting," he said, brows raised. "But hardly worth pulling me in for."

"Are you familiar with Emilio Cordova?" Deacon asked.

"Drug lord," he answered. "He's taken over most of the day-to-day operation from the Black Widow. If I recall, her health has declined in the last year or so, and she doesn't trust her son enough to hand over the reins. Cordova dabbles in a little bit of everything, including weapons and priceless artifacts."

"Which would certainly explain his obsession with finding King Solomon's table," Axel said.

"Well," Dante said. "Now you have my attention."

Miller had always had an instinct about people, and rarely was she ever wrong. But there was something about Dante that wasn't quite as it seemed. He was more polished than the others—more practiced. His accent was British and his attire and manners always impeccable.

He wore three-thousand-dollar shoes and business suits that could pay a year's rent for most families in Last Stop. He was handsome and he knew it, and of all the men, he was always ready to flash a smile at an adoring woman. He was too practiced. Too . . . calculating. And there was part of her that didn't trust him.

Deacon took a few minutes to bring him up to speed, and no one interrupted this time when he mentioned the idea of her and Elias traveling to the Galápagos Islands to retrieve her brother, and possibly the treasure.

"Ahh, well," Dante said. "I knew it was too good to be true. We'll never get approval for this. You all know as well as I do that this is outside the scope of our parameters. It's best left for a paid-for-hire contractor. Finding Justin Darling isn't a threat to the world as we know it."

"Or maybe someone should step up because she's

our friend and that's what friends do," Tess said, the anger vibrating in her voice. Her skin was flushed and her red hair practically sizzled.

"I'm not disagreeing with you about friendship, darling," Dante said, giving Miller a nod. "My statements are based in reality. Eve will never approve an op like this, nor will she fund it."

"The men who broke into her house tonight were professionals," Deacon said. "They're a threat, and they could become a bigger threat. Once Levi is finished with the one we have in detainment, we'll know more about their purpose. We need to find out as much as we can about the mess Justin has gotten himself in. What's the story on this table he supposedly stole?"

"He didn't steal anything," Miller said.

"That's why I said 'supposedly,'" Deacon said. "It's admirable to defend your brother, but he's not in this situation because he did everything on the up-and-up. He's a SEAL, so he can handle himself in most situations, but dragging his sister into it is dangerous and shows a serious lack of forethought."

Elias snorted again, but Miller ignored it. There were large screens on the walls, and Miller jumped when they came on by themselves and a woman's face graced the screen. She was beautiful. Her Asian heritage was strong in her bones, and her jet-black hair was pulled back starkly off her face. It didn't detract from her beauty, but enhanced it. Her lips were slicked red, and despite the fact it was after midnight, she wore a black suit. She had on no jewelry, but she didn't need it. It wasn't until Miller looked into her eyes that she realized beauty was only skin deep.

She'd never cowered before anyone. But there was something about the woman on the screen that made Miller want to take her chances with Emilio Cordova and the men she'd just evaded.

"Eve," Deacon said, settling back in his chair. "Sorry to interrupt your sleep."

"I was up," she said coolly.

The tension in the room had ratcheted up about a hundred degrees with the appearance of Eve Winter, but by outward appearances, no one would know it.

"Status report," she said.

"At approximately seventeen hundred hours, a package was delivered to Miller Darling's door containing the finger of a male, possibly her brother. We later confirmed it when we ran the prints. Darling's classified military files came up, so there could be a possible flag at the Pentagon."

"I'll take care of it," she said. "Continue."

"Also inside the box was a handwritten letter from Emilio Cordova. It seems he feels Justin Darling stole a priceless artifact from him, so he's sending little pieces of Justin to his sister in hopes she can help recover the missing treasure. He's been searching for close to twenty years. He must want it pretty bad, and Darling is all that stands in his way."

"I'm familiar with Cordova," Eve said. "He doesn't get out of bed unless he knows he'll make close to eight figures, so yes, I'd say he must want it pretty bad. Working for the Black Widow has treated him well. I can think of very few artifacts that would fall into the eight-figure category."

"Rumor is Darling has a piece of King Solomon's table," Deacon said.

"And for a man like Cordova," Eve interjected, "a piece won't be enough. I'm familiar with the legend. Without the entire table, its power is impotent."

"I'm sure Cordova is trying his best to convince Justin to talk. It'd be hard to put a number value on something like that, but it would far surpass his standard eight figures. Justin sent a letter to his sister separately, and we believe it contains clues on where to find the treasure. We currently have the letters and Justin Darling's ring in our possession for testing."

"That's all fascinating," she said, "but the last I checked we're not treasure hunters."

"No, but a group of cartel members using military tactics and equipment descended on Last Stop tonight. We were able to defuse the situation and rescue Justin's sister, and take one of the attackers captive for questioning. Local police are currently looking into the damage, but they have no leads and nothing to go on. We'll take care of dealing with them."

"Good," she said. "Then I'm not sure why I'm wasting my time here. It seems Justin Darling can reap the consequences of his actions. Quests for glory and treasure rarely lead to staying alive. There's always someone out there who is more dangerous and who wants it more. It sounds as if Emilio Cordova wants it more."

"If the table ends up in Cordova's hands, then it will definitely become our problem," Axel said. "Because if what legend says is true, then Cordova and the Black Widow will become the kind of evil that's rarely defeated."

"That's all fascinating," Eve said, "and I'm sure we'll deal with Cordova at some point or another, but as of now, neither Cordova nor the Black Widow are in our line of sight. There is no mission where they're concerned."

Her black eyes met each face around the table, but they skimmed over Miller as if she weren't there. "What I'd like to know is why you've brought this woman into HQ? We keep secrets for a reason. Her life and her choices are her own, and they have nothing to do with the missions you're currently assigned, nor the ones you'll have in the future. By rescuing her instead of letting Cordova's men take her and the situation resolve itself, you've put the organization at risk. And that's unacceptable."

"Bullshit," Elias said, coming to his feet, his knuckles resting on the table. "We're not monsters. It's not our job to let innocent people suffer because it doesn't fall in line with the *mission*."

"You don't answer to your conscience, Agent Cole. You answer to me. And you answer to The Directors. Sometimes the few must suffer for the majority. It's the way of war."

"It's also the way of assholes. We do our job here. We do it better than anyone else in the world could hope to. You think Cordova is going to stop hunting her because she managed to escape his men tonight? What about the fact that Tess was with her? Are we supposed to let one of our own die, *anyone* die, because it doesn't fit within the parameters of the mission?"

"He won't kill her," Eve said coldly. "At least not until he has what he wants from her. The Gravediggers are not babysitters. Put her through debriefing, erase her memory of the events, and then set her free. I won't give the same orders twice."

The screen went black, and Miller felt the bottom drop out of her stomach. She looked around at the faces at the table, the urge to run thrumming through the pulse in her veins. This was real. This wasn't a book or one of her dreams. These were real agents who had a real job to do, and she wasn't the job. The sacrifice of the few for the safety of the many. Isn't that what Eve had said?

She pushed her chair back, and Tess grabbed her arm, keeping her in her chair. Miller looked at Tess like she'd never seen her before. They'd been best friends their entire lives, and Tess felt like a stranger. She didn't know this part of her life. What secrets she had. Or how far she'd go to keep those secrets. She couldn't trust her, not after the orders Eve just gave.

"Don't panic," Tess told her softly. "I can see all the scenarios going through your head. No one is going to let anything happen to you. We've all gotten quite good at working around Eve's direct orders."

"Elias," Deacon said, saying more in that one word than he could in a sentence.

"Fuck," Elias said, pounding his fist against the table. "I'll do it. I've got vacation time coming." He was still vibrating with anger after his conversation with Eve, and Miller had a feeling there was something deeper there to cause that kind of hatred for someone. And make no mistake, it had been hatred in his eyes when he'd looked at her.

Deacon nodded. "I was just thinking you looked like you needed a vacation. I'll submit the paperwork to The Directors, and I'll date it as of yesterday. Sometimes I'm bad about filing paperwork," he said, shrugging.

"Careless of you," Elias said, finally relaxing back in his chair. "Is it worth Eve's wrath? We won't be able to keep it from her for long. Hell, she probably already knows. Damned witch."

"I'll let Tess deal with her," Deacon said. "They've come to an understanding of sorts, and Eve hasn't tried to have her killed yet."

"I haven't tried to have *her* killed yet either," Tess said. "That's a two-way street. I do *not* like that woman."

"If it makes you feel better," Dante said, "I doubt she loses any sleep over it."

"No, that really doesn't make me feel better," Tess said dryly. "I'd prefer she appreciate my wrath like the rest of you do."

"I don't understand any of this," Miller said. "Who you are, what you do, where I am, how I'm supposed to save my brother, or why the hell Elias is taking vacation time."

"We're The Gravediggers," Axel said.

Miller rolled her eyes. "Yes, that's very helpful. Thank you."

"She gets snarky when she's scared," Tess said. "Or hungry. Or when she hasn't had coffee."

"I think they get the point," Miller said, glaring at Tess. "Of course I'm scared. I had a bunch of masked men break into my house, and then I was rescued by Mission Impossible."

"She makes a lot of movie references," Elias said to Tess. "Is that normal?"

"She says movies help cleanse her writing palate. She watches a lot of them."

"I'm actually sitting right here," Miller said. "It's weird you're talking around me."

"Just giving you a chance to settle some," Tess said.

"The Gravediggers are an elite ops team. Our agents are the best representatives from all over the world—MI6, Mossad, ASIS, CIA, SEALs—the best of the best working together to fight terrorism. We all had former lives, and we died in those lives so we could do what we do now."

Elias rubbed a hand across his rough cheek and leaned back in his chair. "And sometimes it's worth it."

Miller looked at the men around her in awe, but she felt the struggle from each of them. There had indeed been a sacrifice, and they each wrestled with those demons silently. She watched as Tess took her husband's hand and squeezed, and she felt a lump form in her throat at the connection they shared. Axel and Dante stared off, not making eye contact with anyone, but Elias stared straight at her, almost daring her to look too close. It unnerved her, but she didn't break his gaze.

"We're The Gravediggers because that's how we're reborn," Elias said, finally looking at her. He looked resigned. And sad. "When we go from our old life to this one, we're dug up from the ground and new life is breathed into us."

Miller felt the blood drain from her face. "Well, that sounds awful."

"It wasn't my best day at work," he told her. "To answer your other questions, you already know where we are. Our HQ is beneath the funeral home. That information is yours to keep, and if you can't keep it, the memory serum Eve talked about does exist, though I wouldn't recommend it. It's not pleasant."

"I'm starting to miss the days of 'ignorance is bliss,'" she said.

"There's something to be said for it," Axel said. "It's still a possibility. We can take care of Emilio Cordova and the threat presented there. And you can go back to writing your books and drinking wine with Tess."

"What about my brother?" she asked, afraid she already knew the answer.

"Your brother made his own path," Dante said. "Even if we take care of Cordova and his men, it doesn't guarantee we'll find your brother. Or that he's even alive at all."

"You can't find him without me to decipher the letters," she said. "If I go back to the way things were, then I'm leaving him to die. And I can't do that."

Elias nodded. "Which leaves us with your final question about why I'm taking vacation. The team can't defy direct orders from Eve. Not unless we've been assigned the mission. But I can do what I want on my own time, and I've got plenty of vacation days stored up. We're not on an active mission right now, just preliminary research, so now is as good as any a time to take it. I guess you found your John Cena after all. Though, for the record, I could kick his ass."

"This is all grand in theory," Dante said. "But how are we going to get them out of here without the sheriff or Cordova's men being able to pick up their trail?"

"How are you going to keep this from Eve?" Miller asked. "I don't want you to get in trouble because of me."

Tess snorted out a laugh, and it was the first time Levi had an expression other than an impassive scowl on his face. His mouth twitched with a smile before settling back into its usual grim lines.

"Eve knows all, sees all," Elias said. "And she could stop us before we even got started. But Eve has a weakness. She likes to play with her pawns. She's a mastermind at the game. And she'll watch and wait and see what we do and what we discover before deciding what to do with us or what actions to take. You think she wouldn't want King Solomon's table if it was handed to her on a platter?"

"Frightening thought," Deacon said. "But before you can be her pawns, you need to get out of here without anyone else noticing."

"Actually," Tess said. "I have an idea on that."

CHAPTER SEVEN

He'd been here before.

Most people didn't know what true darkness felt like. There was always some source of light streaming from somewhere, giving a person the ability to let their eyes adjust to the darkness. This was the kind of total blackness that eyes could never adjust to. The absence of all light.

Elias kept his breathing even, knowing that panic would only make the time go slower. His pulse was rapid, but under control, and a light sheen of sweat coated his body. His finger rubbed in a slow circle across the satin lining of the casket, just so he knew he was still there and hadn't faded into existence. They'd be able to breathe for five and a half hours before the oxygen ran out. They'd used up more than half of that driving to their destination.

He could do this. It was much easier than last time. The serum each of The Gravediggers were given to end their life so they could be put in caskets and transported to the United States without questions wasn't easy on the body. It was a paralytic, and it slowed the heart to the point where a pulse couldn't be found. But true hell was the brain waking up before the body, gasping for air and praying that they remembered to dig you back up before all the oxygen disappeared.

There'd been no serum this time. He and Miller had each voluntarily climbed into the caskets and let themselves be closed inside. He'd watched Deacon's face disappear as the lid came down and entombed him in total darkness. And he'd listened as the locks clicked into place. He had the key to open it from the inside, but it was amazing how loud those clicks could be as the casket key cranked round and round, sealing it completely shut.

He'd felt the disorienting sway as the casket had been lifted and slid into the back of the cargo van. He couldn't hear voices or even the sounds of the highway as they traveled, and he found it ironic that the caskets were soundproof. He was alone with the darkness and nothing but his own thoughts.

The plan was that the van would take them out of Last Stop and drop them at the nearest safe house. The safe houses were there for any agent at any time, but there was a seventy-two-hour limit before having to move to the next safe house. It was for the agent's protection and the agency's protection. And then The Shadow would come in and make sure nothing had been compromised.

He knew where they were going. The routes they were taking. The caskets had been brought through the underground tunnel leading from HQ to the empty field, and the van had been waiting for them there, just in case the sheriff stopped them and asked questions. But lights and sirens could still be seen down at Miller's house—every on-duty cop in the thick of things—so chances of being seen were slim.

They'd been right about the sheriff coming to question them first. A sleepy Tess had answered the door in her bathrobe with Deacon at her side, and she'd calmly explained that Miller was out of town for a research trip and she wouldn't be back for at least another week. Cal had told Tess to have Miller call him as soon as she could so he could let her know her house had been burglarized and considerable damage had been done.

Cal had never trusted any of them, and he'd run background checks on each new employee Tess hired. Not that there was anything to show in a background check. They were all exactly who Eve Winter wanted them to be. And they tried not to think too hard about the fact that she could change her mind on a whim if she got irritated enough. He wondered how far this little stunt was going to set him back with her. Maybe too far. But he found the longer he was with The Gravediggers, and the more under her thumb he became, the less he cared.

They'd never seen eye to eye on anything, not since she'd betrayed him and ripped everything he'd ever worked for and loved out of his grasp. She'd ruined his life. All for the purpose of making her team of handpicked agents. Eve always got her way. Even if it meant killing an innocent man and hanging another out to dry. Though he guessed he wasn't so innocent either, since he was the one who'd pulled the trigger. It was a nightmare he'd live with forever.

His heart pounded faster in his chest, and a tightness settled there as he struggled to calm his breathing. Thinking of Eve always brought on a rage he had trouble controlling. She knew it too, but all she did was stare at him out of those cold eyes, never offering an explanation or an apology. Maybe defying her direct orders would be the one thing to finally push her over the edge so she'd take him out completely.

This kind of life wasn't really living. He'd had a life. A family. A girl he'd been interested in. A hometown with friends on every corner who'd saluted him and thanked him for his service whenever he was in town. He'd been quarterback and homecoming king. He'd been an idol. Now they all thought he was a traitor to his country. A murderer. And there was no one to tell them any different.

His parents had finally moved from the town they'd both grown up in—fallen in love in—married in—and planned to be buried in. His mother had been unable to go to the grocery store without the shame of his name bringing her to tears. He'd never thought this would be his life. He was thirty-five years old, and he'd still had some good years in him as a SEAL. He figured he'd either die in the field or retire with honors and go back to his hometown. He'd eventually settle down and have a family so his mother would stop talking about grandchildren, and then he'd open a private business of some sort so his skills didn't get rusty and so he didn't die of boredom.

The best laid plans . . .

The day of his death had only been a year and a half ago, but it seemed a lifetime. Every day he spent as a Gravedigger was a reminder that loyalty and trust meant nothing. And that there were evil people in the world who needed to be brought down. It was the only reason he stayed and hadn't ended his own life. He'd thought about it. He'd held his weapon in his hand and stared at the matte black finish, the weight familiar in his hands, knowing he could pull the trigger. Knowing that if he did, not one soul would care.

The only thing that had kept him from taking his life was knowing that if he didn't take down Eve Winter, then no one else would. She was the definition of evil. She'd wanted him for a Gravedigger, and she'd orchestrated his demise. And her power was so great that no one could stop her. No one could know the truth of the heinous crimes she'd committed. But he was going to prove it. Somehow. Some way.

His only purpose as a Gravedigger was to destroy Eve Winter. And he'd gladly accept whatever consequences came from it. So he worked and trained daily. He'd formed a bond with his brothers, and he'd do anything for them—die for them. But he never took his eye off the prize. There was no room for anything inside him other than vengeance.

And then he'd watched Miller Darling stroll into the funeral home for the first time, bold as you please, a sassy grin on her lips and a hand cocked on her lush hip. And warning signs started flashing in front of his eyes. Her beauty was unconventional, but it was her smile that mesmerized him. Her mouth was wide, her top lip slightly fuller than the bottom. Her nose was small, but slightly crooked at the bridge as if she'd broken it at some point. And her eyes dominated her face, the color of aged whiskey, flecked with gold, and rimmed with thick black lashes.

When they'd first met, her dark hair had been long, almost to her waist, but he'd come to learn that it never stayed the same for long. She'd gotten it cut short not long after, and it had been vibrant red. And then it was a little shorter and a darkish blond he'd thought complemented her eyes beautifully. And then a few weeks ago he noticed it was miraculously long again, only shoulder-length this time, black again with bold blue streaks. He liked it. It suited her. They *all* suited her. But this style too would probably change before long.

He'd gotten to know her over the last year and a half, despite the fact he'd been determined to keep his distance. She drew him like a moth to a flame, and when she was on the premises he couldn't help but stop what he was doing and make a pass-through, just so he could see her face-to-face.

His attraction to her was more than skin deep. She was smart, and her mind was like a machine. She never forgot anything, including passages of books she'd read and the pages they were on. Her humor was dry and sometimes cutting, but it always made him laugh. Laughter was something he hadn't known much of in his adult life.

He knew he'd gotten to see a rare glimpse of her because of the closeness of her relationship with Tess. She didn't like to be in the mix of crowds, and she definitely didn't like to be the center of attention. When he'd seen her at viewings, or once when he'd been dropping off something at the Clip n' Curl and she and Tess had been there with a room full of women, Miller always sat to the outskirts and watched. But when she had something to say, people listened, and oftentimes they didn't understand they'd been taken down a peg with her subtle way of using words.

He'd let himself become weak where she was concerned. He'd taken his eyes off the prize, and in that moment of weakness, he'd let himself touch her. Let himself hope for something more than he knew he could ever have. He'd always been so careful not to touch her. And once he had lost his mind. Her body had been made for his, as if he'd never touched another woman but her. If he'd taken her that night, there would've been no turning back. His passion for vengeance would've turned to passion for her. There was no way to sustain both. He had to choose. And he could never subject her to this life, especially not when he didn't expect to come out of it alive.

But here he was. Voluntarily putting himself in her path. He didn't know if he was punishing himself or her for being such a temptation. His only thought was that he had to protect her.

He felt the jostle as the casket was lifted from the back of the van and carried some distance away before being hefted up a little higher and abruptly set down. Traveling by casket wasn't comfortable, and he wondered how Miller was doing. Some of the toughest men he knew wouldn't have been able to withstand what they were doing. Deacon, for instance. He said he'd rather let Cordova's men try to take him than ever close himself in that box again.

Deacon worked every day to overcome the claustrophobia that had almost crippled him from being able to do his job. And still there were days that were easier than others. Deacon had been the first of them to come over. An experiment. And the serum that had kept him in "death" had worn off long before he'd been dug up from the grave. It had been a kind of torture worse than many of them had already endured.

There were two sharp raps on the top of the casket. It was the signal they were in their final location and that they were on their own. He'd been holding on to the casket key in his hand, wanting to make sure he knew exactly where it was at all times. It would do no good to escape only to suffocate in the next hour.

Elias was a big man, skimming right at six feet, but he was broad through the shoulders and chest. That was going to be the challenge—getting his arm in a position above his head so he could fit the casket key in the tiny hole in the corner, which he had to find in the dark.

He brought his left arm across his chest and then moved it straight so the key pointed to the top of the casket. He slowly extended his arm, his grip on the key firm. Sweat drenched his brow and his body, and there was barely any room to get his arm where he needed it to be. But he aimed the key for the top corner where the hole was, and when the key touched the satin lining of the casket, he slowly slid it back and forth until he felt it slip into the tiny keyhole. Once it was in place, he began to crank the slim handle of the key until he heard the locks *snick* open.

When he pushed open the top of the casket he gulped in air and immediately took stock of where he was. This particular safe house was inside a railroad car, and it made the trip from north to south Texas on a regular basis. They'd gotten lucky that it had arrived at the station the night before and was ready to make its early morning run.

There was a sudden lurch as the train began to move at a slow and steady pace. He heard the whistle at the station and hit the button on his watch to light up the time. Six o'clock on the dot.

The train picked up speed, and he was jostled inside his makeshift bed. He undid the clasps for the bottom half of the casket and opened it up so he could get out. Then he took a flashlight from a pocket in his BDUs and clicked on the high-powered beam. His breathing came a little easier as he stood.

The railcar was locked down with the same security they used at HQ. The car was reinforced steel, and only the correct passcode and retinal scans could open the sliding side door to enter or exit the car.

He found the palm plate for the lights on the wall and placed his hand against it. Bright overheads came on, and the computer system began to come to life. He shoved the flashlight back inside his pocket and hurried to the second casket, kneeling at the top end. He placed the key in the small hole on the outside and cranked it quickly, and then he lifted the lid, unsure what state he'd find Miller in, but prepared for anything. Or *mostly* anything.

He found her completely still, her arms folded across her stomach and her eyes closed, her lashes fanned across her pale skin. Her hair was snarled around her face. Panic swelled inside him and he felt for her pulse, finding it in the soft thump in her neck beneath his two fingers. He released a breath and let his hand linger on her skin. She was asleep.

He'd been worried sick about her and she was asleep, snuggled inside the casket like it was a Sleep Number bed. He found that incredibly irritating.

"Miller," he said, shaking her.

Her eyes opened slowly, and she blinked a couple of times, and then she looked at him grumpily and tried to roll over to go back to sleep.

"Oh no, you don't," he said, reaching back into the casket to shake her again, but she swatted away his hands and made a growling noise that had his brows rising. "You can't possibly be sleeping right now. You're in a casket, for God's sake."

Her head turned ninety degrees and he wondered if he was about to see a remake of *The Exorcist*. And then he shook his head because she'd gotten him comparing everything to movies just like she did.

Her tawny eyes opened fully and he swore he saw a flame somewhere behind her pupils. Or it might have been the glare of the lights. And then, almost as quickly as it began, her face relaxed and her eyes softened.

"I'm in a casket," she said, looking around as if she'd just noticed.

"And you were sleeping. I can't believe you were sleeping."

"What else was I supposed to do?" she asked, surprised. "I haven't slept in days. I've been on deadline. I think I was asleep before they closed the lid. This thing is pretty comfortable. I should get one for my office. It'd freak people out. That's probably the best sleep I've had in a couple of years."

It wasn't often he was speechless. But Miller made it a habit of making him shake his head. She was a constant surprise; she never did what he expected her to.

He gave her a hand and she surprisingly took it as he helped her out. He tried not to think about what her skin felt like against his. Just the touch of her hand—something so simple and innocent—was like being on the edge of a dream—familiar and comforting, but not quite within reach.

He couldn't help but stare at her, but she didn't notice. Her hair was a tangled mess, and her face was free of makeup. There were dark circles under her eyes and her clothes were rumpled. But she captivated him in ways that were unexplainable.

"Why does it feel like we're on a train?" she asked, lurching slightly as she caught her balance.

"Because we're on a train." He let her go and took a step back. "This is our safe house for the moment."

"Cozy," she said.

"Well, it's no casket. But it'll do." He closed her casket lid and pushed it against the back wall, and then he did the same with his. "Watch this," he said. He put his hand against a flat metal plate in the wall, and the railcar began to transform.

"No way," she said, watching in awe as wall panels flipped to reveal hidden treasures beneath. There were narrow spaces for sleeping stacked on top of each other on part of one wall, and a kitchen area opened up next to it. Weapons of every make and size—from knives to submachine guns—fit in their assigned spots.

"This is going in a book too." And then she stopped for a second and the blood drained from her face.

Elias took a step toward her, afraid she might faint, but she looked at him with sheer panic in her eyes. "I left my laptop back at the funeral parlor." Her voice was barely a wheeze.

"Okay," he said. "I'm sure Tess will take good care of it while you're gone."

"We've got to go back and get it."

"No," he said. "I did grab the box of letters from your brother so we can go through them again. And seriously, you can't put all this stuff in a book. Eve would kill you. Probably."

"I can't write a book with a freaking box of letters." She looked at him like he was an idiot. "I need my laptop. I need it right now. I'm on deadline."

"I don't mean to sound critical, but you look like a deranged person. And your hair keeps getting bigger."

She glared daggers at him. "You don't mean to sound critical? Can you not see I'm having a crisis here?"

"You're about to go on a mission in tropical waters, where a dangerous band of terrorists will be hunting us, and you think you're going to have time to write a book? Much less carry a laptop around without it falling in the Pacific?"

"I've written a book while I've had the flu and I've written a book in my hall closet while tornadoes were touching down all around us." She looked fierce and a little scary, and he wondered what was wrong with him that he found that to be a turn-on. "I can write a book anywhere."

He was, once again, at a loss for words, so he decided on a plan of action and took two duffel bags from one of the hidden slots. They weren't airline regulation carry-on bags, but military-style duffels that could hold long-range weapons or an average female body.

"In this bag," he said, laying his hand on top of one of them, "are passports, cash, and credit cards. Grab a passport booklet from Australia or Canada. We can alter your hair and eye color. We have the equipment here to process your photo and add information. I can even give you a few stamps from other countries since you're such a world traveler."

"That would've been handy when I was in high school," she said, shaking her head.

"I won't lie," he said. "It comes in pretty handy as an adult too."

"What about yours?" she asked.

"Just grab mine from whatever country you choose. How are you with accents?"

"Terrible," she said. "The magic happens inside my head and on the page. When my mouth gets involved I usually get in trouble."

His gaze dropped to her full lips, and he hardened in an instant. He knew firsthand exactly how much trouble her mouth could be. He'd been helpless to withstand it. When his eyes met hers again, he noticed her cheeks were flushed and the pulse in her neck was thrumming wildly. As angry as she was, and as much as she wanted to shrug off the attraction, it was still there—still sizzled between them.

He placed his hand on the other bag. "There are clothes in this one. Should be something in there that fits both of us and will work for where we're headed. We can pick up extra clothes once we get to the island. You'll need layers. It's a temperate climate, but we'll be on the water, and the rain comes in every afternoon."

She eyed the two bags as if whatever was inside them gave her hope for what was to come.

"I don't understand this," she said softly. "I mean, I understand what we're doing and that people like you exist. It's a lot easier to conceptualize something that should be fantasy that's become reality than it is to understand Justin's thinking. I don't understand how he got to this point. It's that same kind of compulsion an addict would have. Why is he doing it? Why is it worth the cost of his life? For treasure and riches and glory?"

He knew she was right. He'd spent more time with Justin and knew him better than Miller could ever hope to. His obsession with Solomon was an addiction, and one he seemed willing to give his life for.

"You'll have to ask him when we find him," he said. "Maybe he'll have an answer you both can live with."

She nodded and started digging into the first bag, pulling out the stacks of passports and credit cards. She was hurting in ways he'd never understand. He'd never known what it was like to not have his parents when he'd needed them. He knew, even if he'd stayed "alive" and come home as a disgraced soldier, they'd have both greeted him with open arms along with their disappointment. But the love would have been there as well.

She'd never had that reassurance that the people who were supposed to love and support her the most never had. Even though she'd been blessed with a friend like Tess, it was impossible to fill that void where parental love should've been. Whether he'd wanted to be or not, Justin had become her parental figure once her parents had died. And he'd abandoned her just like they had.

Miller had a tough exterior. She was funny and personable, and anyone looking at her might think she had all the confidence in the world. But she was insecure when it came to love and relationships. Any kind of relationship. He'd been an ass, and all he could think is that his mother would sorely disapprove of how he'd treated Miller. But he'd only been thinking of protecting himself, and he should've been thinking of how to protect her heart. He'd failed miserably.

He wanted to take her in his arms. Hold her. Reassure her. But instead he watched her and waited until she looked at him, hoping she'd instinctively know every emotion rioting through his body.

"What?" she asked him.

And he drew a blank as to what to say. "There's a brush in that bag if you want to contain the beast."

He turned his back on her and contained his laughter, expecting the brush in question to hit him in the back of the head at some point. He might not know what to do about the future, but he could at least have a good time while he was trying to figure it out.

CHAPTER EIGHT

"I've never changed my identity before," she said once she'd gone through both bags. "This is so empowering. There was this kid Chad when I was in high school. He drove a Corvette and he was the *man*, if you know what I mean. He sold fake IDs to all the kids. Made a fortune. And then all the kids with fake IDs would head into Dallas and try to get into the clubs."

"A real entrepreneur," Elias said dryly. "Wonder what he's doing today?"

"He's a deputy at the sheriff's department. They always say criminals make the best cops."

"Who says that?" he asked skeptically.

"I read it somewhere," she said, narrowing her eyes. "That's not my point, though."

"I didn't realize you had a point."

She growled and watched his smile grow. Aggravating man. He was doing it on purpose, and she was falling right into his trap. But she couldn't seem to help herself.

"I can't remember my point now," she said. "You got me off track. I was only saying that I can see why it was so popular. There's something exhilarating about getting to become someone else for a night. To let go of any worries or stress and pretend your life is something completely different. To let your inhibitions go and just be free."

"You'd want to pretend your life is something completely different?" he asked. "You're not happy?"

"Of course not," she answered immediately. "I have an amazing life, and I'm incredibly blessed to get to do something I love to do, even when it brings me stress and worry. But I can see the appeal of escape and fantasy every once in a while."

"Isn't that what you do with your books?" he asked, really stopping to look at her now. She wasn't sure when the conversation had turned so serious, but the tone was different now. Something had shifted along the way, and her footing wasn't steady. "As the writer, you get to escape into these fantasies that you create. Seems pretty cool to me."

"That's very perceptive," she said. "And yes, it's exactly like that. It's part of the reason I write romance. In my head, they can go on any adventure. They can conquer any challenge. And they can overcome any obstacle, no matter how big. And they get to do it together. In four hundred pages, I can make reality disappear and give my readers the possibility of love and hope in any situation. There are no disappointments in the end. But there's love, and a hope for the future. How many people really get that in real life?"

"Not many," he said softly.

She watched the expression on his face turn blank and flat, and she realized his hope for a future was locked into being a Gravedigger, and never knowing if he'd survive one mission to the next.

He cleared his throat and she diverted her gaze to give him a minute.

"All I'm saying," he said, "is that this isn't a vacation. You seem much too excited about all of this."

She took a deep breath and decided to get things back on track. Emotions were running high, and something had changed in Elias since he'd woken her from the casket. It was time to get back in control. They were going to be in very close quarters for the next few days at least. There was no need making things harder than they were already going to be.

She smiled as she put the clothes they couldn't use back in the duffel bag. "Every adventure is an opportunity for great research."

"Yes, until you die," he said. "It'll be hard to write those pages from six feet under."

"Isn't that why you came along?" she asked. "To keep me alive?"

"No," he said. "I'm just not fond of relaxing vacations where I can lie in a hammock and do nothing but drink beer and watch the waves roll in for two weeks. That's boring. I'd much rather be doing this."

"I'm sensing sarcasm in that statement," she said.

"Huh," he said. "And I thought I was hiding it so well."

Elias stood in front of the rows of weapons, carefully making his selections and placing them on the table. She wondered how they were going to carry them all.

"Make sure you get one for me too," she told him. "I'm not going anywhere unarmed."

"Can you shoot?" he asked. "Or am I going to have to worry about a bullet in the back?"

"If I shoot you," she said sweetly, "it'll be in the front. You don't have to worry about that."

"That's good to know." He took down a Sig P229 that was just like the one she had at home, grabbing a couple of extra magazines to go with it. "Good thing you don't hold a grudge."

"Isn't it?" she agreed.

Being in the same room with Elias for this extended period of time was taking up more energy and concentration than she had. Her brain and her body were warring back and forth between jumping his bones and giving him a swift kick to the backside.

When he'd helped her out of the casket earlier,

just the simple act of his hand touching hers had her heart fluttering like a teenager in love for the first time. The shock wave of a binding connection shot through her body, and she'd tried desperately to look everywhere but at him, afraid she was the only one who felt it. And how pathetic would that be? The man had already made up his mind. If a man could stop that close to sex, he must *really* not want it. The sting of rejection was harsh, but she could deal with it. She'd always dealt with it.

"Don't think about it," she muttered under her breath.

"What's that?" he asked.

"Nothing. What were you looking for when you said I could change hair and eye color? I don't want to wear a wig. Seems like it would be a pain in the ass to keep up with the whole time if we're going to be schlepping through the jungle. And hot."

"Simple changes are best. Hairstyle, makeup, eye color . . . things like that. And dress and pack appropriately. You'll want to dress in layers. The weather is odd. The Pacific waters are cold, but there will be a few hours in the day where it's hot, and then the Pacific winds will blow in with the rain and drop the temperatures drastically. They're volcanic islands, so there are areas that are also completely barren."

"Probably not something they like to promote on their tourism brochures."

"It's not Hawaii or the Virgin Islands. We'll put it that way," he said. "The train will stop in San Antonio. Then we'll charter a flight to the islands. We'll take the cash and I'll have our new names printed on a couple of the credit cards."

"Man, working for the government is awesome," she said. "It's like free money everywhere."

"Think of it as your tax dollars at work."

"Yeah, that doesn't make it near as fun. I pay a lot of taxes."

"And now you finally get to benefit from it," he said. "That's if Eve decides she wants to let this scenario play out and not cut off all our funding or try to have us pulled out of the country. She could make things very interesting for us there. The last thing we would want is to end up in an Ecuadorian prison run by the drug cartels. The bullets in your gun would be better used putting us out of our misery."

"Well, that's something to look forward to," she said. "I'll make sure to leave that part out of the book. Not really happily ever after material."

"Not much of this job is," he said soberly. "She made certain of that."

"You really hate her," she said. "Eve, I mean. What'd she do to you?"

"She killed me and brought me back to life," he said, the bitterness evident in his voice. "She should've just left me dead. You'd better get ready. We've got a few more hours on here, and we still need to do some recon."

"Oookay," she said, guessing he didn't want to talk about it. "I don't suppose there's a bathroom on this train?"

"Press that green button behind you."

With that, he turned back to his weapons cache. Despite her anger and resentment over the way he'd treated her, it was impossible not to hurt for him. Not when hurt poured from him in waves at the very mention of Eve Winter's name. And as much as she wanted to harden her heart toward him, seeing his very real pain and not even knowing the circumstances of it made her soften.

She must be a glutton for punishment. Elias Cole was going to break her heart, and she could see it coming a mile away. Miller took the things she'd selected from the duffel bag and hit the green button on the wall. A door slid open silently and she was greeted with a perfectly roomy bathroom, complete with everything a woman needed to change her identity.

She caught sight of herself in the mirror and winced. Casket traveling hadn't been kind to her. And maybe Elias had a point about her hair. It was out of control, and needed more than a simple brush could do.

"I can fix that easily enough," she said, dumping the things in her arms on the table next to the sink.

She stripped down to her underwear and then found a brush and worked it through the snarl of tangles. She hesitated only a second at grabbing the scissors. It would always grow back, and it had been a while since she'd shaken things up with her hair.

"No time like the present."

Her hair was thick and a general pain in the ass, and it took forever to blow dry, so she didn't mind making her life a little easier. She snipped away until there was nothing left but a short cap that fringed around her face. It made her eyes look bigger and her cheekbones a little sharper, and if she said so herself, she didn't do a half-bad job. It was always good to know she could have a career to fall back on if writing didn't work out.

Everything in the duffel bags had been top-of-the-line, and she didn't recognize the style or brand of hair color. Must be government issue. She said a little prayer and applied it, hoping government issue didn't turn her hair green, and then she took care of other necessities.

She gave the hair color a good half hour of processing time before she checked it and decided it needed more time. Her hair was dark and bleaching the color out wasn't going to be easy. But she'd done it before, so she knew the outcome should be okay. And it was a lot easier to bleach such a small amount of hair.

She showered, enjoying the multiple jets and the

steam before she got to the business of scrubbing. And when she got out of the shower and looked in the mirror, she was stuck between complete awe and a sigh of relief that she didn't look like an orangutan. It was always a crapshoot when going from brunette to blonde, but her hair had always held up, no matter how much torture she put it through. And much like the fake IDs and endless supply of cash and credit cards, government-issue hair color was pretty much the best thing ever. Her hair didn't even feel like straw. It was nice and soft.

She'd only found a couple of items of clothing in her size, and she tried them all on just to make sure. A pair of capri jeans and a red-and-white striped shirt worked, as well as a pair of black yoga pants and a ridiculously soft hoodie in pale blue she hoped she could keep.

The makeup case was ridiculous and had more options than she'd ever seen in her life. And she didn't know how to apply half of it. She was a pretty basic kind of girl—powder, blush, eyeliner, mascara, and lipstick. And not a whole lot of any of it, otherwise she started looking like she belonged in the circus. She didn't see a point of wearing any makeup at all other than a quick swipe of tinted moisturizer. No one she knew would've recognized her at first glance. She doubted a bunch of cartel members with a photo would be able to either.

She eyed the contacts with curiosity and decided she'd try those later. No point putting them in and having them irritate her eyes for the rest of the trip. Now she just had to face Elias and see what he thought.

When the door slid open, he turned to face her. His body tensed and his expression went unreadable. She didn't know how long they stood facing each other in silence.

"What do you think?" she finally asked. "Will this work?"

"I think it will more than work," he said, his gaze slowly roaming from the top of her head down her body. She went warm all over, as if his hands were touching every place his eyes landed.

"I definitely like the blond."

"It's going to take some getting used to. I scared the hell out of myself when I got out of the shower."

He'd gone stock-still, and his body was fraught with tension. She couldn't even tell he was breathing. But there was nothing he could do to hide the erection that pulled the front of his BDUs taut, and he didn't bother to try and hide it.

Her body reacted, like an animal sensing her mate. Her nipples hardened to tiny buds and chills broke out across her skin. She crossed her arms over her chest and hoped he didn't notice how he affected her.

"What's the plan?" she finally asked, breaking eye contact. She moved so the table was between them, trying to ignore the tension that seemed to be building at an alarming rate.

"We'll fly into Baltra as a couple on vacation," he told her. "That's the only airport that will allow private aircraft. In the last decade or so, the cartels have started using the Galápagos as a transport location. They'll bring big loads of cargo in and divide it up into smaller aircraft. Then they'll fly off to various locations and drop the drugs. The drug trade there is growing at an alarming rate, and no one has figured out the best way to shut them down yet. There's a lot of politics and red tape involved. There are pockets of safe areas where most of the tourism takes place, but outside of those areas can be very dangerous."

"Let me guess," she said. "We're not going to the tourism areas?"

"I doubt your brother is sitting by the pool drinking a mai tai."

"I'd be happy if he was sitting anywhere," she said. "As long as he's alive. He's the only family I have left. And he's the only one who knows where Mama and Daddy's plane went down. He said he found them. We never got their bodies back for burial. There were just two empty coffins and a room full of mourners. As a child, it was easy to pretend that they'd come back someday. That they weren't really dead, but living out a life of secrecy for one reason or another. My imagination kept that hope alive with scenario after scenario, until one day, I finally realized they were *never* coming back. It's time there was closure. Closure in a lot of areas of my life."

"Then that's what we'll do," he promised her. "Even if something has happened to Justin, I'll help you locate where your parents went down. Twenty years ago, these were still very deserted islands. There are regions that are mountainous and still uninhibited. I promise you I'll do whatever it takes to find them so you can have that closure."

Her throat went dry and she struggled to get a grip on the tears that wanted to fall. "Thank you," she said, hoping he didn't noticed the quiver in her voice. She needed to toughen up her armor. They had a long trip ahead of them.

"I . . . umm . . . am done in the bathroom. I can put the contacts in now if you need them for the passport photo. Otherwise, I'll wait. I'm too tired to mess with them."

"Just leave them," he told her. "It'd be a shame to cover up your real eye color."

Her brows rose in surprise and she felt heat rush to her cheeks. Good grief. Her hormones must be wonky. She was acting like an idiot just because he gave her a compliment.

"I'll only be a few minutes cleaning up," he said.

"They don't know me, so it's not as important I change my appearance, but I'll let my beard grow the next few days. You need to start going through your brother's letters. There's a pad and pen there on the table. Write down anything you think he might be trying to tell you in some kind of code. We'll do the best to match everything up to the map."

"How long do you think we can hide out as vacationers before Cordova's men figure out who we are?"

"Hopefully, for a few days at least. If we're lucky, more. We'll be staying on a boat, so that will give us some freedom. The islands are still small and sparsely populated, so there are only so many resorts. A big part of their tourism comes from renting boats for people to stay on."

"Boats," Miller said, feeling the bottom drop out of her stomach. "I hate boats."

"I remember you mentioned that," he said. "I don't want to be insensitive, but you should probably conquer that fear pretty quickly."

"Sure, no problem," she said. "Hell, I'm thirty years old. That's a pretty full life, right? I mean, a couple hundred years ago I'd be ready to die of old age."

He rolled his eyes and said, "You're being a little dramatic, don't you think?"

"No," she said stubbornly. "Just make sure you have the mop and bucket handy for cleanup."

"You get seasick?" he asked.

"'Seasick' is too kind a word for it. You'd be better off just throwing me overboard to feed the fish."

"When was the last time you were on a boat?" he asked, narrowing his eyes.

"1998," she said. "I was on a Girl Scout trip and they had to bring me back to shore and rush me to the hospital. The boat captain said he'd never seen anyone throw up as much as me."

"You haven't been on a boat in almost twenty years. What kind of boat were you on?"

"A fishing trawler," she said.

"Seriously?" he asked. "Popeye would get sick on a fishing trawler. It's time to give it another chance. You're going to be on a yacht that's more expensive than a Manhattan apartment. Try being dropped into the middle of a turbulent ocean from a helicopter and then talk to me about seasickness."

"Considering that's your job and not mine, thank God, I don't have to worry about it."

"Modern medicine is amazing," he said. "You'll love it. And I won't have to throw you overboard unless you deserve it."

She narrowed her eyes. "I wish I could tell if you're kidding."

He smiled, but didn't say anything as he went into the bathroom and closed the door behind him.

She stared after him a few seconds and let out the breath she'd been holding. "This must be some kind of test. I did something horrible, and now I'm being punished. Though I have no idea what it is I could've done. I'm mostly a decent person. I give to charity. I hardly ever flip anyone the bird when I'm in city traffic. And I talk to myself when I'm alone, so I know I'm a great conversationalist."

She didn't see how this could possibly end well. He drove her crazy, and still, all she could think about was getting him naked. And now she was going to be thinking about it even more because he'd made the prediction that's how they were going to end up.

"Gah!" she said, throwing up her hands and heading to the box he'd placed on the table.

Miller looked around for a place to sit, and realized there were stools efficiently tucked beneath the table. The letters were filed in the box according to date, not that there were a whole lot of them. Seventeen in all. When Justin had been a SEAL, all of the envelopes had been exactly the same—small and rectangular, and of fairly good quality.

She brushed her fingers over the tops of the ivory envelopes until she reached the one she wanted. She pulled out a single-sheet letterhead from the Hotel Coronado. It wasn't a hotel she was familiar with.

Miller,
*   I'm letting you know I've retired from the*
service with full honors. I've actually been

*retired for a while now, but it takes some
adjustment returning to civilian life, so I've
spent some time out on my own. I hope you don't
mind some company for a little while. I'm hoping
to come home within the next couple of months,
but there are some things I have to settle first. I
don't want to intrude if now isn't a good time,
or if you don't want to see me. I understand if
you don't. I'll be at this address for the next few
weeks, so write me back and let me know if I'm
welcome.*

*I look forward to seeing you in person instead
of on the back of your book covers. You look just
like Mama.*

Justin

Miller caught a sob in her throat and slapped her hand
over her mouth. She knew she looked like her mother.
But it was somehow different when Justin said it. She
took a deep breath and shook her head, refusing to let
her emotions intrude on the task at hand.

"Ecuador," she said. Justin's return address was
in Ecuador, but the address didn't match that of the
Hotel Coronado, where he'd borrowed the stationery.

She wrote down his last address, thinking maybe
whoever he was staying with would know something.
Or maybe he'd made friends or spoken to someone
about his plans.

Researching was her life. She knew how to dig for information and read between the lines, so she quickly reread Justin's letter that had arrived with his finger and copied the passages she thought important.

> *I could hear y'all a mile away, and see your*
> *wide eyes through that crack in the rock. You*
> *were always a horrible spy.*

He'd mentioned the Triangle Islands and her use of them in one of her books. That was one of her earliest books, when money for travel and research had been scarce, so she'd not been to the places she'd described. Google had been her best friend during that book.

> *In your book, you call them the Triangle*
> *Islands, but I've seen them for real. They exist*
> *by another name, and everything is just as you*
> *described it, right down to the waterfall.*

What she remembered about the Triangle Islands was that the terrain changed from one side of each island to the next. One area might be volcanic and rocky, and the other might be lush with thick green jungle. There were a multitude of waterfalls on the islands, so that really didn't help pinpointing a location of where Justin or the rest of Solomon's treasure might be.

*Do you remember the miniature replica of
the temple we built that summer? I'd have much
rather been outside playing, but every day, like
clockwork, Dad would have us gluing those
little pieces together and following the diagram.
Remember how hard it was to place the pillars
just right? They kept falling over, and I think the
one on the right eventually stayed that way.*

"Well, that could mean anything," she muttered.

The bathroom door opened and she looked up to
see Elias. He wore another pair of black BDUs and
a dark gray T-shirt that showed a well-defined chest
and arms. Maybe he'd been right to initially refuse
the mission. Being alone with him was hard. Because
she still wanted him.

What she had to figure out was why she was still
so angry over what had happened weeks ago. No, not
angry. *Hurt.* She'd always had the attitude of letting
people go their own way. Of not holding a grudge.
But, dammit, he'd hurt her.

Either way, if she could put the hurt and anger
behind her, maybe they could get naked without any
cares or worries and put the sex behind them so they
could move on.

CHAPTER NINE

Elias was starting to regret his self-control.

Maybe life would've been much easier if he'd taken her that day when they'd both lost their senses, and every day after that. There would've been nothing but heat, because that's all there could have been. He wasn't in a position to ask for or want anything more. And because he'd tried to do the honorable thing, he'd made them both miserable in the process.

The table that had slid out of the wall served a purpose other than that of a normal table. He laid his hand down flat in the bottom corner, and immediately the opaque white top began to glow and become more translucent.

"What the hell?" Miller said, moving her papers.

"Interactive computer," he answered, and then he began calling out commands. "Computer, I need to see a 3-D map of the Galápagos Islands. Topical, plus terrain and landmarks."

Island formations came up from the table and hovered in the air, and Miller gasped and stood up. For the first time in a long while, Elias felt the pride in what he was doing for his country, the incredible inventions that some of the most brilliant people in the world were able to come up with just so they'd have the best technology had to offer to keep them more informed and safer.

The map wasn't just a map. It was real time, using the current satellite imagery, so the ships docked at the harbor floating lazily in the water were actually there. As were the waterfalls and the storm coming in from the west.

"You're kidding me," Miller said. She took her hand and tried to touch the image, but it separated like mist and her hand went straight through.

"The Gravediggers are special because our funding is from the private sector, even though The Directors consist of someone from the Department of Justice, someone from the Department of Defense, and the president of the most powerful weapons manufacturer in the world. It's a mix of government and the private sector. All the cool toys come to us first."

"The Directors?" Miller interrupted.

"They're who Eve reports to, though she's often selective in her reporting. They leave things in her hands for the most part. Probably too much."

"So seriously," Miller said, excitement lighting up her eyes. "She's like M is to James Bond."

"More like what the senator was to the Jedi," he answered. "She just hasn't destroyed us all yet."

"Nice one," she said, nodding in approval. "I didn't think you watched movies."

He pointed to the image of the white yacht docked on the island of Santa Cruz. "This is ours for the next two weeks. Trident owns it, along with the aircraft we'll soon board, but it's all sheltered through a dummy corporation that has known ties to the cartels. It's the easiest way for us to gain access."

"And Trident is . . ." she prompted.

"Trident is the classified, experimental program created by the Directors. The Gravediggers and The Shadow all work for Trident, under the eye of The Directors, and under the direct orders of Eve Winter. Trident is a domestic organization with international agents, and there's nothing else like it."

"Why would they do that?" she asked. "Why would the agents agree to that? To work for another country?"

"Because it's bigger than any jurisdiction or authority. Domestic terrorism isn't limited to American terrorists. It's international. Who better to teach us how to fight Hamas than the Mossad? Who better to teach us how to take down IRA terrorists on our soil than MI6, and fight against ISIS than ASIS, who've been fighting them on a global scale?"

Miller's brows rose in surprise and she said, "Wow, I never thought of it like that. You'd think if they could come up with something that brilliant, they could figure out a way for us to avoid boats."

He barked out a laugh and shook his head. "This fixation on boats is unhealthy."

"Funny," she said, "being on a boat feels unhealthy to me."

"Having the boat will give us the freedom to move from island to island without too many questions being asked. We can expect to be inspected. They know who owns the boat, but they'll want to see with their own eyes who is staying there and if we pose a threat. Emilio Cordova has a lot of power and influence, and once they figure out you slipped out of their grasp in Last Stop, they'll know you're somewhere on the islands.

"But they'll be looking for Miller Darling, and they won't expect you to have the resources you do now. It should buy us some time. Maybe enough time to get in and out without them knowing."

"You really think that?" she asked.

"No, but I can hope," he said. "I just want you to be prepared for what this could mean for you. If we don't shut Cordova down or give him what he wants, you'll be marked for the cartel. Whether you want to admit it or not, your brother has put you in danger. You're looking at a life lived in hiding at worst, or under constant surveillance at best."

He could tell by the look on her face that she *hadn't* thought of it.

"You've got to prepare to have your life invaded. They'll be tracking your credit cards and passport. They'll know everything about you by the time they're finished. They'll know your strengths and your weaknesses. The people who matter most in your life. And they'll know everything about your parents and your brother, even things that you don't know that they can use against you."

"I hope they don't die of boredom," she said, trying to make light of it. But he could see the fear in her eyes—the understanding that everything she'd known had changed. "I can't imagine it would be very interesting for them to discover that I sit around in yoga pants and work an average of seventeen hours a day. Or that I'm a member of one of those wine-of-the-month clubs. Or that I don't have animals because I'm terrified I'll be lost in a book and forget to feed them. That's kind of how I feel about kids too."

His lips twitched, but she'd given a pretty accurate portrayal of her life. The Gravediggers had already done a full background on her when they'd discovered her friendship with Tess and how much time she'd be spending at the funeral home. He'd spent hours poring over her file. She was an enigma, a woman who enjoyed the solitude of her work. She'd invested her money wisely, paid for her house, which was constantly needing repairs of some kind, and she drove a modest car. She lived her life and enjoyed it. It had also been some time since she'd been in a relationship. She'd been in two long-term relationships, but had never been willing to go the long haul with marriage.

She and Tess had the kind of relationship he understood. He'd felt that closeness when he'd been a SEAL. And he felt it to a degree when he'd become a Gravedigger. But it wasn't quite the same. They weren't there because they had the young idealistic notions of saving the world. Their choices had all been taken from them, and it was different when you knew the real cost of freedom. But they were still his brothers, and he knew they were the only ones he could count on in this world.

"I'm sure they'll be fascinated by your wine-club membership and your fear of starving animals and children," he said. "But the bigger concern is them tracking you down, different hair and identity or not. There's only so long you're going to be able to hide that smile and stubborn chin."

"What's wrong with my smile?" she asked, getting her dander up again.

"There's nothing wrong with your smile," he told her, rolling his eyes. "It's distinctive. And it attracts attention."

"Well, that certainly doesn't make me feel self-conscious at all. Like Julia Roberts distinctive, or the Penguin from *Batman* distinctive?"

"And . . . we're back to the movies," he said, frustrated. "And the answer is neither. Your smile lights up a freaking room. It makes everyone stop what they're doing just so they can look. And that full top lip is so fucking sexy it's everything I can do not to bite it."

"Geez," she said, licking the lip in question and driving him crazy. "As far as compliments go, you have a way of delivering."

"You drive me crazy," he said. "And if you keep licking your lips I'm going to kiss you."

"Right, sorry," she said. "Umm . . . I can't remember what we were talking about."

"We were talking about Cordova tracking you down on the islands."

"It'll take time," she said. "We won't be the only people vacationing there."

"They've got the men and the resources. And the locals know to answer questions when they're asked or keep their mouths shut."

He swiped his finger on the tabletop to change the view. "All the islands together only inhabit about twenty-five thousand people. Tourism doesn't add that much to the population, especially at this time of year, because it's not a tropical destination for people escaping the cold weather.

"Look at this area here," he said, pointing to a

small group of islands to the northeast of the main islands of Galápagos. "These are the Triangle Islands. Or Aguas Mortales, as the locals call them. The way the islands form the triangle lets water flow in several different directions, so the waters at the center of the triangle have a swirling pattern that's dangerous to anyone or any vessel in the water. You can see how turbulent it is through the 3-D rendering.

"This island here is uninhabited. Lots of diving, though, and hikers. It's a volcanic island, so a good part of it is barren and the terrain rough like you see here. But you can also see the treed areas are dense and basically untouched. The inside of the island is mountainous in areas and hard to gain access to. The other two islands are sparsely populated—and I mean *very* sparsely—but they're still difficult to access on the interior of the island because of the waters. We're going to have to do some hiking and camping."

"I'm cool with hiking and camping," she said. "But I should warn you I'm not cool with snakes. I've tried. I just can't deal. You'll be better off shooting me."

"You don't like boats or snakes," he said. "I'll add it to the list of things we're most likely to run into while on the islands. Is there anything else I should know about?"

"I'm not a superfan of active volcanoes or lava, but I figure the chances of that are pretty small. What was that movie with Pierce Brosnan and the volcano?"

"*Dante's Peak*?" he asked, wondering how in the hell he knew that.

"That's the one," she said. "Terrible movie. Gave me nightmares for weeks. I still won't step foot in a hot spring because I don't want to accidentally be boiled alive."

"You have a lot of fears that have very little chance of ever coming to fruition. You must entertain the hell out of your therapist."

She quirked a brow at him and put a hand on her cocked hip. "I'm sure I do. You think it's easy to be a writer? You try having all those voices talking in your head all the time and see how it makes you feel."

"It'd make me feel nuts," he said. "That's my new biggest fear. Becoming a writer."

"You're a laugh a minute," she said. "What was your old biggest fear?"

"Running out of ice cream," he said. "I have to have it every night before bed or I can't sleep worth a damn."

"Wow," she said. "Really not what I was expecting."

"Why? Only a foolish man doesn't have fears," he said. "Fear is healthy. When you stop being afraid, you usually don't survive long in this line of work. And who wouldn't be afraid of clowns and creepy dolls?"

He segmented the three islands so they could be

seen separately. He was going to spend more time studying the mountainous regions. Finding the crash site of her parents was important to her, but he knew the statistics as well as anyone—most small plane crashes were never found.

"This is kind of blowing my mind," she said. "I don't understand how you can get things in place so quickly. Private planes out of San Antonio and boats off of Santa Cruz."

"A lot of cash and a lot of connections," he said. "Just because Eve gave the orders to abandon the operation doesn't mean any of us are going to. Tess and the others are working at HQ and they've been busy securing the things we'll need."

"I don't understand," she said. "Eve gave direct orders. Why wouldn't she try to stop you?"

"Eve is never one to underestimate or try to second guess. No one knows why she does the things she does. She could give Cordova our exact location or make sure we were detained by the Ecuadorian police, just for the hell of it. But she won't."

"Why not?" she asked. "If she's angry enough it would be the perfect revenge."

"Mostly because of her ego," he said. "Revenge isn't her primary motive for anything. She's cold as ice. She was lying about how Cordova isn't a current priority. He and the Black Widow both have been on our watch list since I joined with The Gravediggers.

Our job is mainly to deal with threats of terrorism that occur on U.S. soil, and we've not had a reason to go after them because the cartel hasn't been doing a lot of business in the United States in the last several years. Their drugs and guns still end up here, but they're coming in by other avenues. They do a big business with the Russians, as well as several factions throughout the Middle East and Africa.

"As soon as Cordova's men crossed the border and came to abduct you, it gave us the unofficial permission we needed to go after them. Taking down the Black Widow's cartel, even a small portion of it, will be a feather in Eve's cap. It'll mean increased funding and all kinds of things that give her a little more power. If The Directors don't watch it, Eve will be in charge of everything and they'll be wondering what happened."

"What happens if things don't work out the way you expect?" she asked. "What if she doesn't let you use all these resources and we end up in an Ecuadorian prison? What's the game plan then?"

"We'll deal with that when the time comes," he said, mouth grim. "But you'll be safe. Deacon will see to it."

He looked at the Panerai dive watch on his wrist. It wouldn't be too much longer before they were at their stop, and they'd need to move quickly.

"What did you find out from the letters?" he asked.

"Justin's last known address was in Ecuador. He used stationery from the Hotel Coronado, but it wasn't the same address he listed in the letter. He was there for at least a few weeks, maybe more."

"What's the address?" he asked.

She handed over the pad she'd been making notes on and he called out the address for the computer to locate.

"He was in San Lorenzo," Elias said. "That's a three-day boat ride to the islands, according to the computer. San Lorenzo is a port town. I doubt he stayed there longer than to get his mail, buy supplies, or gas up his boat. His time was better spent on the water searching the islands."

"Where'd he get a boat?"

"There are plenty to rent or buy in the area," he said. "It's become a big business for a lot of the locals. Justin is as comfortable on the water as anyone. He'd know how and where to navigate. And he'd know when to abandon the boat and go in by foot. Your brother isn't stupid. He'd know he was being watched. All divers and treasure hunters are. He'd leave his boat anchored somewhere and find a different way of reaching his destination.

"What else did you find?"

"I just wrote down notes from his last letter. Did you read it?"

His lips twitched and he met her gaze. "Yeah, I

read it. I remember when he read your book out loud. That was most definitely one of those memorable periods in my life. I can't believe Rocket never called you."

Her mouth dropped open in surprise. "You mean he was serious about that? You're telling me a bunch of badass Navy SEALs really sat around and read my book?"

"Technically, one of the guys caught Justin reading it, and no one really believed his sister wrote it." Elias shrugged without apology. "So we stole it and read it aloud. By the time Rocket finished the first chapter we were all hooked and wanted to know what happened. He did a great job with all the voices. And it wasn't all mushy stuff like we thought it'd be. There was lots of action and blowing up stuff. And you obviously did your research on all the weapons."

She stared at him as if she'd never heard a compliment before and then said, "Umm . . . thank you."

He looked over the rest of her notes and the passages, hoping that they weren't pissing into the wind by reading into Justin's letter. Maybe he was feeling nostalgic instead of leaving them breadcrumbs. But his gut didn't think so, and his gut was something he always trusted.

Elias took out his cell phone and laid it on the tabletop, looking at it with derision. There was no chance of them going off the grid. Not even in the remote areas of the islands. His phone and watch both had trackers. But each of them also carried a tracking chip they'd been inserted with during their debriefing.

There was no escaping the hold The Gravediggers had on him. He still had a lot of years left on his contract. And the resources he needed to take out Eve Winter were only available if he stayed exactly where he was. He'd take his vacation time and do this mission. And then he'd take his licks at the end. But he'd never stop searching for a way to make Eve pay for what she'd done.

"You look very serious and angry all of a sudden," Miller said, interrupting his thoughts.

"I'm getting hangry," he said. "I'd have thought you'd have made coffee by now."

"Honestly, I forgot. I sat down and started reading. But now that you mention it, I could use a cup. And a snack."

He went over and started the coffee and grabbed a granola bar. "Want one?" he asked her.

"Is it dipped in chocolate or does it taste like a donut?" she asked.

"No," he said, arching a brow. "It's a granola bar."

"Then I'll pass. Toss me whatever has the most calories."

"You know you'll regret it if you do," he said. "Every time you eat junk food you talk about how much you're going to have to work out to offset the calories."

She narrowed her eyes and held out her hand, and he took that to mean she didn't particularly care about calories at the moment.

"Do you know how many calories fear burns?" she asked. "Besides, I'm going to need my strength for the upcoming boat and snakes."

"Good point," he said. "There's a Snickers bar and a bag of chocolate-covered pretzels."

"Yes, please," she said and took them both from him.

"Before you get chocolate all over your face, I need to take your picture and get your passport ready. We'll be in San Antonio in less than an hour. We'll take one duffel with the cash and weapons and pick up whatever other supplies we need when we arrive on the islands."

"Is it stupid to ask how we're going to get weapons on a plane and into another country?"

"Not normally," he said. "But it would look more suspicious if we came without them, considering who they think owns the plane and the boat we'll be using. There are always ways around the law. That's why the world is as fucked up as it is."

"That's encouraging," she said. "I'm so tired I'm about to get back in that casket."

"You can grab some sleep on the plane," he said.

"Let your chocolate and coffee fuel you. And just so you're not surprised—"

"Usually sentences that start out that way don't end well," she told him.

"I want you to remember Cordova is looking for you. He wants you badly. But I'm an unknown entity. We can buy some time going as a couple."

He took a small black box from his pocket and opened it, and then he tapped the three rings into the palm of his hand. She shook her head and took a step back, but he grabbed her hand before she could get too far away.

"Your passport will say Elise Miller," he told her. "It's best to stay closest to the truth when possible, and since Elise is your middle name, you'll at least recognize it if someone says it. Or if someone calls you Mrs. Miller."

Her eyes went big and round as he slid the diamond solitaire and plain silver band around her finger.

"No one knows me," he said, "so I'll keep my first name to make things easier on you." She snorted out a laugh and he wondered if she'd finally cracked under the pressure. "What's so funny?"

"We're Elias and Elise Miller?" she asked. "That's terrible. We sound more like brother and sister than husband and wife."

"Brothers and sisters don't look at each other the way we do," he said. "I promise that would get a lot more attention if we tried to go that route. We're going to be a couple from the second we get off this train until we step foot back in Last Stop. I sleep on the left side of the bed, by the way."

"Are you sure you're going to be able to stand it?" she asked. "You might have to touch me, and there won't be anywhere for you to stomp off to this time."

His arms came down on either side of her, trapping her against the table, and he leaned in before he could help himself.

"Believe me when I tell you I did you a favor by walking away that night," he said. "You tempt me, Miller. Make me want things I know I can't have."

She stared at him out of wide tawny eyes. "I don't know what the hell you're talking about."

"It's probably for the best," he said.

He took her lips in a kiss that rocked him to the core. He went hard in an instant, and every bit of self-discipline he'd harnessed the last weeks went by the wayside. There was no way he'd be able to keep from touching her. Not when she tasted of the sweetest honey.

Her mouth opened beneath his and he felt her tongue slide sinuously against his. He could've spent hours kissing her. But they didn't have hours. They had minutes, and there was still work to be done.

When he pulled back they were both out of breath, and her eyes stayed closed.

"It's not fair for you to kiss me like that and leave me wanting," she said.

The sadness in her voice broke his heart, and there was no one to blame but himself. "I know," he said. "But I can't seem to stop. Forgive me."

CHAPTER TEN

The train pulled into the station sometime mid-morning. Miller's body was lethargic from lack of sleep, her movements slow and clumsy. Her brain had stopped processing conversation about half an hour before.

As long as she'd stayed busy, she hadn't had time to worry about Justin. But the last leg of their trip had been spent in silence, and she'd had too much time to retreat into her head. To worry and wonder if he was still alive. What if he needed help and she wasn't in time to get it to him?

The train whistle blew and jerked her out of a half doze, and the gradual slowdown made her body sway to the locomotive rhythm. Their bags were packed and ready to go, and Miller had a brand-new passport to her name. Elise Miller, married woman. And not *just* a married woman. But a woman married to Elias Cole. Or Elias Miller. But the result was still the same. It gave her a panic attack either way. And the weight on her ring finger was a constant reminder.

"How are we supposed to get out of here?" she asked. "We're in a crazy futuristic train car with a bag full of guns and cash. Someone is bound to notice."

"Only if you yell it out loud," he said wryly. "It's ten o'clock. Ten o'clock is the busiest time of day for the station. It's pure chaos. The trains come in, and several of them connect to other locations. There will be people everywhere. No one will pay any attention to us."

"Unless I yell out about the guns and cash."

"Right, unless you do that," he said, giving her a droll look. "Try to restrain yourself. Ready, Mrs. Miller?"

"Ohmigod," she said, just as he placed his hand on the wall plate, unlocking the exterior door.

"Better get used to it," he said as the door slid open.

The smell of oiled engines and concrete assaulted her, steam rising from the tracks as the whistle blew again. The sunlight was blinding, streaming in through the glass-topped roof of the station, and she used her hand to shade her eyes until they adjusted. Elias had been right. It was pure chaos. The noise was deafening—passengers switched trains and moved at a frenzied pace that was impossible to keep up with. She suddenly remembered why she enjoyed staying in her comfort zone. She hated crowds.

Elias stepped out and then reached up to give her a hand, surprising her when he just lifted her at the waist, bags and all, and set her on the ground. Then he placed his hand on the outside plate, closing the door, and the railcar looked exactly like all the rest of them. She wouldn't have been able to pick out theirs in the lineup.

"Let's go," he said, taking her hand and leading her through the crowd. "We've got a car waiting for us. I'm anxious to get to the islands. My gut is telling me our time is going to be shorter than we want."

"Maybe you should take some Pepto-Bismol," she said. "You said we have a car waiting for us. Who takes care of stuff like that? Cars and planes and reservations? All the day-to-day stuff."

"The little travel agency in Last Stop. They mostly get all the reservations right."

She stopped in her tracks, people jostling around her, and he looked back at her quizzically.

"You let Martha Danforth make all your travel arrangements?" she asked, horrified. "You know Tess's grandmother tried to do one of those around-the-world cruises about ten years back and she got Martha to do all the booking for her. But instead of the around-the-world trip she accidentally booked Mrs. Sherman on one of those swingers cruises to Amsterdam."

"Yikes," he said, tugging her hand again to get her moving. "I'll never get that image out of my head."

"Apparently everyone on board couldn't get it out of their head either. They made her disembark in The Netherlands. If anyone is bad for erections, it's Tatiana Sherman."

Elias's body shook with laughter, but he kept moving them through the crowd. "I was kidding," he said. "Tess takes care of all the organizational-type stuff. We follow a mission plan for each op, and we always have backup plans, but Tess is great at the details. She makes sure we have everything we could possibly need, and she thinks ahead. It's been nice to have her on board, even though her security clearance is limited. She's become a huge asset to the team."

"So her knowledge of y'all really is recent?" Miller asked. "She hasn't been hiding this from me for a long time?"

"She found out by accident," he told her. "When Levi crossed over from his former life, there were some complications and we thought we'd lost him. Tess found his body, and then it turned out Levi wasn't dead after all. If anyone knows dead from alive, it's Tess, and she isn't stupid. She's also relentless as hell."

"She's got that stubborn redhead's temper. Sometimes it's endearing."

"Ha," he said, grinning. "Y'all have a good friendship. Don't ever take it for granted."

"Believe me, I don't. There's no one else in this

world I can trust like her. She knows everything about me, flaws and all, and she loves me anyway. And I feel the same about her."

They made it to the outside of the train station, and to the right was a long line of taxis and an even longer line of people waiting for them.

"I didn't realize so many people used trains," she said. "I've never thought of it for travel."

"You'd be surprised. It's a great way to commute or a great way to see parts of the country you wouldn't see from the highways. It seems like something you'd love. You should check it out."

It did sound like something she'd love, and it only made her slightly uncomfortable that he would know that. Who was this man that was able to read her so well? It was disconcerting.

A black SUV bypassed the taxis and pulled to a stop in the crowded street. Horns blared, but the SUV didn't budge. Elias headed toward it, opening the back door and tossing their bags in the back. He looked around and gently pushed her to the back passenger door, opening it for her so she could slide in first. She'd noticed that about Elias over the time they'd known each other. It was rare he made eye contact for long. He was always looking around, and now that she knew his true background she understood why.

She settled into the SUV, and Elias got in beside

her. It was then she noticed his weapon was out and he was holding it comfortably in his lap. He leaned back in the bucket seat and laid his head against the headrest. He looked more than comfortable with the weapon in his lap, but it seemed like overkill considering they were in the back of a government vehicle.

An opaque partition went up, dividing the front and back seats, and she could no longer see the driver. And then the driver took off with a squeal of tires out of the train station

"What the hell?" she asked, holding on for dear life. "This doesn't feel safe. Who the hell is that guy?"

"You're just *now* thinking this doesn't feel safe? After masked men broke into your home and you had to escape your hometown in a casket?"

"Don't be so dramatic," she said. "I'm just saying it seems like a bad idea to get in the back of a mysterious vehicle that appears out of nowhere. That should be Spy 101. You didn't even say hello to the driver. How do you know we're in the right car?"

"There's a trident where the car emblem would normally be."

She'd missed that little detail. She needed to pay closer attention in the future.

"And the driver is part of The Shadow," he said. "He gave me the signal before the partition went up. If he hadn't, I would have shot him."

"Holy cow," she said. "*That's* why you have your gun out? You would have shot him just like that?"

"Believe me, if he hadn't given me the signal, it means he'd have been shooting at us first. The signal is necessary. We don't know them and they don't know us. I've never seen the same person from The Shadow twice. Everyone just does their job."

"How does he know where we're going?"

"Tess would've relayed the information. They'll be expecting us at a small private airfield. Money has exchanged hands with who it has needed to for us to travel without any complications. Once we get in the air it should be smooth sailing."

"Oh man," she said. "Don't you know anything? The first person to say something like that in a movie is usually the one who ends up dead. You jinxed us."

He rolled his eyes and looked over at her. "I did not jinx us. Life is not a movie. You should get a grip."

"I have a grip. And I have great instincts," she told him. "Don't be surprised if this guy tries to kidnap us or holds us at gunpoint. We'll probably end up going over a bridge and into the water. I don't want to drown. I can think of lots of ways I'd rather die than drowning."

"Yeah, that one would suck. Especially since I was a SEAL. You should focus on different ways we could die. I'm not going to let us drown. It'd be too embarrassing."

She stared at him for a few seconds and said, "That's really comforting. Great suggestion."

He winked and then laid his head back down and closed his eyes.

"I'm just saying," she said, "if we pass by a large body of water, I'm rolling my window down ahead of time. In the movies, the driver usually gets shot and drives over the bridge, or another car will ram us from behind. I can't decide if I should go ahead and take my seat belt off. I don't want it to get stuck."

"Living in your head must be interesting," he said.

"I keep myself entertained," she said with a shrug. "At least I'll never be boring."

"You're definitely not that," he agreed.

It wasn't a long drive to the airport. Or at least what she assumed was an airport. There was one white rectangular metal building, and in back were a couple of small planes and a runway of cracked asphalt and patches of grass. All of it was surrounded by a ten-foot chain-link fence with barbed wire at the top.

"Please tell me one of those two little planes isn't ours," she said, eyeing the planes with genuine concern. They both had seen better days, and she was preparing to add flying in small aircraft to her list of fears.

"Yeah," he said. "That one that the mechanics are working on is ours. Engine caught on fire on its last

GONE TO DUST × 185

run, so they're giving it a look. But I'm sure it'll be fine."

Her head snapped to look at him, eyes wide, and then she saw his laughter. "Not funny."

"Really? I thought it was." He pointed straight ahead. "Our plane is down there. It's fueled up and ready to go. Pilot is waiting."

The driver stopped in front of a gate and typed in a code at the box, and the chain-link opened to allow them entry. The SUV pulled right up next to a plane that looked to be in perfectly good working order, and she immediately saw the trident on the side.

"Let's roll," Elias said. "Can you carry the bag? I want to leave my hands free just in case things don't go as smoothly as I planned."

"I can do it," she said.

They'd barely gotten out of the SUV and closed the doors when the driver took off. "Wow," she said. "I guess we wore out our welcome."

"That's his job. They're never one for small talk or lingered good-byes."

"Still, my mother always said that it never costs anything to give someone a hello and a smile. You should send Eve a memo so they can work on that."

He barked out a laugh. "She'd love that. I might do it just for the hell of it." He moved in front of her as they went up the short flight of steps and into the plane. He had his serious face on and wasn't speaking.

"Oh, praise Jesus," she said. "There's a couch."

She put her stuff in the overhead bins and looked around, soaking in every detail. She figured this was her last chance to ever be in this type of luxury, so she wanted to make the most of it.

"Stay cool, Miller," she said, trying to calm her excitement.

It was everything she could do to keep from jumping up and down and testing out all the furniture. She'd been in a plane before, but it had been nothing like this one. This one was like a traveling hotel room. And not like the rooms at the Bluebonnet Inn. This was pure luxury.

There were six seats on board, and she guessed she should've realized after seeing HQ and the railcar that everything this organization did was top-of-the-line. She felt much better about the engine not falling out of the plane and them crashing into the Pacific.

It wasn't a large plane—just the cockpit, a small kitchen area, seating, and then a closed door she assumed was the bathroom. The walls of the interior were light gray, and the plush carpet a dark gray. A soft leather couch a color somewhere in between the walls and the carpet was against one wall, and two oversized reclining chairs sat across from it. Two other chairs sat adjacent to the couch, in front of the bathroom door. There was plenty of room to work at each station, and she had to imagine there were some pretty cool electronics concealed like in the railcar.

"It's all going into a book," she muttered. She bounced up and down on the couch a little, too excited to sit still, and making sure no one could see her. "I need to get out more."

She found the fridge was stocked full of the soft drinks she liked when she wasn't mainlining coffee, and she also found a bag of trail mix. She would've given anything for her laptop.

She took her finds back to the couch and stretched out. And then she saw the office supplies stuck in the side of each chair, and reached over to grab a legal pad and a pen. She could still get some work done and transcribe it all later. As long as her notepad didn't fall into the Aguas Mortales.

Elias came out of the cockpit after speaking to the pilot and noticed her snack, and he got a bottle of water for himself and a protein bar. It was no wonder he stayed in good shape. He didn't eat any of the good stuff. Of course, if she didn't eat any of the good stuff, she wouldn't have to work out five days a week, but food wasn't something she was willing to give up. Elias could have his water and twigs with her blessing.

"There's a hot breakfast available if you'd like it," he said. "We just have to put it in the oven. It'll take about fifteen minutes after takeoff."

"How long is the flight?" she asked.

"About five hours."

"Then I'll take the breakfast. It seems like forever since I've had a real meal."

He settled in one of the seats across from her and buckled his seat belt. "I don't want to tell you what to do," he said. "But my suggestion is for you to move to one of the chairs for takeoff. It might be embarrassing to fall off the couch and spill your trail mix."

She pursed her lips together and said, "Believe me, I've done more embarrassing things than that." And then because she was a strong believer in Murphy's Law, she got off the couch and took one of the seats, buckling her seat belt. It would've been a shame to waste the trail mix.

"You'll have to tell me some of those embarrassing stories sometime," he said.

"I'd have to have lots of wine first. Or maybe just give Tess the wine and let her tell them. She was there for most of my brightest moments."

They began to taxi down the runway and she fiddled with the buttons on the seat. "You've said before you're from Texas. Where'd you grow up?" she asked.

"A little town called Wimberley. It's just a couple thousand people, but it was a good place to grow up. It's beautiful country. Lots of hunting and fishing. A place where everyone knows your name and your business. It's a little slice of Americana, you know?

Flags flying in everyone's yard and Friday nights spent at high school football games."

"It sounds kind of like Last Stop," she said as the plane picked up speed and lifted into the air.

"Not far off," he said. "And no offense, but there's all these beautiful areas of Texas, and then it was like God got tired when he reached Last Stop and took a nap instead of finishing creating the earth."

She snorted out a laugh and leaned back, discovering that the seat reclined and the footrest came all the way up. "I bet you were nothing but trouble growing up. They probably had your parents on speed dial at school."

He grinned and a hint of dimples showed. She realized despite his always joking around and seemingly jovial and sarcastic attitude, he rarely smiled a genuine smile. It was all surface.

"I was creative," he said. "You can't put kids like me in the confines of a classroom. I was much better off taking a day now and then to run a trotline. And during hunting season, it was best they didn't even try to keep me there. I never fell behind and I graduated third in my class, so I figure I wasn't missing much after all."

"You miss your home?" she asked. "You're relaxed when you talk about it. The memories there must be good."

"I miss parts of it," he said, shrugging. He unbuckled and went to the kitchen to put the breakfast trays in the oven. "But I outgrew it once I became a SEAL. It's hard to go back to small-town life once you've done that job. Tell me about Solomon's table," he said. "Cordova said in his letter that your brother has part of the table. What size are we talking about? Would he be able to carry it around easily?"

She was a little taken aback at the quick subject change. He was clearly done talking about his past. The second he mentioned being a SEAL his entire attitude changed.

"King Solomon's table is considered one of the most treasured items that was in the temple, along with the Ark of the Covenant. It's said the table was as tall as a man, which in those times was somewhere in the mid-five-foot range. The entire table was made of solid gold, but inlaid in the gold were diamonds, sapphires, rubies, emeralds, and pearls. If Justin has a table leg, I can't imagine it's easy to travel with. Not because of the weight necessarily, but just because of the length and size."

"It's doable if he strapped it to his back. We're trained to carry a lot heavier weight than that."

"But he's injured. He might not be able to manage what he normally would."

"Justin's a SEAL, and he's had worse injuries than a missing finger. He'd be able to manage, unless he has severe blood loss. The issue is going to be conditions. We don't know how long he's been out there. Then there's lack of food and water to consider. There could be any number of variables."

The timer dinged on the oven, and Miller's mouth started watering when the smell of food reached her nose. Her last twenty-four hours had been nonstop, and she hadn't had anything in her stomach but wine, caffeine, and junk food. She pulled the tray from the side of her seat and settled it over her lap.

"Thank you," she said, and then waited until he took his own seat before asking, "Why do you hate my brother so much? You don't talk about him like you do about the others on your team."

She thought at first he wasn't going to answer. He buttered his roll and salted his food like the words weren't hanging between them.

"I don't think 'hate' is the right word," he finally said. "He was my brother. We went through BUD/S and hell week together. We spent ten years together. That kind of bond is stronger than most marriages.

"He'd always had the obsession," he said. "We'd lie in our bunks after a grueling day and fall asleep with him telling the stories of Solomon and Sheba. It was nice at first. You know, everyone had their quirks or things that brought them comfort. It's a rough life, and sometimes there's little solace when you're lying in bed, trying to let the memories of the day fade.

"But as the years went on, his obsession grew. To

the point he'd disappear for hours or a day, and then come back just in time to be debriefed for the mission. He got several slaps on the wrist and a couple of write-ups. But he didn't care. He was always looking for *something*, but he'd never say what it was. I wasn't sure he even knew.

"We were on a mission in Palestine. An eight-man team sent in to rescue Israeli hostages and take out a terrorist by the name of Tariq Pitafi. The timing of it got messed up and we had to move a good twelve hours before we'd planned. But we had to go in with a seven-man team because Justin was gone.

"The rest of us were so focused on every mission. We'd go off from time to time, but we were always ready to move at a moment's notice. For Justin, it was like the mission was an afterthought. I was the team sniper, and because we were down a man I was minus a spotter.

"I lay there on my belly in the hardpacked dirt, rocks digging into my ribs and stomach and sweat stinging my eyes. Live fire started and we got our asses handed to us. I really didn't think we were going to make it out of there alive. I still don't know how we got out of that mess, but we accomplished our goal and there were no casualties. And when we got back to the rendezvous point, there was Justin, bold as you please, pissed because we'd left without him and not giving a shit that he'd left us a man down. I was pissed," Elias admitted. "I punched him in the jaw and kept walking. He got reprimanded and had his rank busted down because he refused to say where he'd been, just that he hadn't been in range for his comm unit to pick up the new orders.

"No one can stay too mad for long," he said. "We work in too close of quarters and have to rely on one another too often for there to be bad blood. But I think from that point, no one really trusted him anymore. He knew it too, but there was nothing to be done at that point. So no, I don't hate your brother at all. He was my friend at one point. I don't know what he is now. But it sounds like he hasn't changed much."

She needed something to do while she thought, so she stood and gathered up their dishes and put everything away.

"You should catch a couple of hours of sleep," he told her. "We can turn off all the cabin lights. It'll be like you're back in the casket."

"Wake me up if anything important happens," she said and burrowed down on the couch with a pillow and blanket.

"We're on a five-hour flight to the Galápagos Islands," he said. "What would constitute something important enough to wake you up for?"

"Like if the plane is going to crash," she told him. "I want to be awake if I'm going to die."

Elias stared at her hard a few seconds and then he shook his head. "You're nuts," he said.

She narrowed her eyes and said, "Stop calling me nuts. I'm eccentric. You're the one making me crazy. You left me so turned on I could've self-combusted, and now you keep kissing me. Make up your damned mind. I think you're the one that's crazy."

"I must be," he agreed. "Sleep tight, nut job."

CHAPTER ELEVEN

Elias shouldn't have kissed her. He knew better. Her taste was intoxicating, and until he settled between her thighs and slid into the welcoming heat, he was afraid sex was going to become a major distraction. For both of them.

He'd done his best to focus on work while they were in the plane, but his eyes kept straying to her prone body on the couch, her deep, even breathing indicating the level of exhaustion she must've felt. He didn't really understand what she did or what it must feel like to have that constant inner dialogue when she was creating a story, but he'd observed her long enough over the past couple of years to see what it did to her on a physical level.

He'd seen her elated at the end of a book, and in a deep depression when she was in the middle of one. He knew she skipped meals, because he'd gone with Tess to take food to her and set it outside her office door in hopes she'd trip over it on the way to the bathroom. He'd seen her cry when talking about characters who didn't exist except in her head, and he'd seen her fall asleep during a conversation because she'd worked herself into exhaustion. She was right. She was eccentric. She was quirky and moody, and though she liked to present the illusion she was tough, she wore her heart on her sleeve.

More than anything, he admired what Miller had made of herself. She'd taken the pain from her childhood and turned it into a way to bring hope and joy to others. She lived quietly, but she lived the life she wanted. She was a contradiction—confident and insecure, outgoing and shy, worldly and naïve. She was smart and successful, but there were pockets of vulnerability in her that intrigued him.

He wanted to know all of her—thoughts, hopes, dreams, and fears—and in between his work, he'd look up, just to make sure she was still there and he wasn't just imagining her asleep on the couch, her fist tucked beneath her cheek and her white-blond hair laying in wisps around her face. She looked softer in sleep, and he'd wanted nothing more than to curl his body around hers and just hold her. But there was work that had to be done, and it was an exercise in discipline that had kept him in the chair poring over maps and papers and research, with the help of the team back at HQ. He wouldn't let her down. And he would make sure, above all else, that she was safe.

They had each found one change of clothes that fit and were appropriate for their final destination. He woke her half an hour before they landed so she could freshen up and change clothes. He'd already taken care of his own change of clothes, having donned linen pants and a black button-down Panama Jack island shirt.

He'd handed her a stack of clothes, and ushered her into the bathroom to change. Miller wasn't someone who woke alert and ready to face the day.

When she came out a few minutes later he wanted to laugh at the disgruntled look on her face. "I look ridiculous," she said. "I would never in a million years dress like this. Cordova and his men will never find me. I look like someone's grandmother."

She was wearing a pair of white capris and a shirt with lime-green palm fronds all over it. It had shoulder pads. He hadn't seen shoulder pads since he was a kid. She also wore a matching green oversized beaded necklace around her neck and a big floppy white hat.

"Umm," he said. "I can most definitely say that you don't look like most people's grandmother. Maybe more like Blanche Devereaux from *The Golden Girls*."

"Blanche was pretty hot," she said. "But I'm pretty sure this outfit is sending me into immediate menopause."

No grandmother he'd ever seen had an ass like hers. And the very formfitting pants she was wearing were going to drive him insane. He'd never thought he had a *type* of woman he was attracted to. But the way Miller filled out a pair of pants made him re-evaluate. And he knew firsthand what it felt like for her legs to be wrapped around his hips and his hands filled with her. She'd filled his dreams for weeks, the thought of her kneeling on all fours and him sliding between the round globes of her ass a particularly favorite image burned in his mind.

His body's immediate response reminded him this was hardly the time or the place for fantasy. It also made it all the more important to get her out of those pants and into something that wouldn't drive him crazy, like a potato sack.

"I've never worn shoulder pads before," she said, shrugging her shoulders over and over again. "If I lean my head over I can use them like pillows. Don't tell anyone about this. My readers will think I've lost my edge."

"Your secret is safe with me. We've got to stop and get supplies and pick up more clothes anyway. Then you can burn what you're wearing." And then he added, "Please, God. Because those pants should've been illegal."

"What was that?" she asked.

"Nothing," he said.

"Tess says I need to work on aging gracefully, but I have a feeling I'm going to go down kicking and screaming."

He could get behind that mentality. "Why would you go down any other way?" he asked. "If you're going down, it might as well be with a fight."

"Sometimes you're a very reasonable man, Elias . . . Miller," she said, remembering his name change.

"I'm going to remember you said that," he said. And then he noticed the roiling black clouds coming in from the west. "Look at that," he told her, pointing in the opposite direction. "It's hot and sunny now, but that afternoon storm is going to blow in the next couple of hours."

The sky was a brilliant cerulean and there wasn't a cloud in sight over the island. But out over the water it was as if a curtain had been pulled across the sky. When they stepped off the plane they were greeted by two armed security men who briefly looked at their passports before leading them through what could loosely be called "customs." Of course, the way had been smoothed by the cash he'd palmed to each of the security guards.

"Do we have another creepy SUV ride ahead of us where we're going to get abducted or end up in the ocean?" she asked.

He rolled his eyes behind his sunglasses. "We have a local driver to take us where we need to go before we head to the boat. Let's reel it in a little on the imagination overdrive."

"Why would I do that?" she asked. "It helps me

think out my plots. I've still got a book to finish, and I might as well use as much of this as I can. I'm writing Solomon and Sheba's story, but it's woven in with my present-day hero and heroine, who are hunting Solomon's treasures."

"So you're basically writing our story," he said, brows raised in surprise. "What happens to us?"

"Not us," she said. "My characters. And their car is clearly about to go over the side of a bridge and into the water. It'll be a narrow escape, of course."

"Thank God it's your characters and not us. The best way to get out of a sinking car is before it actually goes into the water."

"Maybe so, but it's not nearly as exciting," she said.

"Surviving beats exciting any day of the week," he said. "What happens after they narrowly escape death?"

She averted her eyes and color crept into her cheeks. She picked at an invisible piece of lint on her sweater. "They celebrate being alive," she finally said.

He hooted out a laugh and put his hand to the small of her back as he put her just in front of him, so he could move quickly if he needed to. He leaned down and said close to her ear, "There's something to be said for burning off an adrenaline rush." He felt her shiver beneath his touch. "What happens next?"

"I don't know," she said, shrugging. "Hopefully, the heroine doesn't die from seasickness or snake bites. And then they live happily ever after. Unless they die."

"That's sure to perk up your readers," he said.

"I'm trying to decide if kidnapping is preferable to getting on the boat. What do you think?"

"I think you're nuts," he said. "But there's a good chance the boat will be slightly less traumatic than being kidnapped, so I'd go that route. And I've got your meds, so that will help. I'll give them to you in the car, and by the time we get ready to board you'll be good to go. Let's go, Blanche. Maybe you can get a senior discount when we grab a bite to eat."

"Very funny," she said.

There wasn't a luxury car with the trident symbol waiting for them, but instead a white taxi with rust spots and bumper stickers plastered all over it.

"I don't mean to complain," she said, "but if we're projecting an image of private planes and expensive boats, shouldn't we have a car?"

"We're in a different world here," he told her. "Private cars are reserved for government officials and the cartel. They're in short exchange. Santa Cruz isn't a driving city. There are many areas where they still only travel by horse and cart."

The driver was wearing rumpled khakis and an unbuttoned Guayabera shirt over a wifebeater. He went around to the trunk and unlocked it with the key and then stood there as they approached.

"*Hola*, señor," the driver said.

Elias nodded and said in Spanish, "We'll hold on

to our luggage." And then he gave him instructions for taking them to the market for supplies before the storm hit.

"Sure, sure," the driver said in English. "Get in."

One of the passenger-side doors was stuck, so Miller scooted across the seat and Elias climbed in behind her. The inside of the cab smelled like sweat and cabbage, and Elias tried rolling down the window, but it didn't budge.

"Mine doesn't work either," Miller told him. "Do you realize what that means if we go into the water?"

"Yes," he said. "It means I'm going to pull out my gun and shoot the window so we can escape."

"Good thinking," she said, grinning mischievously. "See, you're helping me write a book. I'll mention you in the acknowledgments."

"I'd rather get the happily ever after," he told her. And then he realized what he'd said. It was easy to get sucked into the illusion that being with her was normal. That they could have a normal life. But happily ever afters weren't in his future.

She cleared her throat and they each stared out their window while the driver continued to talk with the other cabbies on the street, as if no one had anywhere to go.

"I don't mean to be negative," she said, "but I've got a bad feeling about this guy. I'm pretty sure he's carrying a gun."

Elias sighed. "I think you're still writing a book in your head. He's got to be close to seventy years old. Have a little faith."

"I have faith," she said. "But I still think he's carrying a gun. He's got shifty eyes. What happens if he tries to rob us, or if he just shoots us and leaves us for dead in the middle of this godforsaken place? No one will ever know what happened to us."

"Sure they will," Elias said. "When I became a Gravedigger they implanted a chip beneath my skin. They'll know the location of my body and whether I'm dead or alive. But if it makes you feel better, I put our passports in the inside pocket of my shirt. As long as we have those we'll be fine."

"If you say so," she said skeptically. "Look, here he comes. Be cool."

He laughed before he could help it. "Sweetheart, I'm always cool."

The driver got in and started up the engine with a sputter and a cough, and they started moving through the congested streets.

"I don't want you to think that I can't handle what we're doing here," she told him, and he squeezed her hand to remind her to be careful what she said. She squeezed back in acknowledgment. "Boats and snakes are literally two of the things I'm most afraid of. And heights. I really didn't like climbing out of that tree. But I'm balls to the wall with pretty much everything else."

"You always put real-life stuff in your books?" he asked. There was no air-conditioning, and it wasn't long before they were both damp from the heat and humidity, but at least the front windows were able to roll down, so there was a little bit of a breeze.

"Always," she said. "I watch everything and everyone, and read as much as I can. You never know when one thing will spark an entire book."

"You use real people for characters?" he asked, brows raised.

She lifted her sunglasses and her laughing tawny eyes met his. "I won't confess to anything on the record, but I had a character in a book once who looked and acted an awful lot like the head contractor who did some of the work on my house. He ended up dying a horrible death with a nail gun. I might have chuckled while I was writing that scene."

"What about me?" he asked. "Anyone like me in your books?"

"How about you read them all and then tell me if you think you're in there."

"I'll take that challenge," he said, nodding. "I like to read. What do I get if I find myself in one of your books? Royalties? Or I could pose for your next cover."

She snorted out a laugh. "People never recognize themselves in my books. Tess, or parts of her, have been in several, and she's never once mentioned it other than she likes that particular character."

"We'll see," he said. "How many books have you written since we've known each other?"

"Six and a half."

"Geez, woman. You need a hobby or something."

"I've got one. I drink wine with Tess and watch movies. And sometimes we put on real clothes and go out for happy hour and drinks and watch all the other people and talk about them. Though we don't do that so much anymore because Tess got married, and marriage has a tendency to put a damper on single-life activities."

"I've heard a rumor this is true," he said.

"You've never been married?" she asked.

In another life and time he'd thought about it. When he could've been an honorable husband. An honorable father. "No, never been married," he said instead.

They crossed over the bridge to the island of Santa Cruz, and the world opened up. The bridge was narrow, barely wide enough for two cars to pass by each other, and as the taxi reached the middle it was almost as if they were driving on the water. Nothing but blue in either direction.

"Oh, wow," Miller said, sticking her face closer to the window. "That's amazing. I've never seen water that color before."

The water went from deep blue to turquoise to aqua the closer to shore they got, and it was unbelievably clear. Boats were anchored in the harbor and others were out in the water, sails at full mast. It was postcard perfect, and not even the dingy interior of the taxi could ruin its effect.

Several resort hotels lined the oceanfront, but the resort area was secluded from the rest of the island. Shops and restaurants and lodging could all be found in one area. They were nestled there along the beach and the mountains rose majestically from behind them, the greens of the grasses and trees as vivid as the water. Everything was in technicolor.

The taxi puttered along behind a mix of other cars in worse shape than it was and pedicabs. The driver blared his horn a couple of times for good measure and then sped around the pedicabs and took a sharp left turn down a one-way street.

Gravity had Miller sliding across the seat and up against Elias. She tried to hold herself in place, but she ended up almost in his lap. He wasn't complaining.

"Sorry," she said, crawling her way back to her seat.

"Anytime," he said.

Elias had been watching where the driver was taking them, having studied the map while on the plane. The car radio was half static, half music, but the driver left it on anyway. Sweat drenched his forehead, even though he was fortunate enough to have the breeze from the open window. His dark brown eyes met Elias's a time or two in the rearview mirror before looking straight ahead again, his fingers tapping on the steering wheel.

When they stopped at the corner, Elias felt a tingle across the back of his neck and reached behind his back for his weapon. It was too late. The driver turned and had a gun pointed directly at Miller's head. He never took his eyes from the driver.

"Put your hands where I can see them," he said in very good English.

Elias could see Miller from his periphery. She was sitting stone still, her eyes on the driver instead of the gun. She didn't look scared. She looked pissed. And he hoped to God she wasn't going to try anything stupid. At least not while the gun was pointed at her face.

Elias slowly moved his hands so they lay on the back of the driver's seat and said, "I'm going to go out on a limb and guess you're not the driver we hired."

The driver shrugged. "Carlo ran into a small accident. He will be fine in a few days and out making drops again. But I knew you were a prime target. Private plane, private yacht, and no questions from customs."

"What do you want from us?" Elias asked.

"Whatever you have," the driver said, chuckling. "You are very rich, yes? Maybe worth a nice ransom?" He handed Miller a roll of Duct Tape and said, "Tape his wrists together. Nice and tight."

She glanced at Elias and raised her brows, and he was amazed at her composure. He nodded for her to go ahead and do as the man said and she let out a little sigh.

"I told you so," she whispered, taking the Duct Tape from the man and strapping it around Elias's wrists.

"Good," the driver said. "Now reach into his back pocket and take out his wallet. And hand over your purse." He moved the gun so it was aimed at Elias. "Keep your hands on the back of my seat."

Elias had to hand it to the guy. He was smarter than most penny-ante thieves. But he did as he was told and kept his hands on the back of the seat while Miller reached down to dig his wallet out of his back pocket. Her hand skimmed over the gun in the back of his pants and lingered there, and he shook his head no, the movement so minute he wondered if she could see it. But she moved past it and got the wallet. And then she put the wallet and her purse in the front seat.

"Good, good," the driver said, his smile displaying several gold teeth. "We're going to take a little drive up the mountain. If you move your hands from the back of my seat I will shoot her. Do you understand?"

"Sure," Elias said with a shrug. Where he put his hands wasn't going to make a difference. Once the opportunity presented itself the man would be dead one way or the other.

"Are you private or do you work for someone?" Elias asked.

"I work for myself," the driver said, kicking open his door. "I'm an entrepreneur."

Miller snorted in derision and the driver glared at

her, his eyes turning mean. "Shut up," he said, jabbing the gun toward Miller's face. "I don't want to kill you, but I will. You're a little older than they like, and your hair is too short and the wrong color, but you have good skin and you're very pretty. You'll bring a good price at auction. And your man, he seems very important. Lots of money. Someone will pay a big ransom for his return I'm sure." The driver laughed and spittle spewed from his thin lips. "I'm going to kill him anyway, but the money will be very helpful to my village."

"It's like community service," Miller said, popping off.

"Miller," Elias warned, shaking his head.

"That's right," the driver said. "You need to teach her some manners. My son is good at such things. I think I'll let him spend some time with you once we get to the village."

Unfortunately, what he was speaking of wasn't uncommon in parts of Central and South America. Entire villages would plan for the kidnapping and killing of tourists, hoping whatever they stole from them or were able to get for ransom would be enough to keep them fed and roofs over their head. He had to deal with the driver before they got to the village and were outnumbered.

The driver kept the gun in his hand but put it back on the steering wheel, looking in the rearview mirror at Elias, and then he pressed the accelerator and the car lurched forward. It wasn't long before Santa Cruz was behind them and the crudely paved roads turned into dirt paths that led higher into the mountains. There were no other buildings—no houses—nothing. Only thick trees and jungle.

The roads were curvy and dangerous, and Elias was biding his time, but they'd been on the road for a couple of hours and he knew the time was probably growing short. The driver had increased his speed and he was getting nervous. He kept looking back at them and pointing the gun in their general direction on occasion. Elias was afraid if anything spooked him he'd end up popping off a shot out of reflex.

They took a curve at high speed and Miller slid toward him again, but she quickly righted herself. The road opened up to a short straightaway, and there was a natural lookout point directly in front of them. There was nothing but ocean and a steep drop off a cliff in front of them.

There was no time to spare. He lifted his bound wrists over the headrest and the driver's head and jerked backward with his thumbs straight and stiff, knowing he'd hit at least one eye. There was an unholy scream from the driver and he dropped the gun as he brought his hands to his face. But instead of pressing on the brake to stop the car, he pressed on the accelerator and they shot forward.

"Shit," Elias said, untangling his arms from around

the man's head. "Reach over me and open my door. We've got to jump. Now!"

Miller shot into action and reached across him, pushing open the car door, and then he grabbed hold of the back of her shirt and tossed her out of the car. He rolled out right behind her, and then looked up in time to see the car shoot out over the edge of the lookout point.

"Oh, hell," he said, breaking the duct tape around his wrists and then sprinting toward the edge of the cliff. Drawing more attention to them wasn't in the plans.

He heard the clunk and crash of the car as it hit the craggy cliffs on the way down. He looked over in time to see it hit the rocks and water below, and there was a hissing noise seconds before the car exploded, sending a fireball of heat and orange flame straight up into the air.

He backed away and headed toward Miller, only to find her on her knees, talking to herself.

"Are you okay?" he asked, approaching slowly.

"Are you kidding me?" she asked. "You just threw me out of a car. No, I'm not okay. Why are you always throwing me? Out of windows, down trees, out of cars? If you want to throw people then go join the damned circus."

He moved toward her and helped her to her feet. Her shoulder pads were skewed, her white pants were covered in dirt, and she had pieces of fern in her hair.

"I don't want to be a Debbie Downer, but have

you noticed how different it seems in the jungle when we're not protected by the safety of a vehicle?" She swatted at a mosquito the size of her thumb.

"I wouldn't exactly call that cab ride safe," he said. "But I get what you mean."

There had at least been some semblance of protection inside the taxi. Without it, there was nothing but them and the jungle. The trees canopied over the tiny excuse for a dirt road, casting everything in shadow, and there was nothing but green for as far as the eye could see. Even the tree trunks were covered with moss. Thick vines hung low from the branches and ferns sprouted up from a tangle of roots and fallen limbs. It smelled of damp earth and mold, intermingled with the sweet scent of honeysuckle and other exotic flowers.

"I'm going to make a bold statement," she said, putting her hands to her hips.

He couldn't help but grin. "Please do."

"I'm not a fan of the jungle. It's claustrophobic. And I don't trust that monkey behind you. He looks shifty, and I think he's trying to steal your gun."

He looked over his shoulder, and sure enough, there was a howler monkey hanging from a branch, dangerously close to reaching his gun. The second Elias looked at him, the monkey hissed and climbed up to a higher branch.

"I like how you make friends everywhere we go," she said.

He turned back to and arched a brow. And then took a step toward her.

She took a step back and put her hand up.

"I know that look," she said. "Don't you dare kiss me."

"Too bad," he said, and tugged her toward him. He breathed in the scent of her—heady and seductive—and the control he held onto so carefully slipped away the second his lips touched hers. She was his every fantasy. He devoured her, his mouth demanding on hers. He drank in her sighs and reveled in the surrender of her body against his.

His hands cupped her ass and he pulled her against him, lifting her off her feet. Her fingers dug into his shoulders as she lifted her legs around his waist.

"Jesus," he said, breaking their kiss so he could catch his breath.

"More," she said, and he couldn't deny her.

He felt the raging heat of her against the hard length of his cock, and if they'd been naked, he'd already be inside her. She made him dizzy, and it was everything he could do to stay on two feet and not take her to the ground. Or maybe that's exactly what he should do.

A crack of thunder rent the air and the first cool drops of rain from the storm that had been moving in splattered against their overheated skin. He swore and moved her so they were under the canopy of trees that lined the road, but it didn't do much good. There was another crack of thunder and the sky opened.

"It's like I'm being punished for something I did in a former life," Miller said with a defeated sigh. Her hair was plastered against her head, and she was soaked to the skin in a matter of seconds.

"What are we going to do?" she yelled. The rain was deafening as it slapped against wide, waxy tree leaves, the sound amplified inside the jungled canopy.

"Start walking," he yelled back. "We're probably more than twenty miles from civilization."

"I was afraid you were going to say that." She started walking back toward the way they came and he followed after her, enjoying the way her wet clothes hugged that lush body. "I'm just going to warn you that I can't be held responsible for anything I say or do without coffee."

"I'm aware," he said, still walking behind her. "I'm hoping things won't get that desperate. I'm just starting to get used to you."

They walked for miles, and the rain never let up. There wasn't an inch of him that wasn't soaked. Water dripped from his hair into his eyes and down the collar of his shirt. Mud caked his shoes, and the temperature had dropped. Miller's lips quivered and she'd started talking to herself about a mile back. He knew enough about women to know that was never a good sign.

"Have you ever seen that movie with Kathleen

Turner and Michael Douglas?" he asked, lifting a branch out of her way as the road began to narrow.

"*Romancing the Stone?*"

"That's the one. I can never remember the name."

"I'm a romance novelist," she said. "Of course, I've seen it. Though I've decided I might need a career change. I was just practicing my interview questions for when I start working at Wendy's."

"Why Wendy's?" he asked.

"Because I wouldn't have to stand in the rain, and I'd get as many chicken nuggets as I wanted. I have to confess, there's not a whole lot I wouldn't do for chicken nuggets right now." She glanced up at him from the corner of her eye.

"I almost wish I could conjure some for you," he said, lifting more limbs so they could pass under them. The rain had made the branches heavy and many of them almost touched the ground, blocking the way that they came.

"What do you mean, almost?" she asked.

"You've been talking to yourself the last hour, and you've got kind of a crazy look in your eyes. My sister used to do that whenever she was about to start her period. I still have bad flashbacks."

She grunted, but he saw the hint of a smile. "If you really wanted to be like Michael Douglas you'd have a machete right now and cut through all this stuff like a real hero. I feel a little cheated."

"I just tossed you out of a moving car before it exploded. That doesn't count as being a hero?"

"I forgot about that," she said. "It seems like days ago."

"I always felt like Michael Douglas's character was underappreciated. Look on the bright side, if you get swept away by a muddy waterfall at least you're not wearing a skirt."

She grinned up at him. And then she vanished with a whoosh of air, and he heard a thud and a scream as a mini mudslide swept her down the road.

"Oh, shit," he said. "I was just kidding."

He moved after her as fast as he could, but he had to be careful so he didn't end up in the same predicament she was in.

Then he saw the problem and he decided to hell with it and moved faster. The road narrowed, and the mudslide was shooting over the edge of the road, down into the dense jungle, like a waterfall. Only this wasn't a waterfall like in the movies. Shooting off that waterfall would be the equivalent of jumping off a three-story building. It would hurt, and there would almost certainly be death.

"Try to grab onto something," he yelled as he cut the distance between them. He didn't know if she could hear him or not.

He only had moments to leap forward and grab her arm as she started to go over the side of the road, his body sliding through the mud and carried along with the current. He caught his foot on a tree root and held onto Miller for dear life, hoping he didn't go over the edge with her.

Her scream was cut off as they jerked to a stop, and she stared up at him out of big round eyes. He pulled her up, scooting back slowly toward the tree root he was still attached to.

He heaved her the last bit of the way until she was sprawled out beside him in the mud, but he held onto her just in case. They lay together, both breathing heavy, the rain pounding against their faces. Miller spit mud from her mouth and then turned her head to look at him.

"I've got to tell you," she yelled over the deafening rain. "I'm kind of hating today."

The comment caught him off guard and he started to laugh. By God, he loved her.

"I can see that," he yelled back. "You'll have to let me know if you hate it more than tomorrow morning when you wake up without coffee."

CHAPTER TWELVE

"We need to stop and make camp before it gets completely dark," he told her. "Try to find some kind of shelter. This isn't just one of the island's afternoon storms. It's going to be here awhile before it finally blows over."

"I can't tell you how excited I am to hear that," Miller said. "I don't suppose you have some kind of crazy secret spy kit in your pocket where you can pull a cord and the whole thing will inflate into a tent with soft feather mattresses."

"No," he said. "But I do have our passports in my pocket. Do me a favor and sit right here on this log. I want to look around without worrying you're going to be swept away."

"Believe me, I'm not going to argue about sitting down. Maybe you'll find an all-you-can-eat buffet while you're looking for shelter."

"I'll keep my eyes open," he said.

He moved quickly since he was racing against the fading daylight, and it took him about fifteen minutes before he found something that would work. A huge tree had cracked in half, the jagged trunk splintered where it had broken, and leaned over in an L-shape. It had fallen on a boulder that was almost as tall as he was and several feet wide, making a crude house of sorts. The ground below wasn't completely dry, but it wasn't a mud bed either. It would have to do.

He hurried back to Miller and almost didn't see her on the log until he was right up on her. She was covered in mud from head to toe—the same color as the log. There wasn't a speck of white left on her pants and her legs were caked with it. She was also missing a sandal. He wasn't sure she'd even noticed.

"I found something," he said. "But we've got to hurry." He thought he might have to toss her over his shoulder and carry her, but she heaved herself up and followed him.

"I think I've got mud in my underwear," she said, walking a little bit like John Wayne.

"Just think of all those women who pay money to be slathered in mud," he told her. "You could pretend it's a spa treatment."

"Or I could give you a knuckle sandwich," she said, holding up her fist. "This cannot be our life. I kind of feel like I'm on that show 24. I'd watch each episode, and I'd say to myself, there's no way that much stuff could happen to a person in twenty-four hours."

"Look on the bright side, at least you haven't had to get on a boat or fend off any snakes yet."

"How is that looking on the bright side?"

"You could be dead," he said instead.

"There you go," she said. "Thank you for saving me, by the way."

"I'm invested," he said, winking. "It turns out I like kissing you."

She blinked slowly at him, and he realized she was almost asleep on her feet. It had taken a while for the adrenaline crash to come, but it was coming hard now. He had his Ka-Bar in his boot, so he cut some ferns to use as bedding beneath the roof of the fallen tree. By the time he was finished, he looked over and saw her sound asleep where he'd left her. He picked her up in his arms and laid her down, curling his body around her to keep her warm. It was a nice feeling. Normal. And he closed his eyes and drifted off without the nightmares of his past lulling him to sleep.

***

HER MIND WOKE long before her eyes were able to open. Or maybe they were just caked shut with mud.

If she kept her eyes closed, she could pretend the moss beneath her was a feather mattress and the screeching howler monkeys were her alarm clock. The only thing she couldn't pretend away was the hot, hard male curled around her, and his very obvious arousal poking at her hip.

"I can't believe you have an erection right now," she said. She tried to stretch, secretly enjoying the way he felt next to her, but her muscles were too stiff and sore. "I'm so caked in mud, the howler monkeys probably think we're related. Men are so weird."

His hand cupped her breast and a hardened chunk of mud broke off into his hand. "I was going to say that there's not much that can keep us from getting an erection, but I'm starting to rethink that statement."

"Stop tickling my leg," she said, swatting at her leg.

"I'm not tickling your leg," he said.

"Yes, you are. I can feel it. I don't like being tickled. When I was in the third grade this stupid boy tickled me until I wet my pants. I punched him right in the face and broke his stupid piggy nose."

"As terrifying as that threat is, I'm still not tickling your leg."

She jerked her head up and felt the crunch of Elias's chin against her head.

"Jesus, woman, I'm seeing stars."

She couldn't focus on the pain. She could only focus on the spider the size of a dinner plate crawling up her leg.

She started screaming and kicking her leg, trying to dislodge it, but it didn't budge. She kicked out again and Elias made an inhuman sound as she kneed him right in the balls. She would've apologized if pure terror didn't have her in its grasp. She rolled around on the ground like a crazy person and then jumped to her feet, screaming the entire time.

When she finally took a chance and looked down, the spider was gone. Elias was curled up on all fours, trying to suck in a breath.

Her lungs heaved as she tried to get herself back under control, and she winced as she realized what she'd done to him.

"I'm so sorry," she said. "I hate spiders."

"And boats," he said bitingly. "And snakes."

"I said I'm sorry." She put her hands on her hips and another chunk of mud fell away. "Maybe if you'd been paying more attention to flesh-eating spiders instead of your erection you wouldn't be in this predicament right now."

"Are you kidding me?" he asked. "How is this my fault? Lady, your typewriter is short of an IQ."

She paused for a second and let it soak in. "That's hilarious, and I'm going to use it in a book."

"Glad I can provide a little humor for you."

More than you know," she said. "That monkey just stole your gun."

They didn't make it to the market in Santa Cruz

until almost two o'clock. Miller decided silence was probably the best course of action. Her body ached in places it never had before, she was hungry, cranky, and she would have committed murder for a thimbleful of coffee.

The mud on her body had dried during the night, and she was caked in the cracking substance. Elias had taken one look at her and read the situation pretty quickly. He'd only spoken when he needed to for the sixteen-mile trek.

"Sweet Jesus," she said, coming to a stop. "Am I seeing a mirage, or is that civilization?"

"It's civilization," he said. "About a mile away. Can you make it?"

"I can be like fucking Usain Bolt," she said, and took off running.

The market was busy at this time of day, but she ignored the looks from the locals and focused on the sweet smells coming from a street cart.

"Hold on," Elias said, grabbing her arm before she could tackle the poor vendor. She turned her head and growled at him, but he only smiled at her. Maddening man. "We don't have any money. I'd prefer we not end up in prison for theft. They still cut off limbs for that here."

Then she remembered that his wallet and her purse, along with their other bags that had been in the cab that had gone over the cliff. And then she remembered something else and started pulling at the buttons of her mud-caked shirt.

"Umm, Miller," Elias said, trying to pull her shirt together when she'd finally gotten the first couple of buttons undone. "I think you've had too much sun and you're a little dehydrated. You need to leave your clothes on, honey."

She looked at him and rolled her eyes. "Stop talking to me like I'm a simpleton and help me get to my bra. I stuck cash in there."

"You put cash in your bra?" he asked, brows raised.

"Of course I did," she said. "I'm from Texas. And everyone knows you never go anywhere without your emergency money stashed somewhere in case you get robbed."

"I'd forgotten," he said, his smile slow. "My mother used to put hers in her shoe. She'd forget when she'd take them off, and I was always finding money in her shoes when I was a kid."

"See," she said. "The problem is getting to it. This mud is like plaster. I can't even imagine taking my pants off. I've probably got an entire mold of my reproductive system."

He barked out a laugh and stood in front of her so she was shielded from the occasional passersby.

"Ah-ha," she said, brandishing it in front of his face.

"If I find you coffee, food, and a place to shower

in the next five minutes," he said, "will you let me kiss you again?"

"If you can find me those things in the next five minutes, I'll let you get the mud out of my molars with your tongue." She grinned at him and felt the mud crackle on her face.

"Tempting offer," he said. "How can I refuse?"

TWO HOURS LATER, they were halfway clean, had groceries, new clothes, and full bellies. She wasn't sure if stripping down to her underwear and being hosed off counted as a "shower," but she was too tired to argue with the three-hundred-pound native woman wearing a bright blue flowered sarong and no shoes.

The woman had grabbed her by the arm and shoved her into a straw stall, her Tinker Bell voice completely at odds with her size. She spoke rapidly in a language Miller had never heard before, and she matter-of-factly started stripping off Miller's clothes, as if she hosed down muddy women on a daily basis. Maybe she did.

She still had mud in interesting places by the time it was over, but at least she was clean enough to not scare anyone. The woman gave her a purple flowered sarong, tied it at the shoulder, and then threw her muddy clothes and underwear in a big metal trash bin.

She had to hand it to Elias: he'd delivered on his promises. He must have wanted to kiss her really badly. She had a plastic cup of steaming black coffee in her hand, and though she hadn't found chicken nuggets, they'd had the most delicious street tacos she'd ever put in her mouth.

"I don't think my feet can handle anymore walking today," she said, shifting the shopping bags in her arms.

"You want another cab ride?" he asked.

"No, but maybe you could rent us a donkey or something. Or maybe we could just rent a room somewhere close by."

"Why would we do that when we have a perfectly good yacht to sleep on tonight?" he asked.

"This obsession you have with getting me on a boat is unhealthy."

"I'm just trying to help you conquer this fear. And give you top-of-the-line meds from a government facility no one else in this world has access to, so you don't throw up your lunch all over the deck.

"How about we take a pedicab instead of a donkey. They'd have to be insane to try and kidnap us and pedal that thing up the mountain."

She was too tired to argue about the medication. It would either work or it wouldn't. Only time would tell.

Elias flagged down a pedicab and negotiated a

price, and they rode to the docks, the sun beating down overhead. Just like the day before, the gray clouds waited in the distance.

"This weather is insane," she said. "Is it always like this?"

"What? Molten hot, followed by freezing rain?" His mouth quirked at the corner. "Pretty much."

It took about twenty minutes in the pedicab to make it to the docks where their yacht was berthed. Miller couldn't move. Just the way it bobbed up and down in the water made her stomach churn.

"Uh, oh," he said. "How can you already be green? We're just standing on the dock."

"Just a hidden talent of mine," she said deadpan.

"Hold on a second and I'll get the medicine and bring it back here. I'll take the groceries up with me and put the cold stuff away. I don't want the ice cream to melt."

"I can't talk about food right now," she said, pinching her lips together and swallowing.

"Right," he said. "Be right back."

He wasn't gone long, and she noticed how easy he made it look going up and down the ramp to the boat. He had a black plastic box in his hand, and when he reached her he opened it and took out a syringe with a ridiculously long needle.

"Wait a second," she said, her eyes growing wide at the sight of the syringe.

"Your choice," he said. "A little prick now or a lot of vomiting later."

"I'll show you who's the little prick," she said stubbornly.

He barked out a laugh and thumped the syringe to get rid of the bubbles. And then he leaned toward her and captured her lips in a kiss so hot she was surprised she didn't turn into a puddle at his feet. When he pulled away they were both breathing heavy.

"Is that your payment kiss for the shower and coffee?" she asked.

"No, I'll take payment on that later. I just felt like kissing you."

"Good to know."

"At least when I kiss you next time you won't have to worry about getting seasick. Let me get you a Band-Aid."

She looked at the empty syringe in his hand and then down at her arm, which had a tiny drop of blood where he'd injected her. And then she looked back at him again with her mouth open in a soft O.

He grinned at her unapologetically. "Bet you can't think of a movie reference for that piece of action, can you?"

CHAPTER THIRTEEN

Miller would be the first to admit she didn't know a lot about boats—nothing at all really—but it wasn't the jungle and there was a solid roof over her head, so she wasn't going to complain. It probably helped that the nausea had disappeared within a few minutes of the injection, so she was feeling a little more confident as she studied her new lodgings.

Elias had been right. This was an expensive piece of equipment. He'd checked it thoroughly, weapon in hand, before they'd hauled the rest of the groceries, supplies, and new clothing purchases on board.

"I can't believe that people live like this," she said, looking around wide-eyed. "It's bigger than a house. And look at the quality of the floors and cabinets. I keep thinking about *Titanic*. All that opulence and the ship still sank."

"Probably not the best movie reference for the circumstances," Elias said. "The boat's been boarded," he said. "As I'd expect it to be. They left a footprint on the deck. And I found a couple of bugs while doing my search. I'll have the computer scan for others."

"I'm assuming you're not talking about bed bugs and cockroaches," she said.

"No, the other variety."

There was an unassuming panel on the wall, much like in the railcar, and Elias placed his hand on it. The interior came to life, panels opening in the walls and extra control panels appearing with all the gadgets and knobs that she assumed made the boat run.

"Elias Cole, agent number zero zero four," he said.

Agent confirmed by voice recognition . . . the computer said back.

"You're agent 004?" Miller asked. "Seriously?"

He winked and said, "Run diagnostics."

The Devil's Due *was last boarded at twelve-twenty-three p.m. Tanks are full and engine systems are functioning at one hundred percent. Temperature is dropping at a steady and rapid pace, and thunderstorms are expected in exactly twenty-three minutes. It is suggested to find a secure location to anchor.*

"Any signs of tampering or discovery?" Elias asked.

No signs of tampering, and security was not breached.

"We're free to talk," Elias told her. "As soon as I placed my hand on the panel we became shielded. The only place we'll have to be careful is out on deck.

There are so many long-distance listening devices it's always better to be safe than sorry."

"Why would they board? Do you think they know we're here already?" she asked, eyeing the lone footprint.

"Unlikely," he said. "Cordova's men have their finger on the pulse of everything that happens on the islands. They know regular tourists from tourists with 'money.' It's obvious we came in with money. They've got our identities, and they'll put our backgrounds through the paces, so we'll keep our fingers crossed the agency did a thorough job there and aren't going to leave us high and dry."

The clouds rolled across the sky, turbulent and gray, and the wind caused ripples across the water. The boat rocked beneath her feet, but she didn't feel the waves of nausea she expected. She was keeping her fingers crossed that Elias's magic shot would do the trick. Things might be different once they actually got out onto the water.

"I've got to tell you," she said, "I could go the rest of my life without ever seeing rain again after last night."

"I can promise this is going to be a totally different experience," he said. "Unless your *Titanic* premonition comes true, and then we've got other problems to deal with."

The yacht was beautiful and a sleek white with two blue stripes down the side. The trident she'd become familiar with was painted on the hull. Windows surrounded the main living and kitchen area, letting in watery light. White leather bench seats lined the walls in a U shape beneath the windows, and a dining table for six was bolted to the center of the teak floors. The kitchen cabinets matched the floors and the countertops were the same bright white as the leather cushions. There was a spiral staircase that led both up to the top deck and down below to the lower cabin.

"Bedrooms are down below," Elias said. "Take your pick. I'd like to put a little distance between us and the mainland. There's a little cove that's close that backs directly to the mountains. Anyone approaching would have to do so by water. It gives us a little extra time to prepare."

"We're going out there?" she asked, wide-eyed. "Now? What about the storm?"

"We've got twenty-three minutes," he said. "We should make it just in time. Then we can enjoy dinner and see how bad that four-dollar bottle of wine is going to be."

"I'll let you test it first," she said. "That's why I got the beer. It's almost impossible to screw that up." She took her new clothes and toiletries and squeezed herself down the small staircase. She caught her balance and held on to the stair rail as Elias slowly guided them away from the dock.

The downstairs area was huge. There was a common sitting area and game room, and there was a bedroom suite on each side with a private bath. The king-sized beds each faced windows that looked out onto the water, and other than the color scheme—one in blues and golds and the other in purples and silvers—they looked identical. She hoped there were blinds because she'd never been a morning person, and she had no intention of becoming one.

She chose the purple and silver bedroom and put away her new clothes—mostly long pants and layering pieces, along with a few loose dresses like the one she was wearing, and then she realized she hadn't needed to do much shopping at the market. The closet was fully stocked with different sizes and brands of clothing. And the shoes . . .

"Oh, man," she whispered, eyeing an entire wall of the closet. "I could get used to this."

She checked the drawers and saw lingerie and underthings, all with the tags still on them, and she selected some and then went into the bathroom. After the last twenty-four hours, she was never going to take hot running water and soap for granted again.

If she was being honest with herself, she needed some time alone—to reevaluate things. The Elias she'd gotten to know over the last several days wasn't what she'd expected from the man who'd left her so sexually frustrated a couple of months before. She still didn't understand why he'd done it, but she'd come to understand *him* a little better, and she realized he wasn't the kind of man who would hurt her on purpose.

He had a strict moral code, and she could tell by the way he talked about his mom and sisters that he had an appreciation and respect for women. He was funny, and wasn't afraid to laugh at himself, and she loved talking to him. She liked him. And good grief, did he turn her on. If she believed in the happily-ever-afters she wrote about, he'd be exactly the kind of man she was looking for. But she didn't believe. And she wasn't looking. But that didn't mean the physical need for him wasn't there. In fact, the more time she spent with him, the harder it was to resist. Especially if he kept kissing her.

Thinking about his kisses wasn't helping. Her skin was sensitive, her nipples rigid, and her body primed. Even the water droplets sluicing across her skin were too much. It would be so easy to slide her hand down to the damp folds between her legs. To take the edge off. And she realized if she did, it would be Elias's touch she imagined. The substitution would never match up to the real thing.

She turned the water off with a flick of her wrist and stepped out of the shower before she could give into temptation. The towel was soft, but it was still too much against her sensitive skin. Maybe she should just let things happen. It was sex. A physical release. It's not like he had to declare undying love.

All he had to do was follow through and not leave her hanging.

It was best to just let nature take its course, like a mature adult in charge of her own sexuality. The bathroom was fully stocked with toiletries, and she found creams to smooth on her face and body. She'd gotten some sun walking to the market that morning, and her skin had a nice healthy glow to it by the time she'd moisturized.

She put on the panties and then walked back out to the bedroom to the large closet. If she helped Elias make up his mind by slipping on something a little sexier than she'd normally wear, then who was anyone else to judge. It's not like she'd be holding a gun to his head. The choice was his to make.

There was a white sundress that caught her eye, and when she slipped it on and looked in the mirror she knew it was exactly right. It draped loosely, all the way to the floor, and just skimmed her body.

She took a deep breath and headed back upstairs, and she watched him for a second at the helm, completely at ease and in control as they cut through the water.

"Have you ever seen that movie *Overboard*?" she asked, coming up behind him.

"Let me guess," he said. "You saw the shoe closet."

"I might have had a small orgasm. It's the most beautiful thing I've ever seen."

"Pour yourself some four-dollar wine, and get comfortable. I'm trying to move us into a safe location to wait out the storm, and also keep us from getting ambushed in the night. There's a little inlet up ahead, and anyone wanting to board us will only be able to reach us by water."

She took the wine from the refrigerator and unscrewed the top, pouring herself half a glass of the pink liquid and then moving to the windows to see the view. She saw what he meant when he'd said they'd only be reachable by water. There was a small inlet that butted up to a steep cliff, and there were no other boats docked there. She didn't know if that was a good sign or a bad sign.

Elias expertly maneuvered the yacht into the inlet, and immediately the cliffs protected them from the wind.

"Where'd you learn to drive a boat?" she asked. "As a SEAL?"

She saw him wince, and then he cut his eyes in her direction, his mouth open as if he were going to say something. But he just froze and stared at her.

"What?" she asked, knowing exactly what he was thinking. It was written all over his face.

"Nice dress," he said, his gaze lingering on her breasts. And then he blinked and focused his attention back on the water. "First of all, you don't drive a boat. You sail a boat."

"Oh, my apologies," she said, brows raised. "I hope the mariner police don't arrest me."

"Smart-ass," he said, grinning. "But to answer your question, I could handle one of these babies long before I was a SEAL. I grew up on the water. Like I said, I'd have much rather spent my days fishing than going to school. Of course, I didn't get to captain anything like this, but learning on something not quite so nice helped me understand the workings of boats from the inside out.

"I've always been comfortable on the water. So being a SEAL seemed like the natural course I'd take. I couldn't ever imagine myself doing anything else, really. When I take vacation time it's always the first place I go. I've got a boat down in the Keys."

He got them settled and shut down the control panel. "The security here is set up to let us know when anyone is approaching, so we'll be fine. Plus, we've got a great view of the show."

The way the interior of the boat was designed made it look like you were part of whatever was happening outside. And at the moment, Mother Nature was putting on a hell of a show. The rain came down in sheets and visibility was limited too far out, but they could still see the waves crashing violently against the rocks.

"It does this every day?" she asked.

"Afternoon storms. But this one seems a little out of the ordinary," he admitted. "I checked radar and the forecast and it looks like we're in for something a little stronger than usual, but it should all clear off sometime during the night. Why? Are you feeling okay?"

"I'm feeling really good, actually," she said, surprised any medication could've been that effective. Especially considering the hell she went through the last time.

"Good, then watch this," Elias said. "The cliff is blocking the wind, so we should stay dry."

"What?" Miller asked, confused.

He hit a switch, and the row of windows slowly started to slide open. It was a surreal feeling—the sway of the boat made it seem as if she were standing on the water, the precipice of the storm at her fingertips.

The air was cool and she felt the sea spray against her face. "That's incredible," she said.

"Such power. And we're part of it. At least for a time.

"We might as well start dinner if you're hungry. We're going to be stuck here for a while if the radar is anything to go by."

She was surprised when he joined her in the kitchen, and not just to hand her a beer, though she took it gladly. They'd bought fresh shrimp at the market, along with pasta and the ingredients to make a lemon butter sauce, and she set everything out, letting her mind wander as the storm blew in.

"This could be a problem," she said, watching the

lemons roll from the counter to the floor. She was still trying to find her sea legs, shifting her weight to find her balance.

"Put them in the sink until you need them," he said. "The boat is equipped with a stabilizer for the pot on the stove. Just be careful not to fill it too full so the water doesn't slosh out. I'll put the bread in the oven."

They worked with ease, and it wasn't long until the smell had her stomach rumbling. The temperature had cooled things off, but she was warm in the kitchen, and a fine mist coated the all-weather seats beneath the open windows.

"I spent the flight trying to pinpoint various landmarks your brother notated in his letter to you," he said. "We'll need to start out early in the morning, catch the tide so we can get there a little quicker. Time is of the essence."

"Okay, but I can't promise to be awake or fully functional. I'm used to working night shift. I usually only see the times before ten in the morning if I've stayed up all night."

"I'll make sure the coffee is on a timer for you," he said, moving things to the table. It had transformed again, and in the center were indented areas to hold the bowls of food so they didn't slide off the table. Holes appeared next to each place setting indention that were just the right size for drinks.

"I really need to get one of these tables," she said.

"It's a supercomputer, plus a lot of other things," he said. "But at the core she's a computer."

"She?"

His lips twitched. "Her name is Elaine. She's a patented design, and there aren't any other organizations in the world who have technology like her."

You are correct . . . Elaine said. *I am one of a kind.*

"She listens all the time?" Miller asked, slightly freaked out by the thought.

"When she's activated," Elias said. "But she can be put in sleep mode and still have the full capability to know what's going on around us. She also has the ability to answer questions at her discretion, using the data given. Elaine, what's your favorite movie?"

I have thousands of movies in my database, but I have to say, my personal favorite is Rear Window *with Jimmy Stewart. We should watch it sometime.*

"It's one of my favorites too, Elaine." He looked at Miller and asked, "What kind of music do you like to listen to?"

"Depends on what I'm writing at the time. Usually movie soundtracks or the old standards—Nat Cole and Billie Holiday."

"Elaine, play Billie Holiday and form a soundtrack with similar music."

Good choice, Elias. I enjoy the standards. It seems we have quite a bit in common.

Miller raised her brows, certain that she detected

a flirtatious tone in Elaine's voice. Elias winked at her and grinned. "Thank you, Elaine," he said as Billie Holiday came on and asked where her lover man could be.

"That's incredible," Miller said. "And kind of terrifying. I'm not sure I like the idea of a computer that has that much thinking capability."

The expression on her face must have given her discomfort away because Elias said, "Elaine, go to sleep mode. I'll control manually for the evening."

As you wish . . . And Miller would have sworn she sounded hurt at the dismissal. *I will look forward to being woken in the morning. Good night.*

They brought the food to the table and dished it into their bowls, breaking off pieces of crusty bread and making small talk, enjoying the music on low in the background. It seemed so . . . normal. Like they'd done it a thousand times before. And she guessed they had, though it had never been just the two of them. There was always a group.

"What I was saying before we started talking about computers," he said, "is that I've located at least one of the markers your brother wrote about. There's a cleft rock the locals call Corazón Roto. Or 'broken heart.' We can use that as a starting place and venture out from there. The waterfall angle is a little more difficult. Waterfalls are pretty prevalent on the Triangle Islands, but I've marked out the ones that are tourist attractions.

"We've got to remember that during the course of

your brother's journey, he stumbled across the wreckage of your parents' plane. We can assume it was untouched and that it's in a remote location. There are two waterfalls that fit this description that I was only able to see from the satellite map imagery. There's no documentation of them otherwise that I can find. But it looks like the terrain is pretty treacherous, and it's at least a day hike from Corazón Roto.

"I'll get the boat as close as I can to the coordinates, and then we'll have to take off on foot and try to re-create your brother's steps. The bad news is the waterfalls are in opposite directions, so if we choose the wrong one it's going to add at least another day to our journey."

"And if neither of them is what we're looking for?" she asked.

"Then we'll go back to the drawing board."

"What about the pillar he mentions?" she asked.

"I've got no clue on that one," he said. "The mountain areas are pretty dense with jungle, but it could mean anything. A felled tree or something else resembling a pillar. The Galápagos Islands were discovered by the Incans some sixty years before the Spanish ever got here. There are ruins on the main islands, but it's possible there might be some around here."

"Part of me hates him for this," she confessed. "As much as I love my brother, I hate that he's brought this back to the surface. I've spent my whole life trying to forget my childhood. Trying to move past the grief of their death."

"I hate to say it," Elias said, "because God knows he and I rarely saw eye to eye the last couple of years we were SEALs together. But maybe he really does have an explanation worth listening to, like he said in his letter. Maybe there's something bigger that he has no control over."

She shook her head. She was just so angry. Angry at all of them.

"You've got to let it go," he said. "You can be angry at them and still forgive them for what they did to you. It'll eat you up inside if you don't."

"You know this from experience?" she asked.

"I know what it feels like to be eaten up with anger and the need for revenge. And I know you reach a certain point where it gets harder and harder to become the person you were before. Until you become a person there's no coming back from."

She looked away, giving him time to be lost in his own thoughts, and went back to her dinner. It didn't take them long to eat. "I'll clean up the dishes," she told him.

"I've never actually heard anyone volunteer to do that before," he said. "When I was growing up we took turns. My sister Janelle always managed to have band practice, too much homework, or a stomach bug that kept her from getting to experience her turn."

"Smart girl," she said. "And where is Janelle now?"

"She's a schoolteacher down in south Texas," he said. "She's got three kids. She's the middle child, so she has the syndrome. I expect she'll have a fourth kid before too long so she doesn't give her own middle child the same endearing personality traits she had growing up."

"You have a second sister?" she asked, wanting to know more about him. He rarely talked about his personal life, and she could understand why now that she knew they were all considered dead to everyone who'd ever known them.

"Yeah, Katie," he said. "She's just finishing up her last year of college. She's going to take over the world. She was always the bossiest little thing, but she was cute. I was in high school when she was born."

"I bet that made things interesting," she said, imagining how a teenage boy would react to the fact that there was physical proof his parents still had sex.

His eyes laughed as they met hers. "It was mortifying. But not surprising. My parents never could keep their hands off each other. Now that I'm older, I realize how nice that was to see growing up. They love each other like crazy."

The sadness in his eyes kept her from asking any more questions, even though she instinctively knew he'd answer whatever she asked. Miller watched him from her periphery as he cleared the table. When he was done, he grabbed another beer, taking her at her word that she was fine doing the dishes by herself. She appreciated that. Most men would try to impress by insisting on helping. But she could tell Elias had been raised well. He did things without having to be asked, and he did them without fanfare or looking for praise. It was refreshing to see. She'd dated some really interesting "men" who needed constant praise.

She'd always enjoyed mindless tasks where she could let her mind wander. It was the best way to work out a problem or a plot. He grabbed another beer and then turned off the lights over the table, which had transformed back into a flat surface now that they were finished eating, and it cast the front half of the yacht into darkness and displayed the brilliance of the storm to its full potential.

The group of seats were moveable, and he arranged them so there were two pressed together like a chaise, and then he put two more together for her. He dropped back onto the first one and propped his feet up. She'd never seen his bare feet before, though she'd never really had reason to.

"What are you thinking?" she asked as she dried the last of the dishes and put them away. "You don't usually look so relaxed."

"I was thinking it'd be a hell of a time to go fishing."

"You're kidding. You'd fish in this?" she asked in surprise. "That's insane."

"When you go deep-sea fishing, you play the

hand God deals as far as the weather goes. It's a hell of a good time."

Miller grabbed a bottle of water, but she didn't take the seat next to him. She was restless. Her mind wouldn't shut down. All the variables of what could happen. The worry for Justin. The thought of discovering her parents' plane and wondering if she'd come across their bodies.

She lifted her face to the salty breeze and let her senses take over—the smell of the sea and the crash of waves against the rocks—the rain thunderous as it slapped against the water, and Nat Cole singing about being too young to be in love.

"What are you thinking?" he asked, repeating the earlier question.

His voice was close, but she didn't turn around. And then he moved in so their bodies didn't quite touch, and he twined his hands with hers. There was nothing sexual about the connection, but she felt as if she'd never been more intimate with another human being. There was something inherently magical about the moment, and if she could have, she'd have picked this frame of time to last forever.

"I'm thinking this is one of those moments that will still be with me when I'm ninety and my bones are brittle and my eyes cloudy with age."

"It's a good moment," he said, and leaned down to place a soft kiss on the back of her neck.

A shudder went through her at the touch, and he turned her slowly so she was loosely held in his arms. And then he began to move her to the music—Ella this time—her voice heartbreaking as she sang of stardust melodies.

She was floating. It was the only way to describe what it felt like to be in his arms. She'd liked to think herself cynical and worldly and aware when it came to matters of the heart, but being slow danced in Elias Cole's arms was one of the best feelings she'd ever had.

She didn't know how long they danced. The songs changed over time and again, and there were moments she didn't hear the music at all—only his slow, steady heartbeat as she rested her head against his chest.

It was the most natural thing in the world when his lips found hers. Her sigh mixed with his and her heart thudded in her chest, her body pressing into him as if to say *finally*.

It was different than the last time. It wasn't a lust-hazed, frantic kiss. There was tenderness, a care that hadn't been there before, and when his tongue stroked hers she felt the pull of desire low in her belly.

Her hands stroked and caressed, while he made love to her mouth, dancing her slowly toward the chairs he'd moved together. She felt small next to him, his body hard where hers was soft, and the heat of him enveloped her. Her hands roamed across his back and up his broad shoulders, to the muscled biceps that made her want to take a bite out of him. Their mouths parted briefly as he pulled her sweater over her head, but she barely noticed. Her fingers were busy tugging at the hem of his shirt, lifting it so she could feel the taut muscles of his stomach.

She wanted to commit every sensation and feeling to memory. The gentle sway of the boat and the dampness of the rain across her skin. The way his hand felt against her back as he unclasped her bra and left her bared before him, and his soft swear as he helped her take his shirt off. The way her hands fumbled with the button of his pants before she pushed them and his briefs down, and the weight of his body as he followed her onto the makeshift bed.

Hands moved with more urgency, his mouth devoured her lips, her neck, and his lips finally found her nipple, his tongue swirling around the taut bud. She felt every suckle in the pulsing of her clitoris. Her skirt was rucked around her thighs, and she wrapped her legs around his hips, pulling him closer. But he kept kissing his way down, across her stomach and to the elastic waistband of her skirt. He tugged it gently and she lifted her hips, and he pulled it and the black panties she wore from her legs and let them drop to the floor.

"Please don't make me wait any longer," she begged.

He came down on top of her, his breathing ragged as her arms came around him in a lover's embrace.

"No, I won't," he said. "We've waited long enough."

His hands locked with hers, and she reveled in the heat and weight of his body, the hardness of his muscles combined with the coarse hair on his chest that brought new sensations across her breasts. She opened for him, her legs twining around his waist.

"Miller," he said, his eyes steady on her. And then he slid into her, and she saw brilliant light as her eyelids fluttered closed. "No, look at me."

It was too much. But she did as he asked. Her body moved fluidly with his, a different kind of dance this time, but beautiful in motion.

She felt the pressure build inside her, her hips rising and falling to meet his. Their skin was damp with rain and passion, and her hands slid up his back, gripping his shoulders and trying to find an anchor in the storm raging around her. Cries escaped her lips, and she heard him chant her name over and over again.

The orgasm rolled through her, building and building in intensity, and she cried out his name as he finally let go and emptied himself into her.

CHAPTER FOURTEEN

Elias lay in bed, staring into the darkness, long before the sun rose. Miller was curled into his side, her hand fisted on his chest and her breathing deep and even. And as he held her, he realized he was in a whole lot of trouble. Because he loved her. And love and revenge had no future together.

He'd known it before he'd touched her. But he hadn't cared. His carnal nature had far outweighed his common sense. And now that he knew how well they fit together, what true intimacy really was, he knew he could never settle for anything less. Anyone other than Miller.

He slipped out of bed, smiling when Miller didn't even shift. They'd only gotten to sleep a couple of hours before. Never had he spent so long making love to a woman. And that's exactly what they'd been doing. It hadn't been just sex. They'd talked, and touched, and tasted, and he knew every inch of her body and the places that gave her the most pleasure. And she knew his.

He showered and dressed quickly, donning linen shorts and a blue island shirt, and then he went above to make sure the coffee had started. He didn't actually drink it himself, but he wanted to make sure it was at hand. Especially since he wanted to tell her that he thought she should stay on the yacht while he looked for her brother. He couldn't care less about the treasure. But Miller's safety was of utmost importance.

Had he ever put anyone else above himself? His brothers, of course, but war was different. On a personal level, his life had always been about him. What could advance *his* career. What brought *him* the most pleasure. But somewhere along the way in his relationship with Miller, he wanted to bring *her* the most pleasure, whether it was something as simple as making coffee or something as intimate as watching the way her eyes darkened when he slid deep inside of her.

The storm had stopped about the time they'd finally drifted off to sleep, and the darkness was still in their secluded corner. Even the water seemed at peace for the time being. He woke up Elaine, hoping she wasn't holding a grudge from the night before, and he set the coordinates and started up the engine.

He'd always liked the quiet time of night. It had

been his favorite time as a SEAL. The mission rattling around in his head, the adrenaline pumping, but disciplining his body to stay completely still and alert. To wait and watch. Combined with being on the water, he was pretty much in heaven at the moment.

He steered the boat out of the cove and toward the Triangle Islands. They needed to move swiftly. His gut was telling him Cordova was right behind them. And another part of his gut was telling him Eve was going to play games with him.

The sky faded from black to gray, the promise of the sun a hint at ocean's end. He felt her behind him, and when he turned to look at her his heart stopped in his chest. She wore one of his T-shirts, and it hung to midthigh. Her face was free of makeup, her skin flawless and flushed from sleep, and her lips were swollen from the night before.

"Coffee," she rasped. "I beg of you."

The moment was broken and his heart started beating again. "Right behind you," he said.

She grunted something unintelligible, poured herself a cup, grunted something again, and then turned around and went down below again. He chuckled and thought he could get used to this. And then he quickly put the thought out of his mind.

He made sure they were on course, checked their surroundings, and then he followed after her.

The bathroom was efficient and a good size. The floor was large neutral tiles and it was seamless to walk straight into the shower. There were no doors on the shower, and a large rain head spout hung from the ceiling. There were multiple showerheads on each end of the shower and they all sprayed toward the middle. A simple drain in the floor kept the rest of the bathroom floor from getting wet.

Steam billowed, filling the room, and he grinned again as he watched her for a minute. Her head rested against the wall and her eyes were closed, the coffee cup in her hand, and hot water poured over her. And still his body responded. Even after the night they'd spent.

He checked his watch, and then stripped off his clothes in silence. She didn't hear him approach, and he took the coffee cup from her hand before she dropped it and set it on the ledge. She barely noticed. He adjusted the spray and moved in close behind her, his erection pressing against her full bottom, and she widened her stance for him as he probed for entry.

"I thought I'd help you wake up," he whispered against her neck, nipping with his teeth.

"I don't think it's working," she said, and then she gasped as he pushed fully inside of her.

She was tight, swollen, from the night before, but she was ready for him. Her hands pressed flat against the cool tile and her breath hitched with every stroke. His hands grasped her hips and then slid up and around to cup her full breasts.

"How about now?" he asked, his thumb and forefinger tweaking her nipples. He felt her tighten around him and he groaned because it felt so good.

He pushed high inside of her, lifting her to her toes, and a cry escaped her lips. He bit down on her shoulder and he could feel the change in her—the liquid heat that surrounded him, the change in texture as her vaginal walls swelled around him. But still she was stubborn, and held back.

"Not yet," she said. "You'll have to try harder."

"If I try any harder you won't be able to walk for a week," he said.

"It's good to have goals," she panted, making him laugh.

He moved a couple of steps back, pulling her with him, and then he placed his hand between her shoulder blades, pushing her down. He took her hands and wrapped them around the handrail so she was stretched out fully in front of him. He kissed his way up her spine, burying himself deeper inside of her the farther up he got. And when his lips were next to her ear he whispered, "Hold on."

Her cry of pleasure echoed in the small room as he grabbed her hips and pistoned in and out of her.

She came around him with a violence that almost brought him to his knees. And he couldn't hold off any longer. He emptied himself into her with a roar and then they both crumpled to the shower floor.

CHAPTER FIFTEEN

The Pacific wasn't meant for swimming, but the sun was out and brutal, so they'd each changed into their swimsuits. Talk about mistakes, Miller walking around in a bikini made it hard to keep his mind on the task at hand.

They'd gotten a late start that morning after their shower, and it was early afternoon when they finally reached the Triangle Islands. There was a reason Aguas Mortales wasn't a tourist attraction. Getting to it wasn't convenient, and getting on the island was even less convenient. The tour boats wouldn't risk the chance of having their hulls ripped to shreds by the rocks, or letting a group of people off to roam aimlessly on an island with an active volcano and uncharted territory.

"I keep waiting for the afternoon rain," Miller said. "It's hot today."

She was wearing the red triangle bikini and had

one of the silky floral sarongs they'd found at the market tied at her waist.

"The rain will be here soon," he said. "You can smell it."

It had taken almost two hours to circle the three islands so he could determine the best point of entry. There really wasn't one. He finally decided their best bet was to anchor out a little ways and use the Zodiac attached beneath the yacht to make their way toward shore.

The Triangle Islands were a group of three, and a narrow canal ran between each of them, flowing toward the middle where the three islands met. He could've anchored on the middle island, where the shore was a little deeper and the rocks weren't as prevalent, but it would've added an extra day to their hike, and they were already running short.

He was surprised they hadn't been tracked down already. Elaine had been compiling the alerts that other boats were being boarded and searched at will. And extra security measures had been set up at all the resorts, so passports were checked again and each new visitor went through a checkpoint, with an extra umbrella drink in hand for the inconvenience.

He'd calculated it would take several hours to walk to the Corazón Roto, and from there they'd have to try and retrace Justin's steps. Finding and extracting Justin and somehow taking Cordova out of the game so Miller was safe in her own home was the mission. He still wasn't a hundred percent sure that they'd be successful at either of them. The thought of Miller having to go into hiding if they didn't succeed didn't sit well with him.

Elias couldn't have cared less about treasure, but he'd also promised Miller he'd help her find the wreckage of her parents' plane. It could be an impossible task. But he wouldn't quit until his promise had been fulfilled. She deserved some peace in her life. However he could bring it to her.

"They must be slacking," he said, looking through his binoculars.

"What's that?" she asked, grabbing a bottle of water from the fridge.

"Cordova's men," he said. "Cartel business must be down. I've had Elaine compiling numbers to see what our potential fallout is and the probability that we can fight our way out of this if we have to."

"I'd imagine that probability is pretty small since there are likely more than two of them."

Elias snorted out an offended breath and looked at her incredulously. "Lady, I've taken out a twenty-man team by myself, and they never even knew I was there."

"Okay, okay," she said, hands raised. "I'm sorry. I didn't mean to bruise your ego."

"You've bruised a lot of things on me, darling, but my ego hasn't been one of them."

She rolled her eyes and he looked back through the binoculars with a smile on his face.

"It's taken them longer than I thought to track us down to search us. That's a sign in our favor."

"They've found us?" she asked, a flash of fear in her eyes.

"That's what I've been trying to tell you," he said. "A cutter is heading straight for us."

"Am I supposed to know what that is?" she asked, exasperated.

"It's a boat. A fast one. Typically used by the Coast Guard or law enforcement. And cartels apparently."

"You think they'll recognize me?"

"Not if you keep that bikini on," he told her. "The force is with you, young Jedi."

"I'm so proud of you for the reference," she said. "But I can't believe you'd suggest I'd use my body to get out of this."

"I'm not a fan of it myself. I've become rather attached to it. But do you have any better ideas?"

"Other than shooting them all and dumping them overboard?"

"Funny," he said. "I'm glad you can keep your sense of humor." He watched as she slicked on some gloss that made her lips look poutier, and then she plumped up her breasts in the tiny bikini. "Let's not go too overboard," he told her. "I'd really rather not have to shoot anyone and dump them in the ocean. It's more of a pain in the ass than you'd think."

"Everything involves red tape nowadays," she said dryly.

He hooted out a laugh. He'd missed her sarcasm and dry humor like crazy.

"Elaine," he said. "Suppress all classified systems on board. Lock down weapons closet, and power down until only my voice command reactivates the systems."

Complying . . . Stay safe and kick ass.

Miller snorted out a laugh, and Elias grinned as Elaine did as he asked. "Hopefully, it won't come to that."

"What do you think they want?" Miller asked.

"I think it's probably an introductory call," he said. "They're going to be curious about the people using this craft. Be polite."

"I'm always polite," she said automatically.

He arched a brow and she rolled her eyes. "I can be polite when I need to be," she corrected.

"That's more like it," he said. "It's probably best to just stay silent. This isn't a culture where men want women to speak unless they're spoken to directly. And he's probably not going to be able to form coherent sentences anyway."

Elias had experience with the kind of men on the cutter. They were dressed as a kind of law enforcement official, but they were bought men—mercenaries—owned by the Black Widow. They'd expect a bribe, and Elias was prepared to give them one. He'd already prepared an envelope of cash, expecting this visit the day before.

"Ahoy, *Debido del Diablo*," one of the men called out—the one who appeared to be in charge. The others held machine guns at ease with one hand and the strap of the cutter for balance with the other.

Elias answered in English, laying on a heavy Australian accent since their passports gave them that origin. It was best if they didn't find out he spoke the language like a native to the islands. It is always interesting to discover what people will say then they think you can't understand.

"We can board?" the man asked, his accent thick. The look on his face made it clear the question wasn't really meant to be answered. And then his eyes went to Miller and Elias saw red. He looked her up and down like a piece of meat. Like they'd planned. And the man was all but salivating as he took in her every curve. Elias hadn't expected it to bother him as much as it did.

"Sure, mate," Elias said. "My wife and I were just about to anchor for the evening. It's a romantic spot. This is our anniversary trip, and my boss was generous enough to offer his boat."

Reminding him of the man who owned the boat

seemed to be the right tactic, because he became a little friendlier.

"Congratulations, señor," the man said, barely taking his eyes off Miller. "Your boss has always been a generous man."

The cutter cut its engine and drifted close beside them, and they hooked a ramp to the yacht and then hooked the other end on the cutter, so the two boats were connected together. They boarded the *Devil's Due* one by one, the spokesman last.

"My name is Diego," he said, nodding. "You have passports?"

"Of course," Elias said. "Let me get them."

He went to the drawer where he'd put their passports and the envelope of cash and grabbed them both, and he saw Miller out of the corner of his eye watching the other men. They'd spread out above- and belowdeck, doing a full search of the boat. She had a hip propped against the kitchen island, and she stood so the slit of her sarong showed her entire leg to the hip. While Miller was watching the other men, Diego was still watching her.

Elias handed him the envelope and watched as Diego looked inside briefly and flipped through the bills. Then he put it in the inside pocket of his uniform shirt. He barely glanced at Elias's passport, but he studied Miller's a little more closely. And then he looked up at her and gave her another of those long, slow perusals from the top of her head to the tips of her toes. Most people would have been uncomfortable with the scrutiny, but she stared back at him steadily, her posture relaxed.

Elias felt a surge of pride.

"Your picture doesn't do you justice, señora," Diego said, bowing his head slightly.

Miller smiled and Elias watched as Diego took even closer notice. Damn that smile. Miller was uniquely beautiful at a glance. But she was stunning when she smiled. And dammit, she was *his*.

"I heard that every time I had to take a school picture," she said, taking his cue and speaking in her own Australian accent. He shouldn't have been surprised. There wasn't much she couldn't seem to do. "It takes a lot of work for a camera to make me look good."

"Impossible," Diego insisted. "You are *muy hermosa* always. But in person . . ." He put his fingers together and put them to his lips, kissing them. *"Exquisito."*

Diego's men returned from their search one by one, their eyes on Miller as they gathered on the deck, and Elias braced himself for a fight. But Diego gave them orders to get back on the boat and start the engine.

"I hope we meet again soon," he said, nodding to Elias and then Miller. "Take caution during your time on the islands. I'd suggest hiring a guide if you don't have protection for yourself. There are many dangers lurking. You have a great treasure under your care. These are unsettling times on the island, and there is little help for those isolated in areas such as this. Many are never found."

Diego crossed the ramp and they disconnected the boats, and then the cutter was gone as quickly as it had come up on them.

"Well, that was really weird," she said, rubbing her hands down her chilled arms. "I'm not sure if he was telling us to be careful or warning us to stay out of trouble."

"Both," Elias said. "We'll anchor at the middle island for the night. There's a couple of other boats docked there, and it might be best to have company for the time being. You're about to get your afternoon rain."

"How long do you think we have before they're back?" she asked.

"I don't know," he said. "These men are sloppy. If I were doing a search of this magnitude, I'd make sure every one of my men had studied your picture. And then I'd have computer renderings done of what you'd look like with different hair colors and lengths. Not one of those men even thought you looked familiar. I was watching their eyes. But Diego will figure it out. You just had to go and smile at him," he said, shaking his head. "That smile is so distinctive you might as well have a big 'I'm Miller Darling' tattoo on your forehead."

"Oh, for Pete's sake," she said, rolling her eyes. "You've been drinking the seawater. There's nothing remarkable about my smile. Diego was too busy looking at my breasts to notice my smile."

"In that case, he'll probably be back sooner. Those are pretty unforgettable too," he said.

"Funny," she said.

"I have my moments," he said. "In all seriousness, I think our time is limited. Diego wasn't just captivated by your body. He's more seasoned than the others. He spent some time studying your face. And, like I said, your smile gives you away. Hopefully, we'll be lost pretty far in the mountains by the time they start to hunt us."

"Maybe use a different word from 'hunt,'" she said. "I don't like the idea of being anyone's prey."

CHAPTER SIXTEEN

Dawn came early the next morning.

Especially since he'd spent most of the night awake. His mind had been racing, and he'd held Miller close, feeling the rise and fall of her chest against his side. His body had been on alert, waiting for Diego and his men to catch them in a surprise raid. But he had to remind himself that those men weren't SEALs. They wouldn't do things the way he did.

He'd made sure he had a cup of coffee ready for her and the shower was on as he got her out of bed before the sun rose. She took the cup sleepily and stumbled her way into the shower. And when she came out she was about halfway awake and managed to put on her explorer pants, a white tank top, and an overshirt without looking like she'd been dressed by a blind drunk.

He waited for her to wake up completely before he gave her instructions on what to pack for the trip onto the island. When she was finally alert and coherent he realized he'd gotten good at judging how long it would take her to transform into an actual human being in the mornings, and he'd woken her in plenty of time to see the sun rise.

"Watching the sunrise is a lot more enjoyable when you're about to go to bed," she said. "I can't imagine why anyone would ever wake up early to see it." She'd brought extra clothes and socks and any personal items she needed upstairs to lay out to pack. And then they divided up food and water bottles to carry between them.

"It's one of those things morning people like to do, I guess."

She cut a glance at him out of narrowed eyes. "You're one of those morning people. I can tell. You don't have to pretend. I see you running by my house at godawful early times while I'm finishing up my work for the night."

His lips twitched. "You watch me run by your house?"

"I just happen to be standing by my window thinking as you're jogging by," she said.

"Huh, maybe I should start knocking on your door in the mornings," he said. "What we've been doing the last couple of days is a hell of a lot better exercise than running. Easier on the knees too.

"Okay, put on your pack and let's test the weight.

It won't do us any good if you can't walk the first mile."

"You should really stop underestimating me," she said, putting the pack on and adjusting the straps more comfortably. "This is not my first rodeo. I can make fire from sticks and I know my cardinal directions. You wouldn't believe some of the research I've done for my books."

"I would never underestimate you," he said. "You amaze me every time you open your mouth."

He took both packs out to the diving deck and lowered the Zodiac into the water. When he came back inside he reactivated Elaine from her sleep.

"Elaine, reboot programs."

So good to hear your voice again, Elias . . . Rebooting all programs, and waiting for instructions. While I was waiting for your return, I took the liberty of retrieving your file so I could look at your picture. You're a very handsome man, Elias Houston Cole.

Miller snorted out a laugh, and Elias smiled, but he was hoping that was all Elaine said about his file. He knew there were areas of it that were classified, but he wasn't sure how much Elaine had access to.

"Houston?" Miller asked.

"My great-grandfather's name," he said. "He was a Texas Ranger. Elaine, unlock the weapons closet."

Yes, Elias . . . Is there anything else?

"Stand by," he said, moving into the kitchen.

He punched in several numbers on the microwave and then hit the start button. The pantry door slid open, and then it began to rotate so the food that had just been visible was now relocated to the hidden chamber between the walls. In place of the pantry was the small arsenal they'd brought with them. He took the Sig P229s and checked the magazine, and then he handed it to Miller.

"I've got a hip holster that should fit you, and it shouldn't be uncomfortable or get in the way of anything," he said. "I'd prefer you wear it instead of carrying it in your pack."

"I'd prefer to wear it too," she said.

He strapped on his holster, and stuck a sheathed Ka-Bar in his boot, and then sheathed a machete on his other hip because they wouldn't be going through well-traveled paths. He made a few other selections for his pack, including flares and fire starters, though it might be interesting to see Miller using sticks to start their fires. He'd already packed food and water. He hoped to make it to the first waterfall by dusk and set up camp there. But that would depend on the kind of pace Miller could keep up with. It wouldn't be an easy trek, even for an experienced hiker.

"Elaine," he said. "Secure all classified areas and do a continuous scan for threats within a twenty-five-mile radius. Alert me if there are any problems."

What are my orders if any hostiles board me?

"Listen and record," he said. "And scan faces for recognition. We'll see how many we can take down while we're here."

Complying . . .

Once he had everything he needed, he took the smaller hip holster and fitted it around Miller, making the adjustments where he needed to.

"How does that feel?" he asked after she holstered the Sig.

"I'm not going to lie," she said. "It feels pretty damn sexy. I'm used to carrying concealed. It doesn't have near the same impact."

"Funny," he said. "The thought of you carrying concealed scares the hell out of me."

"What should really scare the hell out of you is that most of the people in Last Stop are carrying concealed. Ginger Anderson is almost ninety years old. She wears it on her right hip, and it makes her list to the side so she walks in a circle everywhere she goes."

Elias burst out laughing because he knew exactly who she was talking about. And now that he knew the reason, it was terrifying. She didn't look strong enough to even lift a weapon, much less fire one.

"You're right," he said. "That scares the hell out of me. Remind me to tell Tess we need to start patting people down before viewings and funerals."

"It wouldn't do any good," Miller said, following

him to the dive deck where their gear was. "Everybody knows the best place to be armed is at a viewing or a funeral. People lose their minds when relatives die. You should know by now there's usually at least two good fistfights a year and a lot of ugly family secrets that come to light during funerals and viewings. If you take their guns away, then you'll be cheating Tess out of the opportunity of getting more business. Funerals are hard to come by in Last Stop."

"If I were any other person listening to you, I'd think you needed to be committed. But after living in Last Stop the last couple of years, I can say with certainty that you're speaking the truth. Which is disturbing in itself."

He climbed down the ladder into the Zodiac and started up the engine, letting it run a couple of minutes while Miller handed down the packs and he got everything secured. She came down the ladder and he helped her step into the Zodiac. It could be an adjustment to get used to an inflatable craft. And it was going to be a real test of the medicine he'd injected her with the day before for seasickness.

"Hold on like this," he said, showing her how to wrap her left wrist through straps that could be used to flip the boat right side up if it ever capsized. He figured it was best not to mention that's what they were for.

"I hope that medicine holds out," she said.

"I was just thinking the same thing." He gave her a thumbs-up and then took off from the berth beneath the dive deck of the yacht.

He heard her swear and then grinned as the wind and droplets of water slapped him in the face. It was almost like being home.

CHAPTER SEVENTEEN

Aguas Mortales wasn't what she'd been expecting. There were few palm trees, and there was nothing peaceful about the jagged rocks and crashing waves.

The three islands rose out of the ocean menacingly. The island in the middle was mountainous, completely covered in trees so it looked like little tufts of broccoli had been planted on every square inch. The island on the opposite side was rocky, the volcanic nature lending itself to more of a barren wasteland than an inhabitable space. But there were small cabanas on stilts that had been built along the water's edge and farther up in elevation.

They'd taken the Zodiac to the third island, leaving the *Devil's Due* anchored at the adjacent island because it was too difficult to approach the island where they needed to be. She noticed it also had the broccoli trees, and there was just a thin strip of white sand around the perimeter, along with a whole hell of a lot of rocks.

Elias explained that Zodiacs were built with a kind of fabric that wouldn't tear when out of the water, and sure enough, he'd driven it right across the rocks and up on shore.

"These are the best," he said, patting the side of the Zodiac almost lovingly. "It's what we used as SEALs. We'd load up in the helicopter and they'd take us over international waters. We'd push the Zodiac out first and then each jump in after it. It's very cool to see."

"You lost me at jumping out of a helicopter into the middle of the ocean," she said.

"Never say never," he said. "I got you on a boat, didn't I?"

"You tricked me," she said, grinning. "I don't think even your kisses would be distracting enough to make me free-fall into the ocean."

"Challenge accepted," he said. "It really is incredible. I miss it. There's nothing quite like that particular rush of adrenaline. It takes a coordinated effort to get it inflated and the motor set up. And then we'll take it at top speed toward land. They're made so they can be stored underwater, so we can go in covertly until the land mission is done."

"That's incredible," she said. "Why aren't we doing that? They'll see it if they're looking for it."

"This isn't military grade," he said. "And it would take more than you and me and scuba gear to get it strapped down."

"Good point," she said. "You don't think anyone will bother it if we leave it here?"

"I've got an alert set up if anyone should tamper with it or the *Devil's Due*. But we'll hide it as best we can."

She helped him drag the Zodiac farther up on the shore, and out of sight from anyone coming from the water, and then they dragged it up into the jungled area and put it out of sight as best they could. The dark color of the Zodiac made it camouflaged, and virtually impossible to see unless someone happened to stumble directly across it.

"The good thing about this beach," he said, "is that the waves come up pretty high on the shore. Our tracks will be gone and they won't be able to see exactly where we've gone ashore. With any luck, if Diego comes back, he'll think we're hiking from where we docked the boat."

She looked at the beach where they'd come ashore and saw the tracks where they'd dragged the boat were already dissipating. She hadn't realized how far they'd dragged it, or how steep the incline had been to where they were starting their journey from.

"Cripes, this weather is bipolar," she said. "It was freezing last night and this morning, and now I feel like I'm in an oven. A wet oven." She took off her overshirt and tied it around her waist, leaving her in the tank she wore underneath it. Then she put her pack on over her shoulders and tightened the straps.

"It's an interesting location," he told her. "We're so close to the equator it's fairly temperate when the sun is shining, but you add in things like the rains and El Niño, and when the sun goes down, temperance goes out the window. Plus, the humidity sucks."

He took off at a pace that made her glad she worked out five days a week, and she knew her competitive spirit wouldn't allow her to ask him to slow down if she started to get tired.

Sweat dampened her skin and clothes and the humidity was so thick she could drink it. The canopy of trees kept the heat from escaping, so it was like being inside a slow-cooker. The colors of the jungle were vibrant—a backdrop of green with splashes of purple, red, and yellow flowers for color.

She'd never realized how loud it would be, the chirping of birds and the constant resonance of something that sounded like a herd of amplified crickets. And through the noise and chaos, it felt like something was always watching—always hunting.

Miller noticed Elias's shirt was already soaked. She also noticed that as he led her deeper onto the island, he barely made any sound as they climbed over rocks and branches and went through a small stream. Whereas she sounded like a rhinoceros behind him in comparison. It just showed her how well trained he really was.

"Make sure you're drinking lots of water as we go," he said. "The humidity is going to dehydrate you faster than you think."

"I'm a step ahead of you," she said, drinking from one of the bottles from her pack.

It was a humbling experience trekking through the jungle with Elias. She considered herself to be in good shape. But she felt like a career couch potato after hiking several miles at the pace he was going. He wasn't even breathing hard.

"You doing okay?" he asked her, looking back over his shoulder. "Tell me if we need to stop."

"I'm good," she told him. "Though I'm not feeling too confident about the snake thing. I saw a vine back there that was bigger than my thigh, all tangled together with a bunch of tree roots. I thought I saw it move when we stepped through them all, and I almost had a heart attack before I realized it really was just a vine."

"I guess it's a good thing I didn't point it out to you, then," he said. "Because that definitely wasn't a vine. But chances are it's probably not following us."

"I can't even tell you how unamused I am right

now," she said. "And I'm going to pretend you're kidding so I can keep my sanity a little while longer. How far until we make it to Corazón Roto?"

Elias stopped and took out his phone, and Miller took advantage of the break to sit down a few minutes. The pack was causing a pang in her lower back that nothing but a good masseuse was going to fix.

"How are you getting service out here?" she asked. "My phone has been dead as a doornail since we left Santa Cruz yesterday."

"I have a special phone," he told her. "I get service everywhere."

"That's convenient. Where can I get one of those?"

"I'll put in a good word for you." And then he said, "Elaine, are you with us?"

Yes, Elias . . . she practically purred. Miller almost rolled her eyes, but remembered Elaine didn't actually exist in human form.

It's a lovely day. You've traveled six-point-two miles and your pulse is holding steady at eighty-three beats per minute.

"How in the world does she know all that?" Miller asked.

All Gravediggers are inserted with a special device. It allows me to track them all over the world, and it allows me to assess their health to the fullest degree if they are ever wounded or killed during a mission. I can also determine eating and drinking patterns, anoma-

lies in the body, and sexual activity. For instance, Agent Cole has ejaculated four times in the last twenty-four hours.

Elias burst out laughing and Miller blushed and said, "All righty, then. That seems unbelievably intrusive."

"You get used to it," he told her. "Too bad she's not hooked up to you." He leaned down and nipped at her bottom lip. She was hot and sweaty and still he turned her on like crazy. "I'd love to know how many times I made you come last night."

"I lost track," she said. "And stop fishing for compliments. I think your ego is inflated enough."

He grinned and then kissed her again before returning to his phone. "Elaine, show imaging map, please, and section it within an immediate radius to Corazón Roto."

He held the phone flat and a miniature version of the 3-D map they'd looked at before appeared, only this time she could see the two of them standing in the map, like two little dolls.

"We're still about a mile out from the rock, so not too far to go," he said. "We'll take a break once we're there and fuel up, and then we'll see if we can find any sign that Justin was there."

"You might have to help me stand up," she said. "I think my weight distribution with the pack is most likely to have me falling on my face."

"And it's such a lovely face," he said, pulling her to her feet.

The idea of a break and refueling had her picking up the pace, and she almost wept with relief when the trees cleared and she saw the large rock at the edge of a cliff. She hadn't realized they'd climbed so high in elevation, but she could see the turbulent waters from the sea inside the triangle below. It was a long way down, and it was easy to see why boats and divers weren't allowed in those waters.

She dropped her pack and stretched out her muscles, and then she downed a bottle of water. Corazón Roto did, indeed, look like a broken heart. The rock was taller than she was, and jaggedly cleft down the middle, so it looked like a heart splitting in two.

"There's a dispute over whether or not the Incans or the Spanish discovered these islands first, but the evidence is pretty conclusive the Incans were here well before the Spaniards. There are ruins of Incan settlements on Santa Cruz and a couple of the other islands, but they were pretty much wiped out when the Spaniards showed up. Most of the Incans died of diseases the Spanish brought with them."

"Seems like this would not be the easiest place to try and settle," she said, looking at the overgrown jungle and uneven terrain.

"When people keep taking your land and killing your people, you go where you can to survive. There's a legend that's told about Corazón Roto. When Spanish ships found these islands, the Inca were already well settled, but they were outnumbered, though their strength in battle was brutal and far outmatched the Spanish. But the Spanish were on a mission for gold and land for their queen, and their ships and numbers were enough to conquer everyone in their path.

"The Incan king was wise and knew there was no gold to be found on the islands, so he negotiated with the Spanish general that he would offer his daughter in marriage to him, and that in return, they were welcome to any treasures discovered on the island as long as there was no war. The king's daughter was incredibly beautiful . . ."

"Of course she was," Miller said. "They're always beautiful. You don't negotiate your homely daughter when forming alliances. That's betrothing 101."

"I forgot you were an expert," he said dryly. "My apologies."

She grinned at him, enjoying the break and the banter. There was a smaller rock not far from Corazón Roto with a flat side, and she sat down with her back to it.

"Did she fall madly in love with the general?"

"No, he was old enough to be her grandfather," Elias said, taking a seat across from her. He took a bottle of water from his bag and tossed her a protein bar. "But she fell in love with one of the lowly shipmen, who was, of course, very handsome. Young and strapping too."

"Of course," she said.

"Well, as things tend to go when kings and generals are involved, the young lovers were discovered before she was able to marry the general. The king dragged the shipman before all the people and had him beaten and beheaded for defiling his daughter."

"As one does," she said. "What happened to the daughter?"

"The general decided he'd still marry the daughter, but at sunrise on the morning of her wedding, she threw herself from this cliff and fell to the turbulent waters below. The legend says when her body hit the rocks and waves below, the rock split in two. Corazón Roto. The broken heart."

Miller arched a brow as she finished her protein bar. "You're not a bad storyteller."

He smiled, but it didn't quite reach his eyes. "No one can bullshit like SEALs. It was a good way for us to keep entertained on long nights. Sleep doesn't always come easy."

She'd put off asking him, but she needed to know. It had been eating at her for months, and it hadn't gone away once they'd made love.

"You've got to tell me why," she finally said. "Why you left that night. You hurt me in a way I didn't think was possible." And admitting that made her a hell of a lot more vulnerable than she'd ever been in her life. "I'll be the first to admit I wasn't expecting it. We'd been dancing around it for months, and I thought we'd have some fun and see where things led. But when you touched me . . ."

"It was more powerful than anything you could've imagined," he finished for her.

She nodded because her throat had closed up, and she didn't think she'd be able to talk.

"That was exactly the reason I stopped," he said. "I don't know how I found the strength to walk away."

"It felt like you were able to walk away pretty easily to me," she said, playing with the wrapper in her hand.

"The last thing I'd ever want to do is hurt you," he said. "But I thought it would hurt you more in the long run if we'd followed through. It might have started out as just fun and sex, but I think we both know that after we got our hands on each other it was a hell of a lot more than that."

"If the last thing you wanted to do was hurt me, then why did you?" she asked. She needed the truth. A straight-out answer. If she didn't know for sure, she'd always wonder.

"You've seen what we are," he said. "What we do. My past means nothing. I'm a dead man walking, and Eve Winter owns me lock, stock, and barrel. Our duty is to the mission. There's no room for anything more, and I thought it'd be cruel to you to bring you into a world I couldn't share with you, and for you to always wonder why I could never give you all of me. You're not the kind of woman to put up with that. And I wouldn't blame you."

"What about Deacon and Tess?"

"Deacon's story is different, and not one for me to tell. But they don't have an easy road ahead of them. He's still at the whim of a government organization that controls him for a certain amount of time. They can make things easy or they can make things difficult. And I know Deacon and Tess have plans in place in case anything ever goes wrong."

"Sometimes it's easier to get through the shit when you have someone on your team who's helping you fight the battle."

"I'm starting to realize that," he said softly.

CHAPTER **EIGHTEEN**

"We need to get moving," he said, getting to his feet. "We've only got a few more hours of daylight and from Elaine's calculations, we can make it to the first waterfall just before dusk."

When he reached down to pick up his pack, he noticed the graffiti on the side of Corazón Roto and shook his head.

"Nothing is sacred anymore," he said. "I'm always amazed at the things people do without thinking, and then I remember that a good portion of the population spends a lot of its time not thinking at all."

She snorted out a laugh and glanced at the two names carved on the rock inside of a heart. "When I was at the Colosseum in Rome, someone had spray-painted 'Texas A&M' on the side in Aggie maroon. I'd never been so mortified in my life to be from Texas."

His muscles had tightened since he'd sat down

and taken a break, and he stretched before he put his pack on. And then he watched as Miller did stretches of her own. She hadn't uttered one word of complaint, and he knew he'd set a grueling pace. But his gut was telling him their time to find Justin was very limited.

"Wait a second," she said, dropping her pack back on the ground and squatting down so she could see the names more clearly. "Bull Brazer and Lily Crowe. I know them. Both of them."

"That's not a coincidence," he said. "Now we just have to figure out what the hell they have to do with finding him."

"Well," she said, "I can tell you for sure that they're not in love as the heart suggests. Bull was a friend of my brother's in high school."

"What can you tell me about him?"

"He was dumber than a box of hair and he once broke both his legs jumping off his roof with a sheet tied around his neck like a cape."

Elias's lips twitched, but he said, "Maybe something else that comes to mind will be more helpful."

She shrugged. "I really don't know what I can tell you," she said. "He and my brother were childhood friends. I think Bull moved away his sophomore or junior year of high school. His dad got a job in Oklahoma, I think. The only thing I really remember about Bull is that he was a neighborhood kid. He lived over on North Street, and my brother would ride his bike down there so they could play basketball."

"There it is," he said. "Elaine, which of the two waterfalls is north of here?"

Both of the waterfalls you earmarked for your journey are north of Corazón Roto, though neither are true north. But there is a difference of ten miles between them and an elevation difference of almost a thousand feet. They are also on two separate paths.

"That doesn't help," he said. "What about Lily Crowe? Who's she?"

"I know even less about her," Miller said. "Do you know Charles and Mildred Crowe? He's been postmaster for more than forty years, and she's been a teller at the bank for just as long. Lily was their only child."

"What's their address?" he asked.

"They live over on Mockingbird. It's the little white clapboard."

"I know the one," he said. "You said 'was'. What happened to Lily?"

"They used to hold Fourth of July celebrations and picnics on the other side of the lake from where y'all have your secret entrance to the Bat Cave. A bunch of kids were swimming, swinging from a rope and into the water, and most everyone else was watching the fireworks. It was dark, so kids were coming and going, and no one noticed when Lily didn't get out of the water after her turn. They didn't find her body until daylight the next morning. She was eight years old. But that was well before my time. I don't know anything else about her. People still talk about it because it was such a tragedy, and things like that don't happen often in Last Stop."

Elias thought about it for a minute, trying to remember the Justin he knew and his thinking patterns. He'd know Miller's knowledge of the girl would be limited, and it wasn't so cut-and-dried as a street name.

"Elaine, is one of the waterfalls eight degrees north from here?"

The 3-D image erupted from Elias's phone, and there was a section highlighted over one of the waterfalls.

Affirmative . . . uploading coordinates now.

"Well, I guess we can assume that Cordova and his men will never figure that one out," she said.

"Which is why he wanted you to begin with," he said. "Let's move while we've still got daylight. We've got a long way to go."

"I've got visions of a good night's sleep already in my head."

"You'll have earned it by the time we get there. We're going up pretty high. Let me know if you get light-headed or start to feel sick. It's still pretty warm out here, and it'll be a while before the afternoon rain comes in."

"I'll be fine," she insisted. "Sleep is a great motivator for me. I hardly ever get any, so having that as a light at the end of the tunnel is all I need to make it through."

THE RAIN STARTED four hours later.

Elias hadn't been kidding about the shift in elevation. She felt the tightness in her chest as they climbed higher and higher, though the temperature had cooled off considerably, so much so that she'd put on the all-weather jacket and pulled the hood over her head. It didn't do much good for keeping the rain off, as the droplets hit her in the face and slithered down her neck.

Her calves and thighs were on fire, and the pack on her back got heavier with every step.

"I hope you can appreciate the fact that I've refrained from making any movie references about the One Ring and how heavy it gets as Frodo and Samwise Gamgee get closer to Mordor. This is a volcanic island after all."

"I really appreciate your restraint," he said, using the machete to cut through the thick vines.

She noticed he'd gotten quieter the farther they went, and how difficult it was to forge a path that wasn't there. He was using all his strength and concentration to get them to the waterfall, and it was far from an easy battle. She hoped like hell they were going to the right one, and they hadn't misinterpreted Justin's clues.

"You hear that?" he asked sometime later.

She hadn't heard much of anything for the past couple of miles. Blisters had rubbed themselves raw on both of her feet, and all she could hear was the miserable whining inside her head, and the occasional whimper she let slip. He'd been checking on her often, asking if she was okay, and she always told him yes. She didn't want to slow them down. It was her own stupid pride that was keeping her silent, but she didn't see what good it would do or what would change if she told him what was wrong. It would just worry him, and put them in potential danger. She'd noticed he'd spent a lot more time stopping to listen before it had started raining, and checking in with Elaine to see if the *Devil's Due* had been boarded again.

No one had boarded their boat, but Elaine had reported there were more boats in the water surrounding the islands. What couldn't be deciphered was if the boats contained friend or foe. But Elias had said it was best to always assume the worst and deal with it.

The rain hadn't let up, and it was almost dark. It wasn't often she found herself in the midst of a full-blown pity party. She was the kind of girl who took her knocks and then pulled herself up by the bootstraps and kept going. But she was physically and mentally exhausted, and she just didn't have a lot left in her. They were both soaked to the skin, and water dripped from her eyelashes and the tip of her nose.

"Hear what?" she asked, but she didn't think he heard her.

It took her a minute to focus on what he could possibly be talking about. And then she heard it. The sound of rushing water could be heard through the rain, and she almost collapsed to her knees in relief.

"Oh, praise Jesus," she said, trying to pick up her pace, but her feet wouldn't let her. She would've taken off her shoes miles ago, but the ground was a mix of gnarled roots and rocks. Not to mention she was pretty sure she'd seen a couple of more moving vines, and she didn't want to take the chance of exposing bare skin. At least her boots protected her above the ankle.

"What's wrong?" he said, stopping to look at her closely. "You weren't limping before."

"Blisters," she said automatically, not caring anymore since they'd made it to their destination.

"Dammit, woman," he said, coming toward her. He looked like a madman, coming at her with machete in hand and a vicious scowl on his face. "Why didn't you tell me you were hurt? That's all we need is to be in a situation where we have to make a run for it and you can't take two steps."

She felt her temper bubble to the surface. "What difference would it have made? Would you have carried me the rest of the way? If not, then there's nothing you could've done about it. We still have to go to the same stupid place, whether I've got blisters on my feet or not."

"Take your shoes off," he demanded. "We don't have time to stop and doctor them, but you can at least give them some relief. We've got about another mile to go, but the sun is going down. It's going to get dark here first because we're canopied by the trees. Damn stubborn woman," he muttered under his breath.

"I heard that," she said, narrowing her eyes.

"I meant for you to," he shot back.

"The ground is too rough to take off my shoes. I'll tear up the bottoms of my feet," she said. "And what do you mean we have another mile? We can hear the falls. It's deafening. I thought we were here."

"It's going to get a lot louder," he said. "And you should be fine to walk. The closer we get to the falls, the smoother the rocks are becoming."

The thought of another mile was just depressing, but she sat down and undid the laces of her boots, stifling a sob as she tried to pull the first one off. She didn't quite manage to stifle it when she pulled the second boot off. Her white socks were stained with blood.

"Oh, baby," Elias said, kneeling down in front of

her and gently taking a foot in his hand. "I've got a first-aid kit in my bag." He stood and then held out his hand to help her to her feet. "Take your pack off your back and put it on your front," he told her.

"What?" she asked, confused.

He was already pulling the pack off and shoving her arms through the holes so it rested over her chest. He reached down and grabbed her boots, tying the laces together and then attaching them to her pack, and then with a heroic amount of strength, he put his arms beneath her knees and her back and he picked her up, carrying her like a baby.

She put her arms around his neck automatically, afraid he might drop her, but he didn't even let out a groan as he shifted her weight in his arms.

"You're out of your mind," she said. "You can't possibly carry me a mile in the rain, plus both of our packs. You'll kill yourself."

"I've carried a man twice your size and both of our gear through the desert. This is not such a big deal."

And then he proved his words to be true as he carried her the rest of the way to the falls.

CHAPTER NINETEEN

She was in over her head. And it wasn't like she could blame anyone but herself.

Her entire adult life had been spent observing those who experienced love. Writing it down on paper with a smugness and assuredness that she was above the butterflies in the stomach and the feelings of light-headed bliss.

But she wasn't above it all. She'd had passion before. She'd had great sex and mutual admiration for her partners. But she'd never had the indescribable feeling of *oneness* like she had with Elias. There was so much more to the bond they shared than just the physical. She trusted him with her life—*had* trusted him with her life, and she respected him as a man, and admired him for having a core value system in him that would always do the right thing, even when it caused him hurt.

She loved him.

And it scared the hell out of her.

Because he mattered. And because he mattered, she knew it would break something inside of her when he left. He'd told her his future wasn't like Deacon and Tess's, where they had a chance to love. But even knowing that, she loved him anyway.

Rays of sun shot through the canopy of trees like spotlights, highlighting fallen logs or the exotic fuchsia flowers that bloomed with abandon. A howler monkey had found a sunny spot on a tree branch and was lazily soaking up the rays.

It was the glint of metal that caught her eye, and she strained to get a closer look, but the sunlight played tricks on the eye. There was a huge tree close to fifty yards away, thick with vines and overgrown with foliage, but it seemed as if part of the trunk was make of some kind of iron.

"That's weird," she said, "Do you see that?"

"I can't see anything with the back of your head in front of my face."

"Oh, sorry," she said and relaxed back in his arms. "That tree over there. It looks like the trunk is made of metal."

He stopped and stared for a few minutes. "No, it's some kind of wreckage. A pretty old one, too. The tree has grown around it, so that's why it looks like that."

As soon as he said the word wreckage she knew.

No one had to tell her that a simple piece of metal had belonged to her parents' plane. She just knew in her gut it was true.

"Put me down," she said, thumping his arm with her fist. "Put me down."

"Miller," he said, but she was already crawling out of his arms and on her feet. The pain of walking didn't register as she moved closer to the tree, almost as if she was in a trance.

"It could be anything," he said, coming up behind her.

"You know it's not," she said. Now that she was closer she could see the metal was part of the propeller, and then she started looking for more. "This is the direction Justin came. He said in his letter he found their plane. It would make sense that we come across it too."

Her breath was coming too fast and tears clouded her eyes. She searched frantically for the rest of it, climbing over logs and pulling at vines to see what else the jungle had claimed over the past couple of decades. Her blistered feet sunk into damp earth as she swatted at ferns and tugged at the ropy vines.

She could see Elias out of the corner of her eye, helping her clear a path, but she couldn't hear him because the blood was rushing too loudly in her ears. She swiped at a group of vines and they pulled back like a curtain. And there it was. Or what was left of it. A small, single engine Cessna with a blue strip down the side.

Miller sucked in a breath and took a step back. Tears blurred her vision and she shook her head in denial.

"I can't," she said, taking another step back. "I can't look."

"Oh, baby," Elias said, but he didn't touch her. If he'd touched her she would've broken completely. "I'll do whatever you need. Just say the word."

She realized what he was offering and she felt the sob rise up inside of her. She didn't have the courage to look for their remains. But he would do it for her if she asked.

Miller turned to him, and he opened his arms, pulled her in as she sobbed twenty years of grief against his chest. She didn't know how long she cried, but he picked her up off her feet and held her so she didn't have to stand. And being held in his arms was the most comforting thing she'd ever experienced.

Exhaustion overwhelmed her and she collapsed against him.

"It's going to be dark soon," he said. "You know I'd sit here and hold you for days if I needed to, but we don't want to be caught here in the dark. There are too many unknowns and too many predators looking for a meal."

She nodded her head, but couldn't seem to look

him in the eyes. "I'm sorry about that," she said. "I wasn't expecting to relive it again."

"Don't ever apologize for your grief. You have a right to it. We all do. Expressing it is the only way to heal." He kissed the top of her head and asked, "Do you want me to look around?"

"Yes," she told him. "I'll always wonder otherwise. It's time to bury them once and for all."

He nodded, and picked her up, setting her on a nearby log, and then he disappeared behind the veil of vines where the wreckage was located. She waited for him in a trance, staring fixedly on grooves of the fallen trunk she was sitting on and the trail of ants marching in the crevices. They hypnotized her, and she might have dozed for a moment or two.

He was standing right in front of her before she realized he'd come back.

"There's nothing," he said, taking her hand.

"I guess this really is their final resting place," she said. "Let's go before it gets dark."

———

THEY REACHED THE summit of the falls an hour later.

"I'm not an invalid," she told him. She was emotionally wrung dry, and her nerves were on edge, but when the clearing opened up all she could do was stare in awe.

It wasn't at all what she'd been expecting. What

she'd seen in her mind was a picturesque waterfall that would splash into a gathering pool at the bottom, where they could hopefully bathe without drowning. She imagined they'd set up their camp near the water and enjoy a peaceful night. She should've known better.

It was beautiful. And terrifying.

As Elias had carried her, the elevation had eventually leveled off and she noticed several creeks with rushing water heading in the opposite direction, instead of down the mountain like she'd assumed they should have been. And then she realized they climbed to a peak and all the water was gathering in a large pool of dark water. It wasn't a relaxing pool, but one that seemed to pick up speed as the elevation dipped down toward the other side of the mountain. There were large rocks sticking out of the water, and the sound of the water crashing against the rocks before it roared down the falls was so loud she could barely hear Elias speak.

"Ohmigod," she said, as he set her to her feet. She hobbled a little but was able to stand. Even the time he'd carried her had at least given her a small respite of relief. "I'm afraid to see what it looks like on the other side."

She watched as Elias made his way around the large pool, climbing up on boulders so he could see over the cliff to where the waterfall fell. The rain had started to lighten, but there was still a fine mist that came down. He looked almost small, standing on the precipice of the unknown and looking down. And then she saw him shake his head and turn around and come back toward her.

"What's wrong?" she asked.

"That's at least a fifty-foot drop, maybe more, and unless your brother left any more clues up here, I'm not seeing any fallen pillars to landmark his last clue in the letter."

"If he did leave us something, it'll be impossible to see in the dark and rain, so we'll have to start at first light."

Elias nodded and helped her remove the pack from her front, also removing his own pack. "You need to get off your feet," he told her. "I'm going to set up camp first, and then we'll see about getting dry and your feet doctored."

"It's getting pretty dark," she said. "Do you need help setting things up?"

"Nah, I can do it blindfolded. And faster just doing it myself. Get off your feet," he repeated, and then went about setting up camp.

He found a good flat place in an area not far from the boulders he'd climbed to look over the falls. It was a muddy area, and she watched as he used the machete to cut several soft-looking fronds from what looked to be a fern of some sort, though it wasn't like any fern she'd ever seen before.

He laid the fronds in a crosshatch pattern on the mud, and then he quickly and efficiently erected the tent that had been rolled up in his pack. And he'd done it with no more than the glow of the flashlight he'd propped on one of the rocks.

"It's not too damp," he said. "Go ahead and strip down and then we can put dry clothes on once inside."

He came over and helped her to the tent. She was too tired to argue, and it wasn't like there was anyone around to see, so she stripped out of her wet clothes as quickly as her lethargic limbs would let her. He did the same and just tossed their wet clothes in a pile, unable to do anything with them for the moment, and then he led her into the tent like a child.

He helped her pull on silk long underwear and she fell back onto the sleeping bag. The fronds beneath the tent were surprisingly comfortable, and she felt him rustling around as he put his own long underwear on and placed his gun within easy reach. Then he pulled out the first-aid kit and took a look at her feet.

"The good news is I don't think we're going to have to amputate," he said.

"I'm so relieved," she said, wincing as he put cold antiseptic on each of the bleeding blisters.

"This is not good, baby. I have no idea how much farther we're going to have to hike to get to where we're going. You can't walk in those shoes anymore."

"I don't really have a choice," she said. "We've got to walk forward or we've got to walk back the direction we came. Either way I'm walking. Unless I decide to jump over the waterfall and end it all."

"You're always looking on the bright side," he said. "That's one of the things I love about you."

Her eyes popped open and met his, and neither of them said anything. Had he *meant* to say that, or was it just a figure of speech? She wasn't sure, but by the look in his eyes, he seemed just as surprised as she was.

He finished with the antiseptic and said, "I think the best bet is to wrap you up as good as we can. I'll put on Band-Aids, and then wrap each of your feet in a loose Ace bandage. Then we'll cover them with socks. Hopefully, that makes it at least bearable for you to walk."

"I'll be fine," she insisted. "I'm a lot tougher than I look at the moment. I just need some sleep and a chance to get off them for a few hours. I'll be ready to roll in the morning. And no offense, but maybe we could stop talking and go to sleep now. I'm not feeling very chatty."

She heard him chuckle as he wrapped her feet. "And I was just getting ready to seduce you," he said.

"Listen, buddy," she said, and she heard him chuckle again. "After the day we've had I'd be impressed if you could use it at all. But I'm closed for business until tomorrow."

"At least you didn't use the old headache excuse. People are going to think we're an old married couple."

She harrumphed and let her eyes flutter closed. His touch was surprisingly gentle, and he stroked his thumb down the middle of her foot, pressing gently against the sore muscles.

"Ohmigod," she groaned.

"Don't go to sleep yet," he said. "I want you to drink some water and put something in your stomach."

"Oh, for the love of . . ." she grumbled. "And stop laughing at me. I see nothing funny about the fact that there's not going to be any coffee in the morning."

"Truer words have never been spoken," he said.

He passed her a fruit-and-nut mix, a small amount of jerky, and a bottle of water. Her stomach growled as soon as she smelled the jerky. They sat in silence for a little while, each lost in exhaustion and their own thoughts.

"What's going to happen when we go back to Last Stop?" she asked.

"Do you mean how are we going to go from the romance of this to doing our own laundry again?"

"I mean what's Eve going to do to you for disobeying orders?"

"I'm on vacation," he said, shrugging. "She can either kill me or kiss my ass. I'm not opposed to either of those things."

"How can you be so nonchalant about it all?" she asked, exasperated. "You're talking about your life."

"I'm already dead," he said evenly.

"No," she said. "You're very much alive. And I . . ." She paused, knowing she'd been about to tread on shaky ground. If he didn't care about living or dying, he sure as hell wouldn't care about loving.

"You what?" he asked.

"I want you to keep living," she said. "Eve couldn't possibly be so cruel as to kill you. That's inhuman."

"That's what she is," he said, rolling up the bag of dried fruit and nuts to stick back in the pack. "I was a sniper. Did you know that?"

"No," she said quietly, but she could see the pain he carried around with him. It must've been a terrible burden to take lives, even in the line of duty.

"I'd get a packet before each mission. Inside it would be photographs and intel for me to study. They were photographs of my targets. I had to memorize their faces. Every one of them."

She couldn't imagine what that did to a person, and she ached for the hurt he must carry.

"There was this one photograph, the last one in my packet. Intel said he was a British agent who was selling classified information he'd obtained from the U.S. to the Saudis. He was a traitor, and I never questioned my orders. It was rare to order a hit on an ally country's agent, but in this case, the British weren't

310 × LILIANA HART

taking care of it, so it was left up to us. So I did the job.

"The only problem was the target wasn't a British intelligence officer after all. The target was an American. A CIA agent who'd infiltrated the network and was feeding them false information. He was an American. A man who was doing his job and who loved his country. I'd been given a false intel report. And guess who was responsible for the life of that agent, besides me when I killed him?"

Her throat was dry as dust, but she knew the answer. "Eve," she barely managed to get out.

Half of his face was shrouded in shadow from the light of the flashlight, but she could see him nod in the affirmative. "Eve had plans of her own. It seems she needed my particular skill set for this special ops team she was putting together. An experimental project that was so classified even the President of the United States didn't know about it. She needed me to die so she could recruit me."

"How did you die?" she asked. The food she'd just eaten lay heavy in her stomach, and she kept drinking her water, hoping it would make the feeling go away.

"There was an internal investigation," he said. "And there was no record of that agent being on our hit list. His cover was so deeply classified that only a few knew of it. So then the question was asked, 'How did I know that he was an undercover agent?' So I was court-martialed and brought in for questioning. I was dishonorably discharged and had everything stripped from me. And then I was sentenced to death. That's when Eve stepped in and made her offer for me to become a Gravedigger. I didn't really care at that point. I'd have actually preferred to take the needle. But she got me to sign the contract and made sure it was the serum to make me appear dead instead of the real thing. And then a couple of days later they dug me up in Last Stop, and the woman who'd caused the shame and dishonor of my name and my family was the puppeteer holding all my strings."

Miller felt sick inside. She couldn't imagine the horror of living through that nightmare. "Your parents," she said.

"They had to move from the town I grew up in. They were too ashamed to stay there. They live in the city now, where there's enough people so no one knows their names. My mother hates it."

"How long do you have to live like that?" she asked.

"Forever," he told her. "The contract with The Gravediggers is for seven years. But it doesn't change my past. I can't go back and right the wrongs that have been done. There's still the fact that I killed an innocent man."

"What do you plan to do?"

"I used to know," he told her. "I've spent the last

two years planning every way I could think of to kill her. And knowing that I would probably die with her."

"What changed?" she asked.

He touched her hand with the tip of his finger—just a simple touch—but she felt it to her soul, and then he said, "I've decided that there are things worth living for."

CHAPTER TWENTY

"I'm too tired to sleep," she told him.

"That makes no sense," he said. "Just close your eyes."

"Oh, great idea," she said wryly. "I don't know why I didn't think of that."

"I'm sensing some sarcasm."

"You're going to be sensing a knuckle sandwich if you keep that up," she said, but she found herself smiling. "Why weren't you sleeping?"

"How do you know I wasn't?"

"You were too still," she said.

"Seriously, how come nothing you say makes sense? You're supposed to be still when you're sleeping."

"Yeah, but you were trying too hard." She unzipped the tent door and pushed back the flap, crawling out into the night air.

"And now we're going outside," he said from behind her. She could practically hear him rolling his eyes. "I'm not going to be happy if I have to end up amputating your feet because you're not taking care of them."

There was a break in the canopy of trees, and there were a multitude of stars, brighter than she'd ever seen, and they cast a reflection off the pool of water. She looked back over her shoulder and saw him coming out of the tent. He'd pulled his pants on, but left them unbuttoned, and he hadn't bothered with a shirt. His gun was in his hand.

"I'm sure it won't come to that," she said. "They're already feeling much better. You're a good doctor."

He grunted and she moved closer to the water's edge. The waterfall roared from the other side, and the water was constantly changing and swirling.

"It's beautiful, isn't it?" she asked. "It looks like the stars are dancing on the water." She could just barely see her own reflection, and then his wavered next to hers as he stood close behind her and looked over her shoulder.

"Beautiful," he agreed and kissed her neck, sending shivers down her spine.

His hands reached around and he cupped her breasts through the thin silk, and his thumbs brushed across her nipples. She felt the urgency in him. Gone was the teasing and playful banter. And she felt herself being swept into the same desperate race to claim him as hers.

He stripped her shirt over her head and let it fall to the ground, and then he turned her in his arms so he could kiss her completely. His lips sealed against hers, slanting across them, and he ate at her mouth with a hunger that drove her wild with need.

"You make me crazy," he said, lifting her with one arm in an impressive show of strength and stripping her long johns off with the other hand. She wasn't wearing underwear. "Even when I've had you, I want you again."

She whimpered as his hand slipped between them and cupped the wet heat between her thighs. The heel of his hand pressed against her clit, and his teeth raked across her jawline. She couldn't remember how to breathe. There were too many sensations rioting inside her body, and she was completely under his control.

"You're so wet," he whispered against her ear, sending an electric tingling across her sensitive skin.

"Elias," she said, her eyes rolling back in her head as he pressed a little harder with the heel of his hand.

His finger traced the lips of her vulva, teasing the area around her clit but never touching it. She was moving against him, and she hadn't realized she wrapped her legs around his waist. But his hand was in the way of what she really wanted.

He slid a thick finger inside of her, and then another. She was shaking with the need to come, but he held her back, just on the edge. And then his hand was gone and she was left gasping for more.

"Don't stop, don't stop," she begged.

"Only for a second, baby," he promised.

He carried her to one of the boulders that surrounded the falls. It was big and flat, and kissed by the starlight. He sat her on the rock and didn't waste any time shedding his pants, so he was as naked as she was.

He was beautiful. There was no other word to describe him, and she drank in her fill of him, reveling at breadth of his shoulders and thickly muscled arms. And then down to the ridged abs that made her want to take a bite out of him. And then her gaze dropped lower and she felt the heat of anticipation roll through her.

"You said only for a second," she reminded him.

"I got lost looking at you. You look like a mermaid, sitting on that rock in the moonlight. And if I've never said it before, I'm crazy about your body. You have the kind of body that can be made love to or ridden long and hard."

"And yet you're standing all the way over there."

His mouth quirked and he moved toward her. And then before she knew what was happening he had her wrists in his hand and she was stretched out across the rock like a ritual sacrifice.

"I guess we're choosing the ridden long and hard option," she managed to get out.

His mouth clamped down on her nipple and talking was no longer an option. She arched against him. Her body was no longer her own—sensations sizzled beneath her skin and her cries became desperate.

"I need you," she begged. "Please."

And he didn't keep her waiting. She felt him probing against her, and he took her mouth in a kiss that rocked her to the core as he slid deep inside of her with one thrust. His fingers twined with hers and her legs wrapped tight around him. And then he rocked them both to oblivion.

As EXHAUSTED AS he was, sleep didn't come easy for him that night. He held her in his arms, listening to her soft, even breathing as she slept. He hadn't meant to tell her the truth. And he'd seen the horror on her face as he'd retold the story of his death. He'd never said the words out loud to anyone before, and it wasn't easy to relive the second time around.

He waited until dawn broke to get up and get dressed. He let Miller sleep, and honestly, he wasn't sure if he could've woken her if he'd tried. He wanted to let her get all the rest she could, so he slipped out of the tent and went to the water's edge to wash his face.

His phone let off a quiet beep that started slowly but began to get faster, and he took it from his pocket, seeing the alert from Elaine that the boat had been breached. She'd also alerted that there were signs of incoming aircraft. Even as he saw the alert, he heard the sound of choppers in the distance quickly getting closer.

He'd been expecting it. Diego had been paying too close of attention to Miller, and he would've recognized her photograph when he'd seen it, even with the different hair. There was no doubt he'd immediately alerted Cordova and called in all the reserves they had.

"Oh, shit," he said, and ran back to the tent. "Elaine, pull up all possible escape routes and places we could hide. Caves . . . Anything will work at this point."

Complying . . . stand by.

"Miller," he said, putting his hand on her leg and shaking it.

Her eyes snapped open and she must've heard the urgency in his voice, because she followed him out of the tent on all fours.

"They're fine, before you ask," she said, taking the clothes he tossed at her. He hoped she was telling the truth, but he could only take her at her word. "What's going on? What's happening?"

"Elaine signaled that the boat had been boarded. There's also incoming choppers. You hear them?"

She nodded and, stripping off the long underwear,

put on clothes similar to the ones she'd had the day before. "Do you think they've seen us from the air?"

"The choppers aren't in range for a drop yet, but it won't be too hard to figure it out. They'll see the trail we cut through the jungle, and it won't take too much to figure out we'd probably stop in a clearing like this one for the night. We're covered here for now, and they won't be able to see us from the air."

There were two choppers, military issue, that circled the islands. The boat had been boarded, but there was a good chance they had boots on the ground long before they stepped foot on the boat. Cordova wasn't stupid. He'd known they'd have set off on foot to try and beat them to the punch.

"Those are cartel mercenaries in the choppers," he said. "They're mostly former military who needed to actually start getting paid for their jobs, so when the Black Widow took over this territory, it was easy pickings to hire them. Diego would've gotten back and reported to Cordova that I'm with you, and whose boat we're on."

"Whose boat *are* we on?" she asked.

"On paper, it belongs to Julio Cortez," he said. "The Black Widow's son. He runs a large arm of her business, mostly in Eastern Europe. His holdings are so vast, even he doesn't know what he has, so it was simple for us to dummy accounts and property in his name. Cordova is bringing in the big guns on the chance that I really do work for Julian, and thinking that the son might be trying to overthrow his mother and getting hold of Solomon's table is the best way to do that."

"Lovely," she said. "Eve said that this organization is on her radar. If they're such horrible people, why does she let them keep existing?"

"It's a game of patience and strategy," he told her. "It's not just about taking out Julian Cortez in Eastern Europe, or Cordova in the South American territories. It's about gathering all the intelligence that can possibly be gathered, knowing exactly how many arms of the organization are up and running, and who the major players are before an attack can be implemented. Because if you take out everyone, but you miss one hidden person who has the power and influence to keep things running, then you've got to start all over and wait years before you can orchestrate the same kind of takedown. I can give Eve credit for one thing—she understands the mindset of espionage and covert ops better than anyone I've ever met."

He packed up their supplies and took down the tent on the chance they got lucky as hell and no one saw their tracks up the mountain. And then he shoved everything beneath the roots of a large tree, the gnarled appendages gaping in places big enough for animals to hide.

"Elaine is looking for alternative routes. She's got an infrared of the map, so she'll be able to see areas that are hard to find. Walk around a little and let's see how you're doing."

"I told you I'm fine," she said, walking around in a small circle. "I was stupid for not mentioning it to you sooner."

"Not stupid," he corrected. "But there's a time and place for hardheadedness. Injury isn't one of those times." He looked down at his phone and swore. "Elaine, we're really on a time crunch here. Have you found anything?"

I'm sorry, Elias. You are in a position that is difficult for me to run probabilities. All the water obscures potential hiding places. From what I can see, you are at the top of a cliff. The only escape is back down.

He'd had a feeling she was going to say that. He'd been able to tell as they'd been climbing that escape routes were going to be limited. The falls roared behind him, and he ran back up to the edge, climbing on the large boulders to look down on the other side. It wasn't a comforting sight. The drop was long, and they'd have to jump out far enough to miss the rocks at the bottom and land in the pool. And then there begged the question of how deep the pool actually was.

"Oh no," Miller said, shaking her head when he turned to look at her. "You're out of your mind."

He jumped down off the boulder and came toward

her just as the *crack* of an assault rifle came from his right. He ran toward her and took her to the ground, taking the brunt of the fall, and rolling them across the ground and behind the cover of trees. Another round was shot off and he pulled his weapon, wondering how badly they were about to be ambushed.

But when he looked to the area where the shots had come from, he saw one of the sweetest sights he'd ever seen. Deacon lay high up behind a rock, laying down steady fire as he was able to see Cordova's men coming up the trail Elias had cut the day before. The Gravediggers were there, and he was guessing they'd all decided to hell with Eve's orders of staying out of things.

And thank God they were all on the same side, because even though he'd walked the perimeter through the night and had checked in with Elaine, he hadn't known they were in the area. Though he was going to have to have a little talk with Elaine about not sharing information. Of course, she was programmed to do what she was told, and someone with the clearance to override her system would've had to give the orders for her to stay silent. Which meant Eve was involved. He guessed maybe she'd decided to play her hand after all.

No one in the world was trained like they were. And the mercenaries didn't stand a chance against them, even outnumbered as they were. He knew the rest of the team was scattered strategically, and they'd slowly dismantle Cordova's men so they had the opportunity to escape.

"We've got to go," he told Miller, reholstering his gun.

"What's happening?" Fear laced her voice for the first time since he'd known her. She'd been through hell and back, but this was real, and being caught in the middle of live fire was enough to put the fear of God into anyone.

"The cavalry is here," he said. "And we've got one shot to get the hell off this mountain and get to an extraction point."

"But my brother . . ." she said.

"We'll find your brother. But if he's on this island, he's going to hear the gunfire and stay hidden. He's well trained. He can survive as long as he needs to. Now come on."

Her eyes widened and the fear turned to terror as he pushed her toward the edge of the waterfall. Gunfire rang out from all around them, but he stayed focused on the goal and he sheltered her body with his for protection.

When he got her up on the boulder, her body went rigid. It was a menacing sight—the water was powerful as it rushed over the precipice all the way to the bottom, crashing against the rocks and spewing up mist as it hit.

"I can't do this," she said. "This is the equivalent of jumping out of a helicopter into the middle of the ocean. Except there are rocks at the bottom."

"We're going to jump past the rocks," he said. "I'm going to be with you every step of the way. You're going to have to trust me."

"You, I trust. But I don't trust what's at the bottom of that waterfall."

He grabbed her by the arms and pulled her in close, kissing her with everything he had. "This seems like a good time to tell you I love you. On the count of three," he said. "One, two . . ."

She was so startled she followed his instructions without an argument, and they got a running start and jumped out as far as they could and fell into the unknown below.

CHAPTER TWENTY-ONE

Miller was somewhat certain she was alive. She'd always been under the impression that there was no pain in death, so she *had* to be alive.

Frigid water closed over her head, and she took in a mouthful of water as she tried to kick her way to the surface. The force of hitting the turbulent water had broken her hold on Elias, and she had no idea where he was or if he was okay. And if he was okay, she was going to kill him when she was finally able to draw a breath.

Her lungs burned, and panic started to engulf her just as her head broke the surface. She coughed up water and then sucked in a deep breath, only to be pulled under again by the force of the churning waters. A hand grabbed her ankle and then pushed her toward the surface again, and she sputtered and coughed as she tried to swim to the rocks at the edge. Elias lifted her onto the rocks and she rolled to her back, staring at the sky and trying to catch her breath. He was grinning like a fool. The damned lunatic. He actually thought that was fun.

"I'm really mad at you for that," she said, panting.

"I figured you would be."

"Did you mean it?" she asked. "When you said you loved me? Or was that your way of getting me to jump?"

His grin faded and he leaned down and kissed her. "I meant it. But we've got to move."

Shots could still be heard from all around, and he knew Deacon would probably stay in place since he was playing the role of sniper for the day, but the others would be surrounding and herding Cordova's men into a smaller radius like sheep before they were about to be slaughtered.

"I love you too."

"I know. Let's go."

If she hadn't been so tired she would've laughed. Not exactly a romance novel response. But she rolled to the side and got to her feet, the bandages wrapped around them completely worthless. She reached down to take the socks off and unwrap them, but he knelt down in front of her so she could catch her balance on his shoulders, and he did the task for her.

"Be careful where you step," he said. But she wasn't paying attention to him. Her eyes were glued to a strand of silver hanging from a tree branch, not ten yards from where they stood.

She stepped down off the boulder and headed toward the chain as if hypnotized as it swayed gently back and forth.

"Miller?" Elias asked, following behind her.

She stared at the necklace with a lump in her throat. She was afraid to touch it. Afraid it would disappear if she did. She hadn't seen it in more than twenty years, but she remembered it like it was yesterday. The way the long silver chain hung around her mother's neck, and the way she'd keep the small compass tucked beneath her shirt.

Elias reached up and unhooked it gently from the branch, and then turned it over in his hand.

"There's an inscription on the back," he said.

"'So you can always find your way back to me,'" she said before he could read it. "It was my mother's. My father gave it to her when they got married."

"Your brother's next clue?" he asked.

"It must be," she said. "She was wearing it when they left for their last trip." The sob caught her by surprise. It had been almost two decades since she'd cried for her parents. But all it took was a simple reminder to keep the grief fresh. "He really found their crash site. She'd have been wearing this."

The enormity of that sunk in and he pulled her into his arms and let her grieve anew. He felt safe and solid, and she realized she'd never had that feeling of security from another person in her whole life.

She wiped her eyes with her hands, though it didn't do much good because she was soaking wet.

"It's a locket," she told him. "There's a hidden switch on the side and it opens up." She showed him where it was and used her thumbnail to open it. Inside was a folded piece of paper, and she took it with shaking hands and opened it.

"What does it say?" Elias asked, moving her farther into the trees as another shot rang out from somewhere above.

"It's a riddle," she said.

"I hate riddles," he told her.

"I recognize it. We used to do them when we were kids. Had a whole book of them and spent one summer trying to trip each other up. I was always a lot better at them than Justin was. He hated that. He didn't like to lose at anything."

"That didn't change as he got older," Elias said.

"'This old one runs forever, but never moves at all. He has not lungs or throat, but still a mighty roar.'"

"And that pretty much sums up the reason I hate riddles."

"It's a waterfall," she told him. And then she took a good look at the one they'd just jumped down, and wondered how the hell they were still alive.

She closed the locket and put it around her neck,

tucking it beneath her shirt, and then she climbed back up on the rocks to see how close she could get to the falls without tumbling back into the water. Elias didn't say anything and didn't ask her what she was doing. He knew. And when the boulders got too big for her to climb, he did it and then pulled her up until they could reach out and touch the falls.

Elias sat down on the rock instead of trying to slide behind the falls and risking slipping. He was already wet, so it didn't matter that he got soaked again as he searched for a ledge. One moment, he was right in front of her eyes. And in the next moment, he was gone.

She scooted close, and then his arm reached out and grabbed her, and she stifled a yelp of surprise. Then he pulled her behind the falls and her feet touched solid ground.

She heard him swear as he tried to unbutton the thigh pocket of his pants, but because it was damp it made it difficult. He finally managed it and the high-powered beam of the flashlight came on, illuminating the cave behind the falls.

"This should keep them busy looking for us for a little while," he said.

"I thought the goal was to find an extraction point."

"It is, but we'll let them do a little cleanup first. You'd be surprised how often sheer dumb luck plays a role."

"That's not a comforting thought," she said.

"Not for us, most of the time," he said. "We're skilled enough to adapt to any situation. But for a good majority of ops, there's a lot of improvisation and a whole lot of praying. For instance, even as advanced as our technology is, a cell phone isn't going to survive a dive from a waterfall."

He held up the device that had been their lifesaver during this mess, and she felt her heart sink at the sight of the shattered screen.

"We can't communicate with Elaine," he said, "but they'll still be able to pinpoint our location with the tracking device in me. And there's another backup on my watch." He shone the flashlight onto the floor, noting the sharp rocks. "Hop up on my back," he told her.

"You can't keep carrying me everywhere," she said. "What happens if you get a hernia or blow out a disc? What the hell am I supposed to do then?"

"Put me out of my misery like an old dog," he said dryly. "Do you have to argue about every damned thing? I've pulled in fish heavier than you."

"Fine, but I'm going to be really angry with you if I have to take you out to pasture and shoot you."

He turned around and squatted down some so she could hop on his back, and then he hoisted her up like she was nothing and started walking.

"Just so you know," he said, "if I need to reach for my weapon I'm going to drop you."

"I'll understand completely," she told him, and they made their way through the narrowing cave, her holding the flashlight so he could hold on to her legs.

"I've got to put you down," he said. "It's getting too narrow for us to go through like this."

The walls had been steadily shrinking, and the sound of the waterfall was a good distance behind them, though she could still hear it. The walls were black rock and slightly wet, and the air was damp and cool. There were places where the walls came close to touching, and she didn't think Elias would be able to get his broad shoulders through, but he somehow managed.

"This is not my favorite thing," she said. "It feels like the walls are moving. I'm having visions of Luke, Leia, and Han Solo being stuck in the compactor in *Star Wars*."

"I was wondering when you'd find a movie reference for this," he said.

"That's ridiculous."

"Uh-huh." He got down on his knees and then his belly and Miller followed suit.

The stone was cold and wet beneath her and her body trembled uncontrollably, out of either fear or the cold, she wasn't sure. Her lungs seized and her breath came in shallow pants as the walls pressed in on her, scraping at her shoulders, rocks digging into her knees as she crawled.

She couldn't focus on Elias. She could only focus on one small movement at a time, and not think about the fact that they could get wedged inside and might not be found until it was too late. She could hear Elias's labored breathing in front of her, and she didn't know how he was doing it. He'd shifted onto his side to make it easier for his shoulders to get through, but it seemed like an impossible fit.

And then when she reached the point where she wasn't sure she could keep going, the cave opened back up again, and she sprawled onto her stomach with relief. There wasn't a waterfall at this end of the cavern, but instead it was covered with thick vines that hung down like snaky ropes.

"Thank you, Jesus," she muttered, crawling on hands and knees toward the opening.

The exit was only as high as her waist, but she could see the little peeks of sunlight through the vines, and she'd never wanted to see daylight so bad in her life. Elias crawled through first and stood up and then reached back to help her through.

A shot rang out and Elias crumpled in front of her, and all she saw was the blood on his face.

CHAPTER TWENTY-TWO

"**S**top where you are," a deep voice called out.

Elias pressed his fingers to the cut at his temple and swore. The bullet had hit the stone behind him and shattered, sending shards into his face. He was lucky he hadn't lost an eye.

"Justin?" he called out, recognizing the voice. "You asshole. You could've shot your sister." Miller was still on the ground, but he felt her scramble up to a standing position and gasp in surprise. He kept his arm out and held her behind him until he could completely assess the situation.

They were in a huge clearing, overgrown with green and ancient ruins. An Incan civilization had once called it home.

"Ohmigod," Miller said behind him, peeking over his shoulder. "It's the fallen column," she said. "We found it."

Sure enough, there was a large column of pitted

stone that had fallen haphazardly across the center of the clearing. The other column still stood perfectly erect, and they had obviously once been the entrance to the city.

"Who is that?" Justin called out.

Elias saw a flash of a hand or arm from behind one of the ruins.

"Who the hell do you think it is?" Elias asked back.

"No fucking way," he said. "You're dead." And he finally came out from around the ruins to face him. "Miller," he said. "You need to come here now."

"Umm, how about a hello or a nice to see you too, you big jerk? You scared the hell out of me. I thought you were dead."

Justin looked worse for the wear. His eye was a combination of interesting shades of purple, yellow, and black and almost swollen shut, and his lip and jaw were swollen too beneath several days of beard. His right hand was wrapped tightly, but blood seeped through the bandages.

"Miller, I don't know what the hell you've gotten yourself mixed up in with this guy, but you need to get over here now. I'm not going to tell you again."

"I'm not twelve years old," she said. "Don't talk to me like a child. I can promise you that Elias isn't what you think he is. You need to give him a chance and listen."

"For fuck's sake, Miller. Please tell me you aren't with this guy. For once in your life would you stop being so stubborn and get your ass over here? And what the hell did you do to your hair? You look like Tinker Bell. It's absurd."

"You listen here, Justin Darling," she yelled. Elias couldn't help the smile. He'd been on the receiving end of that tongue and was looking forward to the fireworks. "I'm in love with him. What are you going to do about that? Oh, right. Nothing. Because I'm a grown-ass adult and you can't tell me what to do. Just because you bother to flit in and out of my life once or twice a year doesn't mean you get a say in my love life. And who the hell are you to make comments about who I'm sleeping with? I had to put up with that moron Hannah James at Thanksgiving that year. She laughed at every possible inappropriate time and she kept putting dinner rolls in her purse."

"Miller," Justin warned. "You're overreacting. I have a damned good reason for not wanting you anywhere near that bastard."

"He was your friend," she said, furious.

"Yes, he was. But he's a traitor," Justin called out. "And he's supposed to be dead."

"It's pointless, Miller," Elias said, touching her gently on the arm. "He'll believe the truth when he wants to believe it. My path is set. I don't need to prove my worth to anyone but you."

"You killed an innocent man in cold blood," Justin yelled. "And get your hand off my sister."

"Would a traitor be here to save your sorry ass?"

"That still doesn't explain how he's alive when he was given the death penalty. He died. We all saw it. We were there."

"Maybe there are things bigger than the both of us that you just don't understand," Elias said. "But your sister has been through hell to get you back home safe."

Justin looked back and forth between them and came a little closer. His clothes were torn and filthy and she could see the fatigue beginning to take its toll on him once he let his guard down and realized she wasn't moving from Elias's side.

"The important thing is Solomon's treasure," he said. "We've got to make sure Cordova doesn't get his hands on it."

"Fuck the treasure," Miller said, her voice breaking. "I am so damned sick of hearing about Solomon's treasure. I don't care if it ever existed or if it still exists. It's done nothing but tear our family apart. Look at you," she said. "You've sold your soul to a legend. You don't care about anything else. We're here to save you, putting our own lives in danger, and still that's all you can talk about. I came here for you. If you don't want to come home, then we're leaving."

"You don't understand, Miller," he said, the frustration evident in his voice. "I don't have a choice. Just like Dad never had a choice. It's the greatest honor and the biggest curse to be chosen."

"How do we get out of here?" Miller asked, turning to Elias and ignoring Justin's pleas. "I'm not going through that cave again. There's got to be another way out."

"I can show you the way out," Justin said, coming closer. "But please, just listen to me."

"Like you just listened to me when I told you Elias was innocent?" she asked.

Justin looked at Elias again and then back at her. "Maybe he is," he said. "I don't know. I only know what I saw with my own eyes. But I also know that before all the shit hit the fan, I would've died for him. None of us ever believed it when the charges were brought against him, but it was hard to dispute the evidence. I can give him a chance if it means getting you out of here safely."

"I'd never let anything happen to her," Elias told him. "I love her."

Justin snorted and shook his head, but there was sadness on his face. "God help you. She's got a temper like a banshee."

"So I've learned."

"I'm actually right here," Miller said. "You don't have to talk around me. But I'm so glad you two are having this emotional moment. Maybe we can go now. I've decided I don't need to be a world traveler, and I'd like to go home."

"I found the wreckage of the plane," Justin told her. His gaze was steady on hers—serious, searching. He had their father's eyes, a rich brown that could go from dreamy to determined in a split second.

Elias heard her indrawn sob, and he moved so he could touch her. He hated to think of the pain she was feeling. She laid her head against his back and took a couple of shaky breaths and said, "I saw the compass, so I figured you did."

"I buried them," he said gently. "It seemed like the right thing to do. We never got the chance to have that finality of a true burial. I can take you to see them."

"Maybe," she said. "But honestly, I don't know if I can deal with it right now. I'm a little overwhelmed at the moment. This hasn't been the easiest week."

"At least you have all your fingers," Justin said.

"I'm about to tell you what to do with that finger," Miller shot back angrily, and Elias had to stifle a laugh. Lord, he loved that woman.

Elias looked around, trying to find an escape route where they could be extracted from, and he noticed the two streams on each side of the clearing. It would've been easy access to fresh water for the Incans, and he could see why they'd settled in this particular area.

"Look at the water," he told Miller, ignoring Justin.

"What about it?" she said.

"It's not flowing toward the falls at the opposite side of the cave. It's flowing in a different direction."

"Which means it has to eventually lead to somewhere," she finished for him.

"You can't go out there," Justin told them. "Ever since I escaped from Cordova, he's sent teams of his men to search for me. This place is completely secluded and protected. Those two streams lead into the Aguas Mortales. No one can enter from that direction. The water is too treacherous. And by equal measures, no one can escape from that way either. You and I could probably swim it if we had our dive gear, but there's no way Miller could. The chances of us making it are iffy at best. How embarrassing would it be for two SEALs to die by drowning?"

"Doesn't matter to me," Elias said. "I'm already dead. You're the one who will look like an idiot. We've got an extraction team ready to pick us up as soon as we give the signal. They should've had plenty of time to take care of Cordova's men."

"An extraction team?" Justin asked. "Why the hell is an extraction team here? Who are you? Why'd they fake your death?"

"That's a lot of questions that I really don't feel like answering right now," he said. "My biggest priority at the moment is getting Miller off the island safely. I told her I'd help you find her and that I'd help her find your parents' wreckage. Both of those things have been accomplished. The treasure can go to the devil for all I care."

"Don't say that," Justin said. And then he reached down and picked up his pack and pulled out a cloth-wrapped cylinder. "Do you know what this is?"

"I'm guessing it's the leg from the table of Solomon," Miller said.

"I hear the resentment in your voice," he said. "But you've never understood."

"Understood *what*, Justin?" she asked.

"You have my ring?" he asked her.

"It's back in Last Stop with your finger," she said.

"There are only twelve of them in existence," he said. "It's incredible to see them all together, each exactly the same and forged by one of the greatest kings in history."

"You've seen all twelve?" she asked, eyes narrowed. "Those rings are a couple thousand years old. How could they have possibly survived?"

"Because that is our destiny," he said. "They call us the Shamira. It was our ancestor who Solomon chose to be one of the prophets of the twelve tribes of Israel. Not only a prophet, but a protector of the most sacred items. The items of the most holy rituals. This was a fitting table to hold the Ark of the Covenant."

He unwrapped it and the gold glowed with an unearthly luminance, jewels of every kind glittering in his hands. Elias couldn't describe the feeling that came over him when looking at it for the first time. It was both pain and peace, and he took hold of Miller's hand because he instinctively knew she was feeling the exact same thing.

"When the temple was destroyed and the treasures looted, it was impossible for the Shamira to discover what had been done with it. Many died trying to find it and bring it back to its rightful place. And when those deaths occurred, it fell to the next in line to take up the cause. And on and on for generations, we've been looking for the items that rightfully belong in the temple. We cannot rest until it is done. Until the temple is rebuilt in Jerusalem and the items are in place. This is our destiny."

"Justin," Miller said.

"Don't you see?" he asked. "I had no choice. When Dad died, the duty came to me. He was so close, and he'd alerted the others, and there was great excitement and speculation. But the treasure would have to stay hidden until the temple is rebuilt, so we would become guardians of the treasure once it was found. Dad was close," he said. "And in his notes he led me right to it."

"They abandoned their daughter, and you abandoned your sister," she said. "Maybe if you'd told me sooner, I would've tried to understand. But I'm finding that I just don't give a damn right now. You're nothing but a selfish jerk. But at least you had the decency to not drag a wife and kid into your insanity."

"Mom and Dad loved you," he said softly, the sadness there in his eyes.

"Stop," she said, her voice breaking. "They didn't love me enough."

"I love you," he said. "I didn't know what to do with you or how to handle you. I was grieving too. I don't know how to apologize. How to correct the past."

"You can't, Justin. You just have to keep moving forward. The past doesn't bring anything but pain." She took a deep breath and said, "I really want to go now. I'm glad you're alive."

"Yeah," he said. "Me too."

CHAPTER TWENTY-THREE

The three of them followed the streams for several miles, Elias in front of her and Justin at her back. Nothing was said.

It was easy to see why the Incans had picked that location. It was like a secluded walled city inside the mountain. It was formed like a large vase, the same black rock shaped like a bowl at the bottom and fluted up to a narrow opening toward the top. There were narrow openings, like doorways that would've made it difficult for anyone to attack their protected space.

The sound of crashing waves became louder as they kept going, and she remembered Elias saying that no boats were allowed in the waters at the center of the Triangle Islands. Which made her wonder how the hell they were supposed to get out of there.

The moss and rich dirt of the jungle eventually gave way to white sand that felt good and warm on the bottoms of her sore feet. Jagged rocks jutted up from the coastline and the waves crashed high and loud against them. She could see why boats and people weren't allowed. The water flowed in different directions, almost forming a series of mini-whirlpools.

"I hit the homing beacon for the extraction team," Elias said. "The best thing to do is wait here. It's been hours since I heard shots."

"You're still going to have to explain this whole extraction thing to me," Justin said, eyes narrowed. "You were dishonorably discharged. Court-martialed."

"I was set up, and you're too stupid to see it."

"Maybe," he said. "But there's still a hell of a lot of unanswered questions."

The vibrations from a helicopter put them both on alert, and then they saw the black chopper as it slowly lowered itself over the treacherous waters. It was a delicate act, and one that would take an excellent pilot.

"Shit," Elias said, catching sight of a smiling Emilio Cordova sitting next to the pilot. He had a submachine gun pointed at the three of them. There was at least another one of their men in the back with the doors open.

"Hello, my friends," Cordova said through a speaker. "I'm so glad you decided to take up my invitation to my islands, Ms. Darling. Your brother has been a great deal of trouble, but it's nice to see you all together. It takes some of the work off of us. Go ahead and relieve yourselves of your weapons," he said. "You're not going to need them. And just in case you're thinking of doing something stupid, these bullets will hit Ms. Darling first. Just below the knees, I think. We still need her as a bargaining tool."

Elias and Justin both tossed their weapons on the ground and glared at the chopper. They were helpless. A long strap fell from the back opening of the chopper and it made its way closer to them. It couldn't get too close because the rotors would be in danger of hitting the side of the cliff. But at the same time, they would have to get into the water to reach the strap.

"I'm not sure who you are," Cordova said, speaking to Elias. "But I'm assuming you're part of the team that is laying waste to my men. I believe you're better off alive for the moment. They might want you back, and you might be a valuable commodity. Mr. Darling, make sure you bring that table leg with you. I'm anxious to see it."

"How do you want to do this?" Justin asked. "She won't be able to swim that distance to the strap."

"We'll both swim her out," Elias said, hating the choices he'd been given but knowing there were no other options. They were too far to take shelter back within the safety of the black cliff walls. "You'll take her up with you and I'll wait below until they redrop the strap."

"No," Justin said. "Let me do it. They still need me, and I don't want to risk the chance of them taking off without you."

Elias nodded and took off his shoes, and Miller felt a swell of panic inside of her.

"It'll be okay," he told her so only she could hear. "Your natural inclination is going to be to fight against the water. Let us do the work for you, okay?"

She nodded and they made their way over the rocks and Justin dropped down into the water, his head bobbing back up instantly. And then Elias did the same.

"Come on, baby. I've got you," Elias said.

Justin's head jerked toward him at the endearment, but Miller kept her gaze on Elias's. She could trust this man with her life. She knew that as sure as she knew she was breathing. She stepped off the rock and into the water, and her head didn't even go under. The water was freezing and she understood what Elias had been talking about. The water was pushing and pulling, and she could feel the suction wanting to drag her down, and her instinctive need to fight to stay above water.

Elias and Justin looked at each other once, and she could see a whole world of communication and knowledge between the two of them. They each took one of her arms, and then they pushed off from the rocks and started swimming with the most incredible strength she'd ever seen. They each had only one arm to swim with, and their other arms were holding her up so her head stayed above water. She did what Elias had told her and relaxed, trying not to make their job any harder. They swam in such unison they were almost like one person.

The strap dangled in front of them and Elias grabbed hold of it, and Miller, sticking his foot in the loop at the bottom, and they began to rise as the crank pulled them up into the chopper. The man waiting at the top tugged at her arms and all but tossed her inside, and then he left Elias to get in on his own. The strap was dropped again so Justin could grab hold, and she wondered how he had the ability to hold himself against the strength of the water.

"Sit down on the floor and stay there, no matter what," Elias told her. "Make yourself as small of a target as you can. Got it?"

She nodded and waited in anticipation as the crank lifted Justin into the chopper. The man in back was holding his gun at the ready, and Cordova was turned in his seat, his own weapon ready to fire.

Miller brought her knees up to her chest and curled in as small as she could get, pressing herself between two wooden crates. The second Justin came over the edge of the chopper, there was pandemonium. Elias and Justin moved in a flurry, a well-choreographed dance.

A shot went off, and then another, and she watched in horror as Justin knocked the man's teeth together by hitting him under the chin with the back of his wrist, and then he flung the man out the side door into the rocky waters below.

The pilot was trying to fly the chopper and kill Justin at the same time. He finally let go of the controls long enough to turn in his seat and aim. But he wasn't aiming at Justin. She could see directly down the barrel of the pistol.

"No," Justin and Elias yelled at the same time, and she flinched as Justin's body hurtled toward her to cover her. And then she felt the impact of the bullet as it hit him and he went limp on top of her.

"Ohmigod," she said, pushing him off her so he lay flat on his back. Blood pooled beneath his shoulder out the back, and she looked around frantically for something to staunch the wound with.

She looked up at Elias for help, but he was still embroiled in his own battle against Cordova. Elias had both hands on Cordova's submachine gun, and he jerked hard, hitting Cordova in the face. Blood spurted from his nose and mouth and he smiled, the blood coating his teeth. And then he pulled the trigger.

The chopper listed and she held on to the grab bar and Justin for dear life as she looked around to see what had happened. The pilot sat slumped over the controls, a good portion of the side of his face missing.

Elias lifted the dead pilot by the shirtfront and tossed him out the open door, and then he took his place in the pilot's seat. Cordova was still in the seat next to him, only his neck was twisted grotesquely to one side.

"You can pilot a helicopter?" she asked, finding some old rags thrown in the back of the chopper. She folded them into a thick square and placed it at Justin's exit wound. And then she made another and pressed it against the entry wound.

"Pretty much," he said.

"Pretty much?" she said, eyes wide. She saw Justin's lips twitch and breathed a sigh of relief.

"A little faith, my love," Elias said.

"Always," she said.

Justin studied her face and he seemed very fragile all of a sudden. He'd always been larger than life.

"Justin, if you die on me I'm going to kill you," she said, holding him tightly in her arms. Her tears fell on his face, but he didn't seem to mind.

"I'm so sorry," he told her. "Can you ever forgive me? I should have done better by you. I didn't know how, and that's my own stupid fault. It was easier to leave."

"Of course I forgive you," she said, worried about his color. His lips were tinged blue. "I love you, you knot head. Save your breath. Elias is bringing us down and they'll take care of you."

"He used to be a good man," Justin said. "The best. There was nothing he wouldn't have done for one of us. We were all devastated when the verdict came in. We never would have believed it, but the proof was irrefutable."

"It was a setup," she told him. "He's still a good man. One of the best."

Justin nodded and squeezed her hand.

"Shh," she said. "It's okay. You can tell me all about it at the hospital."

Panic filled her as his eyes went dim. He was slowly slipping away, and there was nothing she could do. He was the only family she had left.

Elias landed the chopper on the roof of the only hospital in Santa Cruz, and a team came out in a rush to greet them with a stretcher and whisk Justin away. Elias peeled himself out of the pilot's seat and pulled her into his arms and she let herself weep—a cleansing through tears of years of heartache. And she loved him all the more because he held her as if she were the only thing in his world.

CHAPTER TWENTY-FOUR

"**H**ow's he doing?" Elias asked, three days later.

Miller looked up from her laptop and smiled. "He's driving the nurses crazy," she said. "I think they're finally going to release him today just so they can get a little peace and quiet."

"I don't see what's the big deal about asking for pudding," Justin said grumpily from the hospital bed.

Elias raised his brows and bit back a smile. Justin looked a lot like Miller did in the mornings before she had her coffee.

"There's nothing wrong with asking for pudding," she said. "Except that you've literally asked for pudding cups thirty-two times. There is no more pudding on the island."

"It's delicious," Justin said, coming close to a pout. "A man with a bullet wound should get pudding if he wants some."

"Agreed," Elias said, winking at Miller. "And I just

saw the nurse. They are about to release him so we can head back stateside."

"What did I miss?" Justin asked.

"Not much," he answered. "With Cordova's death, there's no one to take control of the cartel, so most of them have scattered for the time being. Word on the street is The Black Widow is pissed and looking for vengeance. If Eve was smart she'd order a full-out search and kill for The Black Widow. Get her while the cartel is at its weakest. But we're on total lockdown on this one."

"And who exactly is 'we'?" Justin asked.

"You'll have to wait until we get back to Texas to be debriefed," Elias said. His grin held just a little bit of the devil. "You're going to love debriefing. Everyone does."

Miller snorted out a laugh and asked, "Has my house been put back together?"

"That's what I've heard," Elias said, wondering if he could talk her into stepping into the hall with him. Or the janitor's closet. It had felt like ages since he'd kissed her. Even longer since he'd made love to her.

They stared at each other for a few seconds, the air between them heavy with need. Justin cleared his throat and said, "I'm kind of right here in the middle of you two. You're making me feel very awkward."

"Then it was worth it," Miller said.

"Do you love my sister?" Justin asked, and Miller's head snapped up to look at him.

"Shut up, Justin," she said.

"No, I get to be big brother for once. You shut up."

Elias's lips twitched at how alike some of their personality traits were. "Yes," he said. "I do. Very much."

Justin seemed satisfied with that answer and relaxed a little. And then he asked, "Are you going to marry her?"

Everyone froze at that question, and the discomfort in the room would've been felt by anyone who walked in. Elias glance at Miller once and she was staring at him. He felt the ball in his gut and the lump in his throat as he tried to swallow. And then he looked back at Justin.

"I can't," he said. "I'm a dead man. And dead men don't have futures or get happily ever afters."

He chanced a look at Miller again and saw the devastation in her eyes at his words. But they were the truth. This mission had stirred up the past, and bringing Eve down had become the most important thing in his universe. Even more important than loving Miller.

EPILOGUE

Solomon watched her from the highest point of his palace, watched her caravan as it made its way back to where it came from. He'd sent his best men to travel with her and see to her safety, for there was nothing more precious on this earth.

She'd been true to her word. Before dawn broke, she'd slipped from his bed, leaving him with a soft kiss and words of her love. She'd gathered her things and her envoy and left him brokenhearted.

Unimaginable grief took him by surprise, and he cried out her name as he raced to the very peak of his palace, where he watched from a distance, her shadow growing smaller and smaller the farther she went.

Tears streamed down his cheeks and his heart was shattered in a million pieces. There would never be another like his Sheba. And for the rest of his mortal life and through eternity, she would be the only one who held his heart. For he finally knew the meaning of love.

Miller wiped the tear that had snuck its way from the corner of her eye down her cheek, just as she did every time she thought about knowing what it was to truly love with all your heart and soul, only to find those pieces will always be missing.

"I've got to say," Tess said, stacking the papers of Miller's manuscript, "that's depressing as hell. Why can't you change the story so they get to be together?"

Miller hadn't been to bed yet. The story had possessed her until she'd finally typed the last sentence somewhere around daybreak. Tess had been reading the book as Miller wrote it, and as if she'd known it was finished, she showed up on her doorstep with breakfast she'd picked up from the diner as an even trade for getting to read the rest of the story.

They'd taken up residence in the living room, much like they had almost two weeks before. Miller was as wired as she was exhausted. She'd crash and crash hard in the next few hours, but for now, there was an elation that only finishing a book could bring.

"I can't rewrite history," Miller said. "Their story didn't end with them getting to be together."

"Of course you can rewrite history," Tess protested. "People do it all the time. Look at the real reason we celebrate Thanksgiving, for Pete's sake. We celebrate a massacre by stuffing ourselves with relish trays and dry turkey. It's absurd. There's no reason you can't give Solomon and Sheba a life together on the pages of your book."

"Some things aren't meant to be," she said sadly, thinking of Elias. "And I told you your turkey wouldn't be dry if you'd stick butter under the skin."

Tess's lip curled in disgust. "But then I'd have to stick my hands all up in the turkey. And that's disgusting."

"You have to stick your hands all up in the turkey to get the giblets and neck out anyway."

"What are you talking about?" Tess asked. "What are giblets and necks?"

Miller closed her eyes and shook her head in disbelief. "How about I make the turkey for Thanksgiving?"

"Why are we talking about turkeys instead of this depressing ending?" Tess asked.

"It's not the only ending," Miller said, rolling her eyes. "My hero and heroine fell in love and lived happily ever after."

Though she didn't confess what a struggle that had been to put on the page. Mostly she'd wanted her heroine to stab the hero, who shared entirely too many characteristics with Elias, in the neck with a fork.

"That's true," Tess conceded. "I just think it stinks that Solomon and Sheba didn't get their happily ever after too."

"Real life rarely works out as well as fictional life," Miller said.

"Are you going to tell me what's really bothering you?" Tess asked. "I know you love him. You can't hide that from me."

Miller sighed and didn't bother to swipe away the tears this time. "I just didn't think it would hurt this bad. I knew he'd break my heart from the start. I thought I was prepared for it, and I'd take what I could get for as long as I could get it. But the worst part isn't that I love him. It's that he loves me too, and still chooses not to be with me."

"If it makes you feel better," Tess said, "he looks a hell of a lot worse than you do." There was a knock at the door, and Tess went to answer it since she was already up. Tess rarely sat. She was always full of energy.

"That makes me feel only slightly better," Miller said. "That's probably the UPS man. He's a glutton for punishment. Scare him a little and send him away."

Tess laughed and left the room, and Miller snuggled down in the couch, pulling the throw that hung across the back of it over her. Maybe she was going to crash sooner than she thought. She wasn't worried about Tess. She'd been coming and going as she pleased for as long as she could remember, and she'd leave when she was ready.

Her eyes were heavy, so she closed them, and listened to see who was at the door, but she couldn't hear any conversations. The floors creaked as footsteps grew louder, and she wanted to groan in protest.

"Tess, you were supposed to send him away, not invite him in. The last time he was here he brought me a finger in the mail."

"I'd like that back, by the way," her brother said. "We can give it a proper burial."

Her eyes snapped open and landed on Justin. He still looked worn and gaunt, but he was alive, and he seemed glad for it.

"That's sick, man," Elias said. "I'm not going to a funeral for your finger."

Her gaze went to the man who stood beside her brother, and seemed to catch there. She felt the emotion deep in her chest, and the pain was just as real as it had been the last time she'd seen him. She couldn't do this. Couldn't pretend like everything was as it was. She couldn't be friends and act as if seeing him wasn't like having her guts ripped out.

She looked at Tess in a panic, but Tess wasn't meeting her gaze, so she tossed off the throw and put her feet flat on the floor.

"Don't get up," Elias told her. "We can all see you're exhausted."

"Good grief, get on with it," Justin said impatiently. "Tess is having trouble finding ways to look natural while you beat around the bush."

"Remember our agreement," Elias said. "You don't want to interfere right now."

Justin put up his hands in surrender and took a step

back, so he stood next to Tess, but his smile held both good humor and warning. There were obviously undercurrents going on that Miller had no clue about. Actually, she had no clue about anything at the moment other than she hurt in ways she never thought possible, though now it was compounded by an audience.

She had some time before she needed to start her next book. She'd get a solid twelve or so hours of sleep, and then she could pick up and leave. It was time to expand her comfort zone. Maybe Tahiti or Australia. And it was definitely time to expand the distance between her and Elias.

"Uh-oh," Tess said. "You'd better hurry. I recognize that look on her face. She's about to run."

"Thank y'all so much for all the help," Elias said sarcastically. "But maybe we can have a few minutes of privacy?"

"Nah, I'm good," Justin said. "You broke her heart once. I want to make sure you fix it."

Miller was suddenly very aware that something was going on and she wasn't privy to whatever it was. Her stomach was in knots, and emotion rolled through her when Elias seemed to find his resolve and moved in front of her, kneeling down so he could look her in the eye.

Her hands were freezing and gripped tightly together, but he pried them apart and gave her a comforting squeeze.

"I should probably start out by telling you that I'm a jerk," he said.

Tess snorted, and Justin said, "That's an understatement."

But though his lips quirked, Elias kept his gaze on hers. She was having trouble breathing, and her brain wasn't processing what was happening. Why would he come and reopen the wounds? To apologize? To clear his conscience?

She wanted to say something, but her throat closed. She shook her head as tears filled her eyes. This was a kind of hell she never wanted to experience again.

"But I'm a jerk who loves you," he said. "Loving you is worth every risk, and I realized that letting myself love you the way you deserve to be loved is the only thing that can set me free. I can't promise that it will be an easy life. At least not for the next five years. But I can promise to love and protect you with every breath in my body for as long as we both shall live."

The tears fell freely now. She couldn't help it. And when a sob escaped, she buried her face against their joined hands. He leaned his head against hers and she felt the shudder run through his body.

"Please, love me," he whispered, so only she could hear.

She nodded against him, and somewhere in the background she heard the front door close.

"I do," she told him. She'd never let herself love

anyone like she loved him. She lifted her head because what she wanted to tell him needed to be said to his face. "I've lived my entire life on my own, holding a part of myself back out of fear. I lived, but I didn't know what it meant to *really* live." His thumb stroked her cheek, wiping away her tears. "I can love you and still survive without you. I'd already resigned myself to doing so. It would be easy to move on and live a full life. Even a happy life. But I'd much rather experience the joy of knowing what it is to belong to you. And for you to belong to me. There's faith in a commitment of that magnitude, and it's one I'd never planned on. But I want to be with you."

Elias cleared his throat, and she realized how humbling it must be for a man as strong as he was to kneel at her feet and lay himself bare. And she loved him all the more for it.

"My job has long, unreasonable hours," he warned her.

"Mine does too," she said, noticing the twinkle in his eyes.

"And my boss can be a real bitch."

"I've heard that," she said. "But I've already got my revenge planned. I'll send her a copy once the book is out. Maybe she'll recognize herself."

Elias laughed and pulled her into his lap on the floor. "I'd love to read it. I'm partial to happily ever afters."

Keep reading for a sneak peek excerpt
from the next mysterious, riveting
installment in the Gravediggers series

Say No More

Available Summer 2017
from Pocket Books!

CHAPTER ONE

Nice, France ~ 2015

There were some men who wore elegance like a second skin. Dante Malcolm was one of them.

He guided the cigarette boat through the black water like a knife, sending a fine spray of mist into the air. The moon was full, the stars bright, and the night crisp and clear. The smell of sea salt and lavender perfumed the air. It was the perfect night for a party. And an even better night for a burglary.

His tuxedo was hand-tailored and silk, his bow tie perfectly tied, and his shoes properly shined. His black hair was cut precisely, so that it would fall rakishly across his forehead instead of appearing windblown.

There was something about wealth that had always appealed to him—the glitter of jewels, the smell of expensive perfume, the not-so-subtle way the elite bragged about their latest toys or investments. It was all a game. And he'd always been a winner. But a small thorn had been growing in his side—or maybe it was his conscience—over the past few months.

Liv Rothschild. He was in love with her. Every stubborn, vivacious, persistent, gorgeous inch of her. And that was turning out to be more of a problem than he'd anticipated. Love had never been in the cards for him. Not until he'd crossed paths with a woman whose beauty had literally stopped him in his tracks. Her stunning features had lured him in, but her intelligence had kept him coming back for more.

She knew the world he was accustomed to—the world of the titled and wealthy British elite. Her father had been a prominent member of society, and he'd married an American actress who preferred the drama in her life instead of on the screen. Liv had a sister—a twin—and though he'd only been thirteen at the time, he remembered the news coverage when Elizabeth Rothschild had gone missing.

The guilt Liv carried from that day her sister vanished was what had forged her future. She'd never stopped looking for her. The investigations had turned up no clue to her whereabouts, and even Dante's searches in the MI6 database had returned nothing. Not a hospital visit or a fingerprint taken. The assumption was that Elizabeth Rothschild was dead. He tended to agree.

But Liv had never lost hope, and Elizabeth's disappearance had motivated Liv to go into law enforcement and ultimately join Interpol so she would have the resources she needed to find her sister. What had been a surprise to Liv was that she was a damned good agent. What had been a surprise to him was that he'd started looking forward to their paths crossing from time to time. Fortunate circumstances had combined their efforts on this case.

Which was why they were meeting at the Marquis de Carmaux's château in the south of France. He enjoyed working with Liv, and if he had his way, they'd continue to work together. And play together. In his mind, life couldn't get any better. He *could* have it all. And he did.

La Château Saint Germain was lit like a beacon atop the rugged cliffs overlooking the Mediterranean Sea, a pink monstrosity with towers and turrets and more than fifty rooms that rarely got used. Expensive cars lined the narrow road that wound up the mountain, headlights beaming for as far as the eye could see as their occupants waited for the valets to take the keys. He checked his watch, noting that Liv should already be inside.

Dante eased off the throttle, and the boat coasted up to the dock. He tossed the rope to the valet, who tied it to the mooring, and then he stepped up onto the dock, adjusting his cuffs and bow tie.

The pathway from the dock led all the way up to the château, the grounds divided into three steep tiers. The wooden steps were lined with hanging lanterns, and the trees were decorated with lights. Once at the top, Dante sauntered along the stone-paved walkway toward the house and retrieved his invitation from the inside of his jacket pocket to present to the doorman. It was time to work.

The Marquis de Carmaux had terrible taste in wine and women, but his art was exceptional. His personal collection was going on loan to the Metropolitan Museum of Art in New York City for the next year, so he'd decided to throw a farewell party so the social elite could not only praise him for his generosity, but be envious of something they'd never be able to get their hands on.

Dante had been fortunate enough to be born into the British upper crust where wealth was passed from one generation to the next, easily accumulated with buying or selling real estate, and easily squandered on a whim. He was titled, a lord no less, and he'd been educated at the best schools, one of his classmates being the future king of England. He also had an unusual talent for math—he could solve any problem in his head, no matter how difficult. It gave him a natural aptitude for winning at cards.

He had many other talents as well—an ease with languages and the ability to see patterns amid what seemed to be nothing but random occurrences—which was why MI6 had wanted him so badly. To a wealthy young man of twenty-two who had multiple degrees in mathematics and was quickly getting bored of the party life that all his contemporaries seemed to live for, becoming an intelligence agent for his country had seemed like the right choice.

It had been around the same time that he'd met a man by the name of Simon Locke.

Simon had introduced him to the art of stealing. He'd given Dante something that no amount of money could provide, that seduced him as no woman had, and that international espionage couldn't satisfy, though it came a close second. Simon had given him an adrenaline rush that was more intense than any drug and just as addictive.

Simon Locke had given him a purpose. Dante felt no remorse when it came to taking things that belonged to others. Because he only took from those who could afford to lose what he stole, from those who had taken what wasn't rightfully theirs. His jobs always had a mission. He would collect the item that didn't truly belong to the current owner, and he'd take a second piece of his choosing as his commission.

He'd met Simon in a Belgian prison while on assignment. MI6 had set up Dante's arrest so he could get information from Simon's cellmate, who was suspected of being part of a terrorist organization and supposedly had information about recent bombings in Brussels. Simon had been brought in after the police had done a sweep of drunk and disorderlies. He'd been neither drunk nor disorderly, but in the wrong place at the wrong time.

The cell was no bigger than a small closet, maybe eight by eight feet, and metal-frame bunk beds that had been bolted into the floor sat against one of the stone walls. The mattresses were paper-thin and dingy, and it was best not to think about what was on them. There was a metal hole in the floor for a toilet and a barred window that overlooked the guarded courtyard below. The cell was shrouded in darkness, but every twenty-seven seconds the spotlight from one of the towers scanned across the window, giving light to the shadows of the cell.

Simon stayed quiet while Dante drew information from their third cellmate, who *had* been drunk and disorderly, but fortunately was also loose-lipped. And when the man had passed out and was snoring obnoxiously in a corner, Simon had looked over and said, "It's good to know British intelligence hasn't changed."

Dante had been speaking in flawless French to their other cellmate, but still Simon had known. And then he'd said something that piqued Dante's curiosity.

"I was like you once."

In his twenty-two-year-old arrogance, he'd responded, "I beg your pardon, but there's no one else like me."

Locke had smiled at him and moved into the light. He wasn't a big man—maybe five eight or five nine—and his hair was slicked back and tied at the nape of his neck. Even in the holding cell, his black slacks were precisely pressed and his expensive shirt only slightly mussed. There was a nonchalant cockiness about him that Dante could appreciate. He wasn't screaming about injustice like many of the others down the long hallway. He was calm and cool, his hands in his pockets.

St. Gilles Prison was overcrowded, its nineteenth-century cells never meant to accommodate so many prisoners. The holding cells were in the east tower. MI6 had assured Dante he'd be released early the next morning, but that was still hours away.

"Are they planning your release for the morning, Mr. . . ."

"Malcolm. I'm sure someone will post bond for me in the morning," Dante said vaguely. "And you? Will you be released in the morning? I didn't catch your name."

Simon smiled again and jangled some change in his pockets. Dante was surprised they hadn't confiscated the man's belongings when they'd brought him in.

"You can call me Locke," he said.

"The jailers are getting lax," Dante said, nodding to his pockets, making Simon grin again.

"Not so much. My pockets were empty when I came in. I tend to travel light."

Dante wasn't sure how Locke could have acquired a handful of change, but he was getting tired of the man's vagueness.

"I told you I was like you once," Simon said. "What if I told you there's something more for you than interrogating two-bit terrorists in a moldy jail cell?"

"I'd say they were right to arrest you for drunkenness."

He shrugged. "I was just in the wrong place at the wrong time. It happens. What if I told you I can get us both released right now? A man like you isn't used to places like this. I can see the disgust in your eyes. They give you these jobs because you're young and don't know any better than to take them. But wait until the rats come. You'll learn to speak up then."

The man was beginning to get under his skin, but Dante had to admit he was curious. And the idea of spending even a few more hours inside the dark cell grated against his sense of propriety.

"And how would you get us released?" Dante asked.

Simon took a copper cent from his pocket and held it up to the passing light. "Watch and learn."

And he had watched. And he had learned. Simon had used that copper cent to remove the bars from the window. And Dante had followed him, knowing that he could at any moment be caught and shot, but there had been something compelling about Simon. He'd watched the other man scale the narrow ledges of the prison, counting the seconds before the spotlight would pass, and timing his movements precisely.

Dante had done the same thing, and he'd found it came to him as naturally as breathing. Then they were outside the prison, not a soul the wiser. Before they'd gone a block, Simon had slipped into the shadows as if he'd never been there at all.

Within a day or two, Dante had thought he might

have imagined the whole event—except that he'd had a hell of a time explaining to his superiors why and exactly how he'd gone off book. He'd returned to London and his home, having delivered his report of the information he'd gotten from the terrorist, and when he walked into his bedroom, Simon had been sitting in the chair by the fireplace as if he belonged there.

It hadn't taken long for Simon to convince Dante to become his protégé. He was nearing retirement and only had a few good years left before age caught up with him, Simon said, and he needed someone who was vigorous and sharp of mind.

They had more in common than Dante had expected. But he had drawn a hard line about certain jobs. He wouldn't interfere if Simon targeted something specific on his own, but Dante refused to steal for the sake of stealing. There had to be a reason, and someone had to benefit. Simon had eventually acquiesced.

He'd taken over the persona of Simon Locke ten years before, when Simon felt Dante was ready to go out on his own. Dante hadn't looked back once, and he'd never had a moment of regret.

But Liv Rothschild had been a surprise. He'd seduced her for his own pleasure the moment he saw her. But then he'd found himself being seduced. Interpol had been looking for Simon Locke for years, and as irony would have it, she was put in charge of the investigation.

It had been pure self-preservation that had caused him to involve MI6 in the hunt for Simon Locke. She'd come too close too often to discovering his true identity, and joining his MI6 resources with hers guaranteed that he always knew the steps she was taking. She was good. But he was better.

He could've stopped, of course. But when it came down to it, Dante didn't want to. The thrill was in his blood. But Liv had become his oxygen. He needed both of them to survive, and he had no reason to think he couldn't have everything he wanted.

There was no reason to confess and ruin everything. Some confessions could never be forgiven. Liv was a straight arrow. She was adventurous and liked the thrill of the chase—that was in her blood, just as thieving was in his. But in the end, law and order would take precedence.

He'd always enjoyed the Marquis de Carmaux's château. It had been built in the eighteenth century to honor the palace of Versailles, and everything as far as the eye could see was decorated in French Baroque. It was overdone and gaudy, but as Carmaux liked to say, it was jolly good fun and women loved it. Dante and Carmaux had been friends for years, and he could attest to both of those statements.

The entryway was done in pink marble and was completely open to the second floor. The domed ceiling was painted with cherubs and erotic scenes that most people never noticed, although the other nudes painted in niches along the walls were harder to miss. The double staircase was the showpiece, also done in pink marble and flanked by pink marble columns. Whenever he walked in, Dante always felt as if he'd been swallowed whole and was lounging about in someone's stomach.

He made his way through the growing crowd and into the ballroom—white, thank goodness, with gold-leaf trim and ceilings again painted with subtly erotic love scenes. It smelled of perfume and excitement, and couples were already moving around the dance floor. The ballroom opened up on either side—on one side was the bar and a smattering of high tables so people could rest, and on the other were the doors that led into the courtyard.

What Dante didn't see was the one woman he was looking for. Then he felt her behind him, and his mouth quirked in a smile as he turned.

"You're late," Liv said.

"I'm never late, darling," he said, taking her hand and kissing it. And then he stopped and lingered when he got a good look at her.

Never had a woman had the ability to make his heart skip a beat. He'd always thought the phrase trite and impossible—foolish words of romance. But now he knew it to be true.

She was spectacular. She wore a long column of dark blue velvet—strapless and simple in its design—and the small train pooled at her feet like the darkest part of the ocean. Her white-blond hair was piled artfully on top of her head, and a sapphire the size of his thumb dangled just above her décolletage. His gaze lingered there, and all he could imagine was her wearing nothing but that necklace.

"If you keep looking at me like that, we're likely to get in trouble," she said, her lilting voice husky.

"Only if we do what I'm thinking about in front of all these people." He released her hand and took two flutes of champagne from a passing tray, handing one to her.

"Are you sure he'll be here tonight?" she asked, looking around the ballroom.

"I have a gut feeling. Carmaux has one of the premier art collections in the world, and after tonight, it's going to be under museum security. If Locke is going to make his move, it'll be tonight, when everything is out on display."

"There are close to a thousand people here, and security is everywhere," Liv said, bringing the flute to her lips to cover her words. "He'd be a fool to try to take one of these paintings. And Simon Locke is no fool."

"Everyone has a weakness," Dante told her. "And a challenge like this one is his. He'd go down in history as the greatest thief ever to live."

ACKNOWLEDGMENTS

I'll admit that this was the most difficult book I've ever written, not because of the book itself, but because of what was happening in my personal life. I'm so blessed and honored to have a group of people around who support and encourage me, talk me through the hard times, and carry me through the really hard times. This book wouldn't have been possible without these people.

A huge thank you to my editor, Lauren McKenna, for seeing something in this book when I couldn't see anything, and for fighting for me. I couldn't have done it without her. And thank you to Marla Daniels and the entire team at Pocket for being so amazing to work with. I've enjoyed every step of the process. I also want to thank my agent, Kristin Nelson, for always having a game plan and being the calm in the storm. Thank you to Jillian Stein, whom I adore, because she is the best social media person on the planet. And to Chas and the team at RockStar PR for making my life so much easier. I also want to give a special thanks to my friend Chermaine Stein who helps me put the pieces of myself back together again, a little bit at a time. She also gives me love, encouragement, and a friendship I'll treasure always. I'm blessed.

On the home front, I have to thank my children for their patience and unconditional love. And because they don't mind eating take-out every night while I'm on deadline. I also want to thank my husband, because he sees to the smallest details of life so it's possible for me to write books. He's my hero.